JORJA'S CRYSTAL

By
Annie London

PROLOGUE

In the enchanting realm of Inorac, a land called Enrac with breathtaking expanse and vivid splendour, the climate mirrored that of Earth, with summers that embraced warmth and winters that cloaked the world in icy breath. To the far north, beneath the watchful gaze of twin suns, lay the tenacious nation of Merizgar. Here, Morwenna and her beloved husband Goran nurtured their brood of six. Their eldest, a radiant daughter named Saffran, embodied the brilliance her name conveyed. In contrast, their second-born was a son, Helgi, who bore a name that whispered of peace, yet he grew to be a tempest of turmoil. Even in his youth, Helgi's heart was a cauldron of envy, simmering with bitterness toward his sister.

As the seasons turned, Helgi's jealousy morphed into a shadowy obsession. At the tender age of fourteen, he severed ties with his family, traversing the treacherous mountains to carve out his new realm. With a heart hardened by ambition, he enslaved the villagers, compelling them to erect a grand palace worthy of a sovereign. From the strongest among them, he forged an army.

The war he unleashed raged like wildfire, consuming all in its path as Helgi vowed to obliterate his family. The fateful day arrived when the final clash loomed. Saffran stood resolute at the gates, her heart heavy with dread as she watched her forces falter. Helgi was the first to breach their defences.

With urgency coursing through her veins, Saffran grasped her mother's arm, pulling Morwenna into the sanctuary of the nursery. She placed her newborn child into her mother's embrace, a silent plea echoing in the air. Understanding the moment's gravity, Morwenna stepped through the portal, cradling the infant. Yet, as she turned, she witnessed the horror unfolding. Her heart shattered at the sight of her son, her own flesh and blood, plunging a blade into Saffran's chest.

And then, the portal sealed shut.

CHAPTER ONE

Jorja, a kind-hearted and gentle soul, resided in the quaint little village of Whitstone, nestled in the countryside alongside her beloved grandmother, Lissa. Their humble abode, a cosy bungalow, served as their sanctuary where love and contentment flourished. During the frosty winter months, the crackling fire within their home enveloped them in warmth, while the verdant garden, with its lush foliage, provided a refreshing shelter from the scorching heat of summer.

Despite the abundance of comforts surrounding her, Jorja was unassuming, appreciating the simple pleasures bestowed upon her. Whether taking a leisurely stroll through the neighbouring woods, where the sound of chirping birds created a soothing symphony or indulging in a cup of homemade tea while lost in the pages of a novel, Jorja found solace in life's quiet moments. Her humility shone through in the way she treated others, always offering a listening ear or a helping hand without seeking recognition. Even amidst the hustle and bustle of daily life, Jorja's unassuming nature remained a constant, a beacon of peace and tranquillity in a world often consumed by materialism and self-promotion. Her actions unknowingly inspired those around her to embrace simplicity and find joy in the little things that truly matter.

In their serene oasis, a charming trampoline in the garden and two sets of wheels in the shed - a bike and a scooter - were the sources of her daily joys. A trusty laptop for her studies and a sizeable TV in the serene blue-hued confines of her bedroom were the sources of her daily joys. The colour blue held a special significance in Jorja's world. It adorned her attire, room and even school uniform, reflecting her fondness for its calming hue.

Furthering her journey through adolescence, Jorja embarked on her educational pursuits at a prestigious secondary school in the little but bustling town of Launceston. The school's exceptional standards of education resonated with Jorja, fostering a nurturing environment that she wholeheartedly cherished. Amidst the academic rigours, her heart found solace in the company of her dearest companions, particularly her lifelong confidantes, Megan and Millie. Since their early days of shared innocence in preschool, Millie's captivating afro curls had drawn Jorja in, forging an unbreakable bond between them. Together, the threesome revelled in the simple joys of childhood, frequently indulging in impromptu playdates and cherished moments that transcended the confines of the schoolyard. Light-hearted laughter intermingled with heartfelt discussions in their intimate conversations, enriched by the genuine camaraderie they wholeheartedly shared. The joyous echoes of their laughter reverberated through the serene surroundings, symbolising the innocence and purity of their unyielding friendship.

As the end-of-term exams approached, Jorja felt increasingly pressured to perform well and secure good grades, enabling her to advance into the prestigious top group of Launceston College Senior School. On the other hand, her friend Megan, who excelled in mathematics, seemed unfazed by the impending exams. Jorja, aware of her challenges in the subject, knew that she needed to work harder and put in extra effort to keep up with her peers. Millie was a middle-range student in maths and, like any good student, tried her best.

The morning of the math exam arrived, and Jorja's nerves were at an all-time high. She carefully focused on a particularly challenging question, her pen in hand, only to witness a strange occurrence: the pen inexplicably started twirling two centimetres above the desk on its own. Astonished, Jorja gasped in disbelief, inadvertently drawing the attention of the vigilant teacher, Miss Campbell. Acting quickly, she snatched the pen from the air and pressed it firmly onto the desk, hoping to avert any unwanted attention and avoid potential consequences for this peculiar incident.

Disoriented and unsettled, she tried to continue her exam without further interruptions. Miss Campbell had put a mark on her pad, and she knew that it was not a good sign. One more mark, and she would be sent to the dreaded reflection. Reflection was a cold room where the naughty students went to reflect on their behaviour.

As Miss Campbell signalled the end of the exam and students began to take a much-needed break, Jorja felt relief wash over her.

However, her peace was short-lived as Jago approached her with his persistently grubby appearance and thick Cornish accent. His unwelcome presence loomed heavily, and Jorja's unease heightened as she was unsure of his intentions.

"I know what ya did when we woz in the test with ya pen. I saw ya," Jago said, speaking in a broad Cornish accent. "Jago, go away and leave me alone, please," Jorja responded. "Ya're a witch, ain't ya?" he continued. "I have no idea what you are talking about, Jago, and I've asked you to leave me alone!" she said louder, hoping someone would hear her. "Ya made that pen float in the air. I is gonna keep an eye on ya, makin sure there ain't no more funny business" he retorted.

Jorja tried to think of an answer, and an idea popped into her brain. "Oh, that...well, my uncle showed me a magic trick. If you are nice to me, I will show you," Jorja lied, hating herself for it but feeling it was justified.

Jago's words cut through the air, accusing her of using magic during the exam, claiming he had witnessed the pen floating mysteriously. The image of Jago accusing her of witchcraft weighed heavily on her mind, leaving her feeling defenceless and cornered. Despite desperately trying to focus on taking a break and to find her BFFs, the implanting accusation gnawed at her concentration, making her small task impossible. Feeling the weight of Jago's accusatory gaze, Jorja attempted to divert the conversation, dismissing his claims with unease festering in her mind. However, as Jago persisted, she knew she had to think quickly to defuse the escalating situation.

Crafting a deceitful tale about a family magic trick, Jorja had pacified Jago, hoping to appease him and bring his accusations to a close. The weight of her lie settled heavily on her conscience, but at that moment, she saw it as a necessary means to protect herself from Jago's relentless scrutiny. The web spun by her words and the façade she created hung between them, a fragile barrier shielding her from further accusations and suspicion.

During the next exam, which happened to be History, one of Jorja's favourite subjects, Jago positioned himself strategically close to her, appearing to be engrossed in the test but, in reality, keeping a discreet watch over her. The term 'funny business,' as he casually labelled it, was nowhere to be found. Yet, his eyes scrutinising her bore down on her, causing her to grapple with maintaining her focus amidst his unrelenting observance of the teacher.

Mr Lanyon, the history teacher, observed Jago's behaviour and reprimanded him, asking him to focus on the task.

At lunchtime break, Jago subtly intercepted her path to the bustling canteen, a move that did not go unnoticed by Jorja, who couldn't help but feel a pang of unease at the unexpected turn of events. The way he appeared so unexpectedly heightened her unease, casting a shadow over her thoughts as she grappled with the unsettling nature of their meeting and pondered the reasons behind his intentional interference.

As Jorja approached Jago, who was blocking her path with playful stubbornness, she could not help but notice the mischievous glint in his eyes. "Any more funny business?" he asked, a hint of challenge in his voice as he held his ground.

Politely, she appealed to Jago, "Jago, please let me pass. " Her tone carried much impatience at his antics. However, Jago was not easily swayed and demanded, "Not until you show me that trick again. " His insistence was evident in his words.

With a resigned smile, Jorja explained again, "It is only a dumb magic trick my uncle showed me. I have told you this already," a touch of exasperation seeping into her response. But Jago, determined to have his way, resorted to more aggressive tactics and threats: "If you don't show me, I'll tell everyone you're a witch." His voice raised a notch for emphasis.

Refusing to be intimidated, Jorja maintained her composure and countered, "Jago, stop being silly. No one will believe you, and I am hungry. Please move." Her words were laced with a mix of patience and reasoning.

Just then, their friends Megan and Millie arrived on the scene, their curiosity piqued. "What's going on?" Millie inquired, breaking the tension in the air.

Dramatically, Jago exclaimed, "She's a witch!" causing Megan and Millie to burst into uncontrollable laughter, further irking him. Sensing the need to intervene, Megan stepped in and dismissed Jago's claim, asserting, "Don't be daft, Jago. Jorja's not a witch. I have known her all my life. I would know if my best friend were a witch," as she gently nudged him aside, allowing Jorja and the girls to pass.

With a deep sigh of relief, Jorja felt immense gratitude for her friends' steadfast support. The three of them then collected their lunch trays and ventured to their familiar nook at the far end of the canteen, eager to savour their meal and the warmth of each other's presence.

"Tell us what that was all about?" Megan asked, her kind gaze fixed on Jorja's uneasy face, which displayed the telltale signs of nervousness: a dry throat and clammy palms. Sensing Jorja's reluctance, Megan's encouraging tone softened her resistance, assuring her, "You know you can tell me anything; we are here for you."

In a moment of vulnerability, Jorja confided in her friends about the unsettling accusation made against her by Jago, revealing how an innocent trick her uncle had shown her inadvertently embroiled her in misunderstandings. The weight of the accusation lingered heavily on her shoulders, casting a shadow over her usual cheerful disposition. However, the unwavering support of Megan and Millie provided a safe sanctuary for her confession, easing the burden of her secret.

As the school day progressed, Jorja found herself navigating through the maze of emotions and challenges, culminating in the final test in English. Strategically, positioning herself at the back and one side of the classroom, shielded by Megan's comforting presence on one side and the protective barrier of the wall behind and to the right of her. Milie's deliberately seating arrangement in front of her was a silent shield against Jago and his insidious whispers, ensuring a buffer zone from his accusatory glances and malevolent intentions. Jorja found solace in her friend's strategic plan and silently thanked them.

Despite the lingering tension in the air, the trio's united front exuded a silent strength that fortified Jorja's resolve as she delved into the test, her focus unwavering and her determination unyielding. The steady rhythm of her pen against the paper echoed the resilience of her spirit as she navigated through the challenges of the exam with a newfound sense of fortitude. As the final bell rang, signalling the end of the test, Jorja exhaled a sigh of relief, her heart lighter knowing that she had faced the day's tribulations with the unwavering support of cherished friends by her side.

Jorja readied herself to head home after this eventful day. Jago carelessly brushed past her, causing her rucksack to slip off her shoulder with an abrupt thud onto the ground. "Remember, I'm watching ya," he whispered with a sly grin, making Jorja feel uneasy and embarrassed about her extraordinary powers that she now found she had. Her mind swirled with complex emotions as she longed for a sense of normalcy, wishing fervently that she could somehow shed this unconventional burden.

Awaiting her as always, her grandmother stood outside, a comforting presence amid Jorja's inner turmoil. The young girl was practically bursting at the seams, eager to relay the day's startling incidents to her trusted confidante. "Nanny, you'll never guess what happened today!" she exclaimed, momentarily forgetting the decorum and manners that her grandmother had instilled in her over the years.

With a twinkle in her eye, her grandmother gently teased, "Jorja, are you perhaps forgetting something?" It was a reminder that brought a warm smile to Jorja's face as they walked together towards the familiar car that would take them back home. "Sorry, Nanny. Hello, how was your day?" Jorja asked politely, leaning over, she placed a loving kiss on her grandmother's cheek. "I love you so much," she added with heartfelt sincerity, knowing deep down how fortunate she was to have such a caring and understanding figure in her life.

"Ah, you are so much like your mother," her grandmother chuckled as they settled in for the fourteen-mile journey ahead. Jorja struggled to contain the bubbling excitement within her, determined to keep the recent extraordinary event hidden for the time being. Silent yet brimming with anticipation, she allowed her thoughts to wander, conjuring up whimsical daydreams of the day's earlier happenings.

Lost in her reverie, she barely noticed her grandmother's amused voice breaking through her thoughts. "Earth to Jorja," she chuckled softly. "Were you off in the land of make-believe?" The light-hearted comment snapped Jorja back to reality, prompting her to consider the forthcoming revelation she was itching to share with her grandmother. "Nanny, there's something I need to tell you, though I fear you may find it hard to believe," she sighed, preparing to disclose the extraordinary truth unfolding before her eyes.

They arrived at the quaint bungalow, a charming little oasis surrounded by lush, vibrant gardens. Feeling the weight of the decision ahead, Lissa took a moment to gather her thoughts and compose herself before broaching the topic with Jorja as she settled into a cosy chair and glanced over at the puzzled expression on Jorja's innocent face, a pang of uncertainty tugging at her heart. Was Jorja genuinely ready for the revelations that awaited her, or should Lissa allow more time for her young charge to mature and grasp the magnitude of her newfound abilities?

Despite Jorja's outward appearance of youthful innocence, Lissa knew all too well that in their realm, she had already reached the age of understanding and responsibility. The child's magical crystal continued to emit a soft, ethereal glow, a tangible reminder of Jorja's destiny once she fully embraced her powers. Yet Lissa was torn between the situation's urgency and the desire to shield Jorja from the overwhelming truth and hesitated to reveal the crystal's secrets too soon.

Seeking a moment of respite, Lissa retreated to the cosy kitchen with its comforting warmth and the gentle hum of the Aga stove. The vibrant red kettle sang a melodious tune as it began to boil, filling the room with a soothing rhythm that matched the steady beat of Lissa's pondering heart. With practised hands, she prepared a velvety hot chocolate, the rich aroma mingling with anticipation as she carried the drinks back to the inviting lounge, where Jorja awaited, her eyes filled with curiosity and uncertainty.

"Jorja, we need to have a little chat," Lissa said in a gentle yet firm tone as she carefully placed the delicate cups on the polished wooden table with an air of solemnity. She then motioned for her granddaughter to come and sit beside her, patting the cushion as she did so, a gesture of comfort and familiarity. "Now, tell me all about it," she said, her voice tinged with both worry and intrigue, seeking to comfort Jorja, assuring her that she was present to lend an ear and provide counsel for any troubles that weighed upon her heart.

"Oh, Nan, you're never going to believe me!" Jorja sighed wearily, a hint of resignation in her voice as she braced herself to recount the extraordinary events that had unfolded before her eyes.

"Try me, dear. I think I can manage it," Lissa replied with a knowing smile, her eyes twinkling with a blend of wisdom and mischief. As she raised her teacup to her lips, she brought the spoon to life, a subtle display of her magical abilities that went unnoticed by Jorja in her preoccupied state of mind.

Lost in thought, Jorja was momentarily unaware of her surroundings until a sudden cough from Lissa broke her reverie, causing her to startle and inadvertently knock the cup from her grandmother's hands in a moment of panic.

"Oh my gosh, Nanny, I am so sorry! Did I burn you? Are you okay?" Jorja exclaimed in a flurry of apologies, her worry evident as she rushed to ensure her grandmother was unharmed by the mishap.

With practised ease, Lissa utilised her magic to prevent the teacup, saucer, and spoon from meeting an unfortunate fate on the floor. She orchestrated a seamless dance of liquid mercury as the contents flowed back into the cup, and the spoon resumed its rhythmic stirring, a graceful demonstration of her control over the mystical forces at her command.

"Nan, am I a witch?" Jorja's voice quivered with uncertainty, her eyes brimming with unshed tears as she sought reassurance and clarity from the only maternal figure she had ever known.

"My darling, you are no witch, but you are a Princess," Lissa declared solemnly, her words carrying the weight of a long-kept secret now unveiled. Jorja's initial scepticism was met with a mixture of misunderstanding and uncertainty from her grandmother, who had always vowed to protect her granddaughter at all costs.

"Nan, this is not a joke or one of the bedtime stories you told me when I was four. Please tell me the truth," Jorja implored, her voice tinged with desperation and a fervent plea for honesty in a world that suddenly seemed filled with secrets and mysteries.

Lissa grappled with the weight of her decision, torn between shielding Jorja from a reality she might not yet be prepared to face and the necessity of revealing the truth that had long been kept hidden from her. Ultimately, she knew that the time for secrecy had passed, and it was time to unveil the magnitude of Jorja's destiny.

"Jorja, darling, now listen to me. I am not some kooky old disabled woman, you know." With those words, Lissa rose from her seated position; in her usual way, she bent over and slowly made her way out of the room, leaving Jorja momentarily stunned by her departure at such a crucial time. In a matter of moments, the stooped figure of the grandmother known as 'Nan' was replaced by the regal stature of a Queen, resplendent in a magnificent gown that shimmered with an otherworldly radiance. She no longer stooped and stood tall and regal.

As Jorja's gasp of astonishment echoed through the room, she was confronted with a truth that shattered the illusions of the past and revealed the hidden depths of her grandmother's existence. Little did she realise that behind the façade of a frail woman in need of care, Lissa bore the mantle of royalty and the responsibility of shaping Jorja's future with a legacy of power and magic long-lain dormant, waiting to be awoken. And when Jorja ventured off to school, unaware of the enchantments that unfolded in her absence. She would soon discover the extent of her grandmother's dual existence, forever changed by the revelation of her royal lineage and the legacy of magic that now flowed through her veins.

Lissa left the room again, her long, flowing gown swishing gently as she moved, an air of mystery surrounding her. When she returned, she had hold of an odd-looking crown that seemed to shimmer under the soft glow of the room's lights. The crown was a sight to behold, a stunning creation crafted from a dazzling blend of intricate gold and gemstones that glistened in hues unfamiliar to Jorja. It exuded an otherworldly elegance, a beauty that seemed out of place in their earthly surroundings - at its heart rested a magnificent purple jewel that radiated a mesmerising glow, casting a spell of awe over the room.

In her other hand, Lissa carried a glowing crystal necklace, its ethereal light dancing in delicate patterns that seemed to whisper secrets of distant realms. Placing the crystal delicately on the nearby sofa, just beyond Jorja's reach, Lissa's eyes held a knowing gaze as she spoke softly, her words weighted with a hint of destiny, "Jorja, you and I are not from here."

Jorja's world seemed to spin at the revelation, emotions swirling within her like a stormy sea. Overwhelmed, she rose from the sofa and fled to her room, tears streaming down her cheeks uncontrollably, her heart heavy with the weight of newfound truths.

Lissa observed with a blend of worry and determination, weighing the choice between pursuing Jorja or allowing her the solitude to come to terms with the newfound truths at her own pace. With a sorrowful heart, she opted for the latter, retreating to the kitchen where a profound silence enveloped the space.

As she prepared dinner using her magic, which seemed to infuse the room with warmth and comfort, Lissa could not shake the worry that gnawed at her. Had she crossed a line that should never have been breached? The line between truth and fiction blurred, leaving her questioning the wisdom of her actions. Yet, in the depths of her soul, she knew that the path chosen was the only one she could tread now.

An hour passed, each moment heavy with unspoken words and unresolved emotions. Tentatively, Lissa approached Jorja's door, her knuckles rap-tapping lightly against the weathered wood. "Dinner's ready, darling," she called out softly, the words reassuringly.

Only soft, rhythmic breathing greeted her ears from within the room, a lullaby of peace amid turmoil. Steeling herself, Lissa pushed the door open; the creak of old hinges was a melancholy reminder of the passage of time. As she entered the room, the scene before her tugged at her heartstrings – Jorja lay curled up on the bed, her tear streaked face peaceful in slumber.

Sitting beside her granddaughter, Lissa reached out and stroked her arm tenderly, the gesture a silent offering of solace amid upheaval. Leaning in close, she whispered, "Wake up, little one. It is time for dinner. I love you."

A murmur of affection slipped from Jorja's lips in her hazy, half-asleep state, a faint echo of love and trust in the darkness. "I love you too, Nanny," she murmured, the words a fragile bridge between their hearts.

As Jorja stirred awake, her eyes heavy with remnants of dreams half-forgotten, a sense of sorrow clung to her like a shadow. With a gentle effort, she lifted herself from the bed, feeling the burdens of existence press down upon her. The enticing scent of a beloved dish drifted in from the kitchen, its rich flavours intertwining to create a comforting and nostalgic allure that called her to rise.

The kitchen welcomed her with open arms, the scent of onions, garlic, herbs, and tomatoes swirling around her like a warm embrace. It felt like home, like safety, enveloping her senses in a cocoon of familiarity and love. The rich aroma filled her lungs, drawing her closer to the source of comfort and solace awaiting her.

Seated at the table, Jorja savoured two generous bowls of her grandmother's famous spaghetti Bolognese, each bite a symphony of flavours that danced on her tongue. The meal was a balm to her soul, a reminder of the enduring love that bound them together through these moments of joy and sorrow. With each mouthful, the heaviness in her heart eased, replaced by a sense of contentment that could only be found in the embrace of family, the warmth of a shared meal, and the enduring bond between a grandmother and granddaughter.

Her granddaughter's bold inquiry took Lissa aback: "Are my parents dead?" A heavy weight of uncertainty had long settled in her heart. With a tender embrace, she held Jorja close; her eyes reflected a mixture of tenderness and melancholy. In a soft voice, she began, "My dear child, the truth lies hidden within the mists of time, cloaking the fate of your parents in a perplexing enigma. The echoes of your childhood may not reveal the undeniable truth you seek.

Though I long to soothe your heart, the shroud of uncertainty looms large between us and the answers we desire."

With a sense of quiet resignation, Lissa settled into recounting the events of that fateful day, their memories hanging in the air like unspoken whispers of the past. The tale unfolded slowly, each word a bridge to a distant moment when the threads of fate had been woven with unfathomable complexity. As she wove together the tapestry of events from 12 years ago, a tapestry frayed by time and unanswered questions, Lissa's voice carried the weight of a long-held secret, a burden she had shouldered in the silence of her thoughts. And in that sacred shared history between grandmother and granddaughter, the past unfurled like a scroll of forgotten truths, beckoning them both to confront the shadows that lingered on the fringes of their understanding.

Grandmother looked up at the clock, astonished to see it was 8 pm; the hands of time seemed to be moving quickly as she delved into the memories she held close to her heart. With wide eyes brimming with curiosity, Jorja hung on to every word that fell from her grandmother's lips, the air crackling with a sense of magic and wonder. With a gentle smile displayed on her face, Lissa's presence exuded a sense of comfort and reassurance, enveloping Jorja in a warm embrace of love and understanding. As the aroma of freshly brewed tea wafted through the room, mingling with the sweet scent of the cake that materialised before them, the bond between grandmother and granddaughter grew more substantial, confirming the unbreakable connection transcending time and space.

Lissa watched as Jorja's eyes widened with curiosity, her young mind intrigued by the mysterious glowing crystal that Lissa held so protectively. The room seemed to hold its breath as Jorja tentatively asked, "Please tell me about that crystal, Nanny?" A pang of nostalgia tugged at Lissa's heart as she recalled the days of her youth, grappling with the weight of royal responsibility tied to the very object that now glistened in her hand.

Taking a deep breath, Lissa embarked on the tale, which had been passed down through generations of their royal lineage. She explained to Jorja that the crystal, radiant and pulsing with otherworldly energy, was more than just a pretty trinket - it was a vessel of life force, an ethereal link between the royal bloodline and the cosmic forces that shaped their destiny. As she spoke, the room seemed to shimmer with an otherworldly light, casting dancing shadows across the walls.

Lissa revealed the ancient tradition that bound the royal children to their respective crystals in a hushed tone laden with solemnity. Jorja listened intently as her grandmother explained that at the tender age of eleven, each royal child would be presented with their crystal, a pivotal moment that marked the threshold between innocence and obligation. With a steely gaze, Lissa warned Jorja of the gravity of the choice that lay before her - a choice that could alter the course of her life irrevocably. No one else can hold a person's crystal, as it disrupts the balance.

As the weight of Lissa's words settled upon the room, a palpable tension hung in the air, mingling with the faint scent of incense that always lingered in Lissa's home. Jorja's gaze flickered between the crystal and her grandmother, a storm of emotions brewing beneath the surface. Would she choose the path of royalty, with all its splendour and burden, or would she opt for the simplicity and freedom of a life unshackled from the expectations of the crown?

And so, amidst the flickering candlelight and the soft rustle of silk, the fate of a young princess hung in the balance, poised on the delicate precipice of choice. Lissa could only hope that her words had impressed upon Jorja the gravity of the decision that awaited her, guiding her with a steady hand as she navigated the intricate web of destiny that lay woven before her feet.

Lissa often found herself caught in a timeless dance with the clock, the minutes and hours passing by unbidden, unheeded until they demanded acknowledgement. On this particular night, as the clock's hands crept towards midnight, Lissa cast a fleeting glance at it, and with a declaration, she set the stage for the day's final act - bedtime. With a gentle hand, she ushered her granddaughter Jorja to her room, a promise of morning revelations hanging in the air like the faintest wisp of a dream.

As the night unfurled its cool embrace over Lissa's home, the matriarch sought solace within the sanctuary of her bed. The darkness did not bring with it the soothing balm of sleep but rather the sharp sting of contemplation. Her thoughts wandered through the corridors of possibility, pondering deeply the weight of responsibility that came with the knowledge she possessed. To train her granddaughter or not, this was the question that echoed through the chambers of her mind, reverberating with each passing moment.

Meanwhile, deep in the realm of dreams, Jorja grappled with the enigmatic tapestry woven by her subconscious. Strange and surreal images danced before her mind's eye, their meanings as elusive as shadows in the night. The visions that haunted her slumber were not of the comforting kind but rather a tangled web of unease that left her waking in a cold sweat, disoriented and unsettled.

CHAPTER TWO

With the first rays of dawn painting the sky in hues of pink and gold, Jorja's eyes fluttered open, her body heavy with the weight of restless sleep. She entered Lissa's room in a daze, seeking the familiar comfort that only a grandmother's embrace could provide. Clambering onto the bed with the ease of long practice, Jorja found herself enveloped in Lissa's arms, a warmth that banished the lingering chill of her nocturnal ordeal.

Under the covers, a playful moment unfolded as giggles and tickles filled the air, the bond between grandmother and granddaughter woven ever tighter with each shared laugh. Time slipped away unnoticed in the innocence of the moment until Lissa's glance at her phone shattered the peacefulness, revealing the lateness of the hour.

The reality of missed swimming lessons loomed ahead,

disrupting the day's schedule by the unhurried pace of their morning. Jorja's jest about Lissa's royal heritage sparked a playful exchange, their banter reflecting their unique bond. Despite the formality that protocol demanded, the affection between the two transcended titles and ranks, grounding them in the simple joy of companionship.

They put on their warm, cosy slippers, a perfect complement to the chilly morning that greeted them as they shuffled into the inviting warmth of the kitchen. Lissa, mindful of the early hours, decided to leave the kitchen blinds drawn, adding to the intimate atmosphere as she proceeded to work her culinary magic. With a flick of her wrist, she ignited the Aga, filling the room with a comforting glow that danced on the walls.

A feast fit for royalty soon greeted hungry appetites as Lissa effortlessly whipped up a hearty breakfast that included sizzling eggs, crispy bacon, succulent sausages, golden toast, and a steaming pot of flavourful tea. The fragrant aromas wafted through the air, tempting their taste buds and beckoning them to the table, where they eagerly savoured each delicious morsel until their hunger was fully sated.

Amidst the murmurs of contentment that lingered, Jorja, unable to bear the silence any longer, finally broke the tranquillity with a thoughtful inquiry. "So, I have a question," she began, her curiosity piqued. "Where did you learn to cook, Nanny?"

With a soft smile playing on her lips, Lissa's eyes glinted with memories of years past as she shared the origins of her culinary expertise. "I first delved into the world of cooking through enchanted cookbooks, experimenting with magical recipes when you were just a child," she explained. "Over time, as you grew older, I transitioned to mastering the art of cooking from scratch, honing my skills through years of practice and dedication."

As their conversation meandered into deeper territories, Jorja grappled with a weighty decision, torn between conflicting emotions. "Nanny, this is an impossible choice to make," she confessed, her voice tinged with uncertainty. "I feel conflicted, burdened by the weight of this decision."

With a gentle hand on Jorja's shoulder, Lissa offered words of wisdom and consolation. "Do not feel obligated, my dear. This decision is yours to make, a reflection of your true desires and aspirations," she reassured. "In these tumultuous times of war and unrest, it is important to consider the impact of your choice on the world around us. Remember, we once lived in peace and harmony, and that serenity can be restored if we choose wisely."

Deep conversations took place in the peaceful atmosphere of the warm kitchen, surrounded by the delicious smells of breakfast and the soft light from the Aga, creating a beautiful mix of love, advice, and reflection.

"Nanny, are dragons real, like in the stories you told me?" she asked, excitement bubbling in her chest, heart racing at the mere thought of coming face to face with a dragon. "Yes, but not as you would know them from TV. Our dragons, called DrakÔns, are kind and caring, much smaller in stature than the ferocious beasts seen in popular media, and possess the extraordinary ability to breathe ice and fire. They dwell in the secluded icy peaks of the mountains, utilising their fire breath to prepare their meals and stay warm amidst the frosty terrain. What sets our DrakÔns apart is their remarkable intellect and wisdom, enabling them to communicate in a sophisticated manner. I have been honoured to have numerous encounters with their esteemed King of the DrakÔns," she disclosed, adding a theatrical pause for emphasis before resuming her narrative.

"A few of these majestic creatures were unfortunate to be captured and subjected to dark enchantments that not only altered their physical form, making them larger, but also twisted their once gentle souls, turning them into malevolent beings, unlike the benevolent drakÔns we cherished. I had the great privilege of serving alongside a revered DrakÔn elder in my esteemed Cabinet of Officials, a group comprised of the most sagacious individuals and extraordinary beings like Erlend and Undines," she elaborated in response to Jorja's curious inquiry.

"Erlend? What exactly is an Erlend?" Jorja inquired, eyes widening with curiosity.

"Erlend is akin to the elegant elves depicted in conventional media, albeit much smaller in size - resembling our diminutive fairies - yet devoid of wings. Endowed with unmatched cleverness and formidable arcane abilities, they eclipse us in their command of sorcery. Our existence flourished in unity until the arrival of the catastrophic conflict." Lissa recounted, her voice tinged with melancholy remembrance.

"Oh, Nanny, this is utterly thrilling. My mind is brimming with many questions, whirling like a tempestuous storm. However, I find myself at a loss on where to embark on this fascinating journey of knowledge-seeking," Jorja expressed, her eagerness palpable. "Is Jorja even my name?"

"Yes, my dear, Jorja was your given name, consciously chosen and agreed upon by both your parents. It signifies attributes of sagacity and authority, though interestingly in our realm, but in this realm, its connotation of a farmer. Jorja signed and stated, "Personally, I am partial to the interpretation of our world, are you not?" Jorja exclaimed mirthfully, a light giggle escaping her lips. "Your naming ceremony transpired that very morning in the esteemed presence of The Cabinet of Officials, where a potent spell was cast to shroud your name from memory for the sake of security. Subsequently, they convened in the designated chamber to commence the creation of the mystical Portal," Lissa relayed with a sense of solemn importance.

Lissa thought deeply about the conversation with her granddaughter, Jorja. She pondered the implications of the mysterious man her grandmother had banished and exiled. The grim thought of imprisoning him within the mountain, guarded by drakÔns, weighed heavily on Lissa's mind. She knew the man was an Erlend of a malevolent nature. The fear that he might be able to disrupt their lives cast a shadow over their peaceful existence.

In considering ways to ensure Jorja's safety, Lissa entertained the idea of changing her granddaughter's name and relocating to a distant place. Despite the hopeful thought that it could shield Jorja, Lissa harboured doubts that such measures would be sufficient. The enchanting notion of a fresh start in a new location enticed her, especially given Jorja's growing involvement in her studies at their current abode. While Lissa nurtured a secret desire for Jorja not to start her education, she could not shake off the worry and apprehension about the looming decisions that her granddaughter might face.

Lissa suggested a bright outing to the beach the following day to ease their discussion's tension. Envisioning a day filled with sunshine and joy, she proposed a delightful plan to bask in the morning glow, savour a leisurely picnic, and revel in the sanctity of exploring the intriguing marine life around the rocky shores. Jorja's eager acceptance of the plan, brimming with excitement and enthusiasm, momentarily lifted Lissa's spirits. Observing her granddaughter's infectious zeal for the day ahead, Lissa could not help but wonder if the tranquillity and joy of Earth might lure Jorja away from the tumultuous dangers that loomed in their hidden realm.

And she hoped beyond hope that this would be the case.

By the afternoon, Lissa was utterly exhausted. The weight of the information she shared with Jorja had taken a considerable toll on her, especially following a restless sleep.

Standing tall and exuding confidence, Jorja declared, "Nanny, I have reached a decision. I aspire to be a princess. "Although a flicker of disappointment flashed across Lissa's face, she composed herself and replied, "If that is your heart's desire, dear one, then your journey of training and majestic knowledge must commence."

CHAPTER THREE

As the following day dawned, Jorja groggily made her way to the kitchen in the dim light. The previous evening had been spent aiding her grandmother in preparing meticulously for their beach outing. To Jorja's astonishment, she observed her grandmother effortlessly orchestrating tasks with an almost magical fluidity that left her awestruck.

Silently, they ventured to the awaiting car, Lissa maintaining her usual gait to preserve a semblance of normalcy in case they were observed. Exiting the driveway and embarking from Whitstone, Lissa straightened her posture and guided the car toward Widemouth Bay. After securing a parking spot for the day, they unpacked the car and settled in their customary position, nestled by the rocks on the far right. The tranquil morning unfolded undisturbed, with Lissa opting to utilise her magic to arrange their belongings efficiently while asserting a protective shield around them as a precaution.

In a matter of moments, a windbreaker, a tent, a barbecue, a fully set table, and a kettle materialised. Lissa put the kettle atop the barbecue to boil, preparing a pot of tea.

"Now, my dear, the time for your instruction has come," Lissa exclaimed, getting up and commencing a series of fluid, enigmatic movements that amalgamated yoga, Tai Chi, and Japanese dance elements. Jorja found herself chuckling, yet a stern look from her grandmother hinted at her need to rise and replicate the motions.

Amidst laughter and a few tumbles, Jorja attempted to mirror Lissa's graceful actions, gradually gaining familiarity with the art form, ' Telm, a martial discipline.

By 06:30, hunger beckoned them back to the barbecue for breakfast. While Lissa rustled up the morning meal, Jorja busied herself, laying out the table and preparing tea. Engaged in hearty conversation about royal decorum and mannerisms, Lissa noticed a passerby accompanied by a dog. With a friendly wave exchanged, the trio acknowledged each other momentarily.

As breakfast drew to a close, their conversation continued unabated. Noticing the dog walker approaching, Lissa employed a loud cough to steer the topic away. "Jorja, would you prefer to explore the rock pools this morning or in the afternoon?" she inquired, casting a firm, though well-intentioned, elbow nudge at Jorja to redirect her focus.

"Hey there, good morning! It looks like it will be another beautiful day," the woman said. "Absolutely! That is why we arrived early to catch the sunrise," Lissa replied. "You did get here early! I woke up at 06:00, and you were already set up. I thought you might have camped out here. I took Barny for a walk around 22:00 last night, and the beach was empty then. You must have been here super early to get everything ready," the woman commented. "We rolled in at 04:00. These new-age tents are a breeze; you pull them out of the bag, and they pop up. Super easy, plus my strong granddaughter helped me out," Lissa said, even though Jorja had not lifted much. "Yeah, I helped set it up. We are pros at this now," Jorja fibbed. Lissa felt a strange familiarity with the woman but shook it off.

"Isn't it sweet to see a young girl helping her grandma? I wish mine had done that. Anyway, enjoy your day! Do not forget the sunscreen; it is promised to be a scorcher," the woman laughed. "We have already put some on, thanks! Have a great day," Lissa replied.

The woman walked away, calling for Barny. Lissa thought rock pooling would be a good way to avoid unwanted attention. She cast a protection spell around their stuff and headed towards the rocks with Jorja. Lissa stayed on high alert; something about the woman felt off, assuring that there was always a shield around them. She did not like the feeling she got from the woman.

During their rock pooling and climb to the top of the small cliff, they engaged in lively discourse about royal etiquette and mannerisms, which continued without interruption.

After their climb, they returned to the tent feeling victorious and hungry, eager to refuel with a satisfying meal. Being thoughtful and organised, Lissa packed pre-made sandwiches in the cool box, a welcome treat that Jorja wasted no time retrieving. At the same time, Lissa busied herself preparing more of their favourite tea. Lissa had grown fond of the drink during their excursions and had even taken to the notion of taking some back home to Enrac with her, a comforting reminder of their adventures. She made a mental note to purchase some plants and seeds to return to Enrac.

Savouring their lunch amid the beach's serene backdrop, they relished the meal and the camaraderie it represented, a shared moment that solidified their bond. With a sense of contentment lingering in the air, they tidied up after themselves, leaving no trace behind as a mark of respect for their cherished environment. Eager to cool off and embrace the refreshing embrace of the sea, they made their way to the water's edge, where the contrast between the scorching sun and the icy Atlantic Ocean offered an invigorating sharpening of their senses. Though Lissa found the sudden chill bracing, Jorja revelled in the sensation, savouring the vitality it brought.

As they swam, thoughts meandered through Jorja's mind, her musings ranging from the practicalities of her training to whimsical notions of magical shortcuts for building muscle. Despite the fanciful idea, she recognised the merit of swimming as a form of exercise, which she genuinely enjoyed. However, a shadow of concern crept into her mind as she pondered the delicate balance between her aspirations and the responsibilities that awaited her beyond the shore. The weight of decisions to come tugged at her heart, prompting thoughts of her dear friends Megan and Millie and the challenges of sustaining those connections amidst a changing landscape.

With conflicted emotions swirling, Jorja hurried back to the tent, seeking solace in the familiar space. Sensing her distress, Lissa's nurturing instincts kicked in, prompting her to offer a comforting presence to her granddaughter. Wrapping Jorja in a reassuring embrace, Lissa gently inquired about the source of her troubles, unravelling the tangle of emotions that threatened to overwhelm the young girl. Jorja's tearful admission about their imminent move and the prospect of parting ways with her friends struck a chord with Lissa, propelling her to reassure the girl with a blend of pragmatism and compassion.

Amidst the backdrop of a bustling beach, Lissa's protective instincts sharpened as she discreetly wove protective spells around their sanctuary, shielding it from prying eyes and unwanted attention. In a moment of vulnerability and trust, Lissa laid out a plan that balanced Jorja's desires with the necessary sacrifices, setting in motion the delicate dance of secrecy and security that would guide their future endeavours. With cautious optimism, Jorja embraced this newfound understanding, pledging to uphold the façade, which allowed her to maintain her connections without endangering her beloved friends.

As the evening sun cast a golden glow over their interactions, Lissa and Jorja found moments of levity amidst the weight of their situation, sharing laughter and light-hearted banter that temporarily lifted the burden of their clandestine dealings. Looking ahead to the next training phase, Lissa unveiled plans for their journey to the Brecon Beacons, a prospect that Jorja found exciting, with a mix of anticipation and trepidation. Despite the looming challenges and uncertainties, the bond between grandmother and granddaughter remained steadfast, offering respite and reassurance in the face of an uncertain future.

On their journey home, they paused in Bude to procure climbing gear for their upcoming adventure in Wales. Lissa deeply admired this place, particularly the stunning sunsets that painted the sky from the hills overlooking the coast. Countless times, while Jorja was occupied at school, Lissa had sought refuge here, yearning to connect with the beauty of nature.

Bude was always a guarantee of finding what you wanted. Being a pretty picturesque Cornish town, Bude was large enough to provide many shops and sports facilities. A surfing hotspot with vintage-style beach huts added to its charm. Despite its popularity, Bude's beauty remained in its small size, retaining its Cornish allure. After purchasing all the required equipment, they headed home.

During the rest of the day, they laughed as they connected. Jorja was frequently curious about her training, balancing her interest between magic and royal training. Lissa understood the importance of both, especially the need for the royal training to engage Jorja in acquiring the necessary skills. Communication was an area that needed development for Jorja, a task Lissa nurtured.

The evening progressed smoothly as Jorja excused herself early to catch up with her friends, Megan and Millie, through a video call. Eavesdropping, Lissa hoped Jorja would not blurt out anything better left unsaid to her friends. Lissa traditionally prepared their evening meal in the kitchen, enjoying the rhythmic cooking process. She created a cosy atmosphere by cutting carrots and potatoes and boiling them.

After Jorja's call, she entered the kitchen, excitedly announcing the finalised plans for Sunday upon their return from camping at the Brecon Beacons. They were organising a day together, with their moms dropping off. Megan and Millie were excited by Jorja's ideas, which enhanced their upcoming quality time together.

When Jorja returned to her bedroom, Lissa could hear Jorja in her room flipping the pages of a book every so often, so Lissa decided to brew a pot of delicious tea. As she brought a warm cup of tea to Jorja, Jorja was lying cosily on her bed, engrossed in a captivating book, her blue laptop open beside her. The screen displayed a video on martial arts training, a verification of her dedication and focus. Proud of her granddaughter's curiosity and willingness to explore new things, Lissa could not help but smile fondly.

Upon sharing her thoughts on meditation and the importance of mental clarity, Jorja sought advice from her wise grandmother on incorporating swimming into her regular exercise routine. Ever the guiding figure, Lissa emphasised the need for holistic muscle strength and praised the benefits of a clear mind through meditation for facing challenges ahead. Jorja, appreciative of her grandmother's wisdom and support, beamed back at Lissa with gratitude before continuing her research.

As Lissa pondered the upcoming adventure to teach her granddaughter in the secluded beauty of the Brecon Beacons, she found herself contemplating a way to ensure Jorja's crystal remained safe. After dinner preparations, an idea struck her to conceal the precious crystal, currently stored in the darkest part of the shed under a heap of garden equipment and bits, under the protective cover of the garden. Opting for a discreet spot beneath the potato plants. Satisfied with her plan, Lissa relished the calm of cooking, a therapeutic activity that allowed her mind to wander freely.

After their evening chores were done, Lissa and Jorja packed essentials for their upcoming camping trip. While Lissa meticulously organised supplies, Jorja enthusiastically sorted clothes and waterproof gear for the adventure awaiting them in the Brecon Beacons. Jorja was excited as she envisioned the endless possibilities of exploring an unfamiliar setting. She also eagerly anticipated the arrival of her closest friends for a fun-filled reunion after their outdoor escapade.

Under the cloak of night, when Jorja was deeply asleep, Lissa stealthily carried out her plan to safeguard the crystal. With utmost care, Lissa sourced the crystal from the shed; she concealed the precious item within a waterproof bag in a secret spot amidst the potato plants, ensuring its protection without arousing suspicion. Pleased with her discreet actions, Lissa returned indoors feeling tired and contented.

Though racked with a moment of doubt regarding the depth of Jorja's understanding, Lissa eventually drifted into a peaceful slumber, finding solace in the tranquil rhythm of her newfound way of life on this planet. As she rested, thoughts of the shared experiences with her granddaughter filled her dreams, creating a sense of warmth and joy that enveloped her in a serene sleep, marking the end of a fulfilling day and the beginning of a hopeful tomorrow.

CHAPTER FOUR

Not a single soul was around when they arrived at the remote spot in the wilderness of the Brecon Beacons after a very long drive. Lissa took the extra precaution of standing for a considerable amount of time, meticulously scanning the vast horizon as she projected her magical energy in hopes of connecting with other mystical beings or individuals in the vicinity.

Once Lissa had fully assured herself that no one was in the vicinity, she effortlessly utilised her magic to assemble the colossal thirty-one-foot yurt, resembling a grand golf ball amid the serene landscape. Inside the yurt, she meticulously set up two fold-up beds complete with cosy sleeping bags, a welcoming lounge area, and an inviting dining space. Lissa cast a protective boundary spell around the camp to further fortify their safety before she and Jorja embarked on a brief hike back along the gravel road to retrieve their supplies from the car, including essential food provisions and a compact camping stove.

Using her magic to carry the items, leaving Jorja to carry her rucksack of clothes. Thankfully, the camping stove was lightweight and conveniently stored in its backpack-style carry case, making it effortless for them to transport their belongings. Before their departure, they had meticulously packed only the essential items, ensuring their load remained manageable and not overwhelmingly heavy. Their journey had commenced early in the day to avoid the congested traffic near Bristol, with only a brief mid-morning break for a light snack being their sole sustenance since their early breakfast.

Upon their return to the yurt, Jorja took charge of setting up the cooking tent. At the same time, Lissa skilfully brewed a comforting cup of tea for them and prepared a delightful meal comprising sandwiches and generous portions of fruit cake. Opting for an outdoor dining experience, Jorja swiftly arranged the chairs and portable table beneath the cool shade cast by the yurt, creating a perfect setting for their relaxing meal amidst nature's beauty.

After their satisfying feast, they mutually agreed to dedicate the remainder of the afternoon to Telm Training, with Lissa gently guiding Jorja through precise movements at a deliberate, unhurried pace. Witnessing her granddaughter's remarkable aptitude for Telm filled Lissa with immense pride, motivating her to emphasise the importance of daily meditation to Jorja for her continued progress. Given the lateness of the hour and their accumulating fatigue, they concluded their training after a condensed two-hour session before preparing, eating and enjoying their meal; they tidied as the day gradually ended.

Lissa, enchanted by the mystical allure of the Legend of Llyn y Fan Fach Lake, made a thoughtful decision to share the captivating tale with Jorja, eager to immerse her granddaughter in the rich folklore and magical essence that surrounded this ancient place. As the sun's rays danced upon the shimmering surface of the lake, Lissa's voice was filled with passion and reverence as she narrated the ancient story, weaving a tapestry of enchantment that captured Jorja's imagination and transported her to a realm where myths and reality intertwined harmoniously. With each word that resonated through the air, the bond between the two deepened, united by the shared experience of delving into a world where legends breathed life into the very essence of nature itself.

"According to one version of the legend, a boy would graze his sheep and cattle around the local lake of Llyn y Fan Fach, which is situated in the Brecon Beacons National Park. He would spend the long hours of the day gazing into the waters of the lake and daydreaming. The boy had been born on the day the first spring flowers opened their petals in the mountains."

"When he became old enough, he was awarded the task of tending the sheep and cattle; he had to take the animals to graze up by Llyn y Fan Fach. He spent many of the years of his boyhood by the lake, reaching an age when he was ready for marriage. As you can see, it is an old love story; I researched it last night when I couldn't sleep," she informed Jorja.

"Now, one day, as a young man gazed dreamily into the cold, clear waters of the lake, he was amazed to see the form of a most beautiful woman slowly walk out of the water towards him. He had never seen anyone so lovely in his life before, and he stood dumbstruck as she moved gracefully out of the water towards him. As their eyes met, he instantly fell in love with her."

"Whether she was a fairy or one of the goddesses of old, he did not know, but she must have been one, or the other, or some other kind of supernatural being. It did not matter to him. He was absolutely love-struck and under her spell. She seemed to be a fountain of wisdom and knowledge and had mystical and extraordinary powers. She presented him with the future she saw for him, explaining that he would become wealthy and respected if he accepted her proposition that the two of them be married."

"The young man was besotted and would have done anything she asked anyway, without the rewards of wealth and respect, so he readily agreed. However, certain conditions had to be followed if they were to be married. The first condition was that he must never strike her three times. The second was that he must keep secret where she had come from and never reveal to anyone the supernatural source of their relationship and good fortune. The young man readily agreed to these conditions. It proved difficult to explain her sudden appearance and their marriage to the small, close-knit Welsh community of Myddfai. Nevertheless, he managed to allay local curiosity, and the couple married."

"After the wedding, the young man's sheep and cattle grew fatter and healthier, and many lambs and calves swelled the numbers and value of his livestock, with exceptional rams and bulls being produced. His livestock increased in market value, and his rams and bulls were in demand for breeding."

"He became good at negotiating the best prices for his animals at the market, becoming a widely respected breeder and successful dealer. Soon, he had his own farm. He began to make small profits, which he invested wisely in buying and renting land out. He branched into horse breeding and gained a reputation as a good and honest businessman who was respected far and wide. Soon, whatever he turned his hand to prospered. He was a friend of many, and his advice was widely sought after by the whole local community, which prospered through his business enterprises."
"Throughout the passage of time, his devoted wife remained a steadfast presence, managing their home with grace. Together, they were blessed with three handsome sons, and she was ever by his side, offering unwavering support. Their love for one another was palpable, a bond that radiated warmth. However, as the young man's

fortune flourished, he occasionally succumbed to arrogance, neglecting old friends and forsaking some of his cherished promises and principles. This shift in demeanour led to a decline in the trust others placed in him, resulting in missed opportunities and dwindling profits, igniting a simmering anger within him."

"One day, his wife went to meet him at the market, but he was angry because the business had not gone the way he wanted. As he seemed upset, she asked what the matter was, thinking it would help him to talk about it. To his shame, he struck her. It was not hard, but he struck her. With great dignity, his wife reminded him of the most important conditions of their marriage. Full of shame, he begged her forgiveness and promised never to do such a thing again. His wife embraced him with the warmth of forgiveness, her heart choosing love over betrayal. But fate tested her resolve once more. He vowed it would never happen again - yet it did. And once more, she forgave him with a quiet strength only the truly devoted possess. To his eternal shame, it happened a third time, but this time, his wife stood up straight and looked him in the eye and told him the marriage was now over."

"She immediately turned her back on him and walked back to the lake, with him desperately trying to catch her. As she walked through their farm, she called all the animals by name and all the sheep, cows, ducks, chickens, and other farm animals followed her as she made her way to the lake. No matter how fast he ran, he could not catch her and his cries for forgiveness echoed off the mountains, but she never turned and said another word. When she reached the lake, she strode gracefully into the water without turning back, with all the farm animals following her into the lake. Her distraught husband and sons were left weeping on the lake's edge, their cries of anguish ringing across the empty mountains."

"Her husband was devastated and spent the rest of his life in regret and remorse. The loss of his animals ruined his farm and business, and all his luck had gone. And he lived the rest of his life in despair, pining for his wife. His three sons stayed with him and looked after him as best they could. Sometimes, the boys would wander around the lake to search and call for their mother. One day, she appeared from the lake and taught them the arts of medicine and herbalism. She told them they would be great healers who would teach the arts of the physician and the herbalist to humans, and they would become known as the Physicians of Myddfai. The End," Lissa said.

As the evening sky painted a canvas of deep hues, Lissa's storytelling prowess illuminated the hearts of her listeners, igniting a spark of curiosity and awe that lingered long after the last echoes of her words faded into the tranquil night. At that moment, beneath the starlit sky, the power of storytelling intertwined their souls, connecting them to the eternal wisdom and magic that dwelled within the whispering waters of Llyn y Fan Fach Lake, forging a bond that would endure through time and tide. Lissa nodded to her granddaughter to get ready for bed.

CHAPTER FIVE

Jorja had woken up with a sense of tranquillity from the clear mountain air enveloping them. She stretched her arms lazily, savouring the morning's peace before the buzz of daily activities began. The soft light filtering through the fabric of the yurt hinted at the promise of a new day.

Jorja tiptoed around the camp, treading lightly as if not to disrupt the calmness that still lingered in the air. The first order of business was lighting the stove, a simple task that nevertheless felt important in their daily routine. She traversed the familiar path to the Lake with practised efficiency, a brief yet refreshing journey connecting her to the Earth's bountiful embrace.

Upon returning to the camp, Jorja began preparing breakfast. The sizzling sound of bacon and sausages filled the yurt and mingled with the promising aroma of freshly brewed tea. As the kettle hummed with readiness, she returned to the yurt to rouse her sleeping grandmother. As she greeted Lissa with fondness and teasing in her voice, she reflected on their deep bond. "Wake up, sleepyhead," Jorja giggled.

Lissa, stirred from her slumber by Jorja's cheerful demeanour, felt a rush of gratitude for the simple joys of this secluded place they had chosen. Accepting the proffered mug of tea with a warm smile, she marvelled at her granddaughter's self-sufficiency, an acknowledgement of the skills she had instilled in her over the years.

The sight of a prepared breakfast table filled with hearty dishes spoke volumes of Jorja's care and dedication.

Together, they sat down to enjoy the morning meal, the flavours mingling with the laughter and memories that floated between them. Lissa's heart swelled with pride as she watched Jorja take charge of the morning chores, a glimpse of the strong, independent woman she was becoming. After breakfast, Lissa embarked on the soon-to-be ritual of fetching water from the lake.

At the water's edge, Lissa shed the trappings of night, embracing the coolness of the lake as a baptism of sorts. The shock of the frigid water jolted her senses awake, a sharp contrast to the warmth of the morning sun that caressed her skin upon emerging. With a sense of invigoration, she filled the bowl and returned to the camp, the glistening droplets of water clinging to her like a cloak of renewal.

Meanwhile, Jorja focused on heating water for washing, and her movements were quick and steady. The hiss of the boiling water mingled with the rustling of nature awakening around them, a symphony of the morning sounds that filled the yurt with a sense of bustling activity. The warm water was distributed, and Jorja and Lissa entered their separate quarters to wash and dress for the day ahead.

Today, on a beautiful morning, Lissa proposed to Jorja the idea of embarking on a challenging adventure up the southern slopes, followed by a delightful lunch at the peak. Excited by the prospect of the scenic hike, Jorja eagerly agreed, anticipating a fun-filled day ahead. However, Lissa could not help but chuckle inwardly as she highlighted to her granddaughter that the excursion was more about strenuous physical exercise and not at all for fun, knowing full well that this might be quite the challenge for Jorja.

Their journey was filled with captivating moments as they strolled by a charming little tarn and marvelled at the breathtaking close-up vistas of the mountains that Jorja skilfully captured with her phone.

As they continued their path, they eventually encountered a junction and decisively veered towards the lake, Llyn y Fan Fach. This picturesque glacial lake, which Lissa believed indeed revealed its splendour from an elevated vantage point, despite the water not quite reaching the edges, added a unique charm to the landscape.

After several hours of trekking, the duo reached their destination and settled for a well-deserved lunch break at the summit. Observing her grandmother catching her breath, Jorja eagerly took charge, serving up the meal and refreshments, suggesting her growing knowledge of Telm Training skills as a form of relaxation for Lissa.

Grateful for the pause and feeling worn out, Lissa joyfully watched her granddaughter execute the intricate Telm manoeuvres, reminiscing about her experiences with the practice. Witnessing Jorja effortlessly recall and perform the routine filled Lissa with immense pride.

"Perfect, darling; I am amazed you have remembered so much," Lissa expressed, her eyes filled with pride. "Now you have mastered the last of the moves. We must make some changes now that you have gotten to grips with it well enough. It will be necessary for you to make the moves smaller in scale and to tighten your muscles as you transition between poses. Effectively, the key is you must imagine that holding a sword will be part of your performance," she explained reassuringly.

The breathtaking views of the landscape were nothing short of astonishing. They encompassed two mesmerising glacial lakes, endless stretches of majestic ridge lines, and awe-inspiring mountain vistas. Subsequently, they made their way to the second lake along the trail, which exceeded all expectations in terms of beauty. Serene, secluded and adorned with pristine, crystal-clear waters, it offered a truly enchanting sight.

Under the scorching midday sun, Jorja could feel sweat running down her brow, prompting her to suggest a retreat to camp for some respite from the heat. The descent back was via a narrower and less groomed pathway, which was particularly challenging for Jorja. It became evident that descending was far more demanding than ascending; with a few slips along the way, she managed to maintain her balance, gradually comprehending the essence of physical exertion her grandmother had emphasised.

Experiencing only one slip herself, Lissa passed on a valuable tip to her granddaughter, advising, "Jorja, engage your core muscles to prevent slipping." Heeding her instructions, Jorja tightened her core, intensifying the workout but making walking easier. Upon reaching the yurt, they swiftly changed into their swimsuits, heading to the lake to cool off and indulge in fun aquatic activities. Jorja revelled in the invigorating swim and the refreshing waters, while Lissa found it a tad too chilly and soon retired to the shore.

"Royal Training begins now," Lissa proclaimed. Jorja, upon emerging revitalised from the lake. Guiding Jorja through the postures and movements expected of a princess, Lissa was met with laughter from her granddaughter. "Though it may seem amusing,

Jorja, this is serious business. You must embody royalty in every aspect of your demeanour - walking, talking, sitting, eating, and greeting," Lissa emphasised, a hint of exasperation evident in her voice.

Jorja observed her grandmother closely and attempted to replicate Lissa's posture and gait. As Lissa observed from her portable seat, Jorja continued to practice; together, they shared moments of light-hearted laughter amidst the seriousness of their training session. Eventually, overwhelmed with amusement, Jorja collapsed onto the floor in a fit of giggles, prompting Lissa to suggest a change in the training regimen.

"You need to channel your focus, dear; concentrate on the spoon - its form, material, and weight. Now, envision it as light as a feather. Excellent. Now, lift it," Lissa instructed. The spoon suddenly soared two meters into the air, to their mutual surprise, before clattering back down to the ground.

"Perfect, Jorja, but this time, I want you to lift it and hold it in the air, bringing it down and placing it gently on the table," Lissa instructed with a tone that carried a subtle mix of challenge and encouragement. With her eyes sparkling with determination, Jorja diligently adhered to Lissa's guidance, ensuring the spoon landed with a feather-like touch as instructed.

"Now let's try something bigger," Lissa suggested, noticing the gleam of excitement in Jorja's eyes. The contrast between the rigid Royal Training and this hands-on lesson was palpable, and Jorja was revelling in this new form of learning.

"Okay, hunni, I want you to lift the saucepan, hold it still for the count of 10, and then gently place it back down again," Lissa elaborated, her voice filled with affection and authority. Eager to prove herself, Jorja accepted the challenge with an enthusiastic nod.

"Okay, Nanny, I'll try," Jorja responded earnestly, her determination shining through. However, fatigue began creeping in, making the seemingly simple task of lifting the saucepan, with her mind, more arduous for the young girl.

"I can't hold it. It is too heavy," Jorja confessed, the clang of the falling saucepan echoing through the room. "Aaarrgghh, I'm so sorry, Nanny, but it was so heavy," she apologised sheepishly, a hint of disappointment in her voice.

"Ah... that is because you forgot to make it weigh like a feather" Lissa chuckled, her eyes twinkling with amusement and wisdom. Jorja, learning from her mistake, took a deep breath and prepared to try again, her determination renewed.

With unwavering focus, Jorja lifted the saucepan off the floor, held it steady with her grandmother counting to ten, gracefully spun it in the air, and placed it back on the table with a newfound confidence. "Did you see that, Nan? I did it! I did it!" Jorja exclaimed, her face beaming with pride and accomplishment.

"Very good, honey, nicely done," Lissa praised, her heart swelling with pride at her granddaughter's progress and resilience. "Nanny, can you show me something else?" Jorja pleaded eagerly, her thirst for knowledge evident in her wide eyes.

"No, dear, we have to be perfect in one thing before we can move on," Lissa gently reminded, reinforcing the importance of mastering the basics before venturing into new challenges.

The day had taken its toll on Jorja and her grandmother, leaving them exhausted as they sat silently to eat before heading to bed. The day's weight hung heavy in the air as they lay in bed, reflecting on their challenges and tasks. Slowly, the exhaustion gave way to the embrace of sleep, their thoughts fading away as they slipped into a restful slumber devoid of dreams.

As the sun rose the next day, it mirrored the routines of the day before, beginning with a hike up the slope and continuing with hours dedicated to Telm, royal and magical training. Jorja observed with growing concern the toll that the intense training was taking on her grandmother, her worry deepening as she noticed the strain on her health. Meanwhile, she felt a burgeoning sense of strength and self awareness within herself, and the natural world around her seemed to come alive in a symphony of wildlife, which sounds more vibrant than ever before. It was as if the creatures of the area had taken a particular interest in her, their melodies harmonising with her thoughts like tiny birds perched on her shoulder, filling her with a sense of connection to the world around her.

Amid the enchanting sounds of nature, Jorja's concern for her grandmother weighed heavily on her mind, prompting her to ponder deeply on how she could offer support and assistance. She was determined to find a way to alleviate her grandmother's burdens and contribute positively to her well-being. As the evening stretched on and the sky dimmed, Jorja's thoughts remained fixed on this critical task, her determination building until she finally settled her mind on a plan of action that she hoped would provide comfort and relief to her beloved grandmother.

Lissa had begun to feel as she used to on Enrac, where the air was crisp and invigorating, filling her with a newfound energy that seemed to wash away the weariness she had carried for so long. With each step, the training she had embraced with determination proved to be a transformative experience, gradually revitalising her body and spirit. This sense of renewal spurred her to encourage her granddaughter, Jorja, to embark on a more challenging path up the slope that day, one that would test their physical capabilities and strengthen their bond even further.

CHAPTER SIX

The next day, Lissa's rigorous training regimen was not merely a means to physical fitness but a reclamation of her inner strength and resilience. As she guided Jorja through the process of donning the climbing equipment, Lissa couldn't help but feel a surge of pride in passing down her knowledge and skills to the next generation. With each harness adjustment and knot secured on the guide ropes, she prepared Jorja for the ascent and instilled a sense of self-reliance and determination.

Despite Jorja's initial apprehension about her grandmother's ability to undertake the challenging climb, Lissa's steely resolve and unwavering confidence in her capabilities shone through. She knew that her transformation was physical and mental as she shed the limitations of the past twelve years and embraced the strength and agility that lay dormant within her. Her newfound sense of empowerment radiated with each step taken up the sheer rock face.

As they navigated the steep ascent, with Lissa leading the way with practised ease, she took the opportunity to impart vital and valuable lessons to Jorja in the form and art of mountain climbing. Drawing on her experiences from Enrac, where climbing was a way of life rather than a recreational pursuit, Lissa shared the wisdom of generations past with her granddaughter, instilling the importance of perseverance and adaptability in the face of adversity. The absence of modern conveniences on Enrac. This fostered a sense of self reliance and communal unity, values that formed the bedrock of their society.

Initially daunted by the challenge before her, Jorja soon found herself grappling with the physical demands of the climb. Despite Lissa's guidance on the proper footholds and hand placements, Jorja's inexperience led to moments of uncertainty and struggle. Each slip and misstep served as a reminder of the arduous journey ahead, but with Lissa's unwavering support and encouragement, Jorja found the strength to persevere. The sight of her granddaughter clinging determinedly to the rocks, her resolve unshaken by setbacks, filled Lissa with a sense of pride and joy that transcended the physical exertion of the climb.

As they reached the summit, a sense of accomplishment washed over the duo, mingling with the refreshing breeze sweeping the rocky terrain. Pausing to catch their breath and quench their thirst, Lissa and Jorja shared a moment of quiet reflection, revelling in the bond forged through their shared triumph. The journey up the rock face had been more than a physical feat; it had been a testament to their resilience, determination, and unwavering belief in each other. And as they sat atop the slope, gazing out at the vast expanse before them, they knew their shared adventures had only just begun.

After both enjoyed a hearty lunch, Lissa carefully prepared for the next challenge by attaching a single rope to three secure clips, fastening them firmly to the crag. She exhibited extreme meticulousness and attention to detail as she repeated the process a second time, ensuring the safety of each participant. She affixed one end of the rope with precision and expertise to herself, deftly tossing the remaining length over the precipice until it gracefully reached the ground below. Turning towards Jorja, she took a moment to explain the importance of safety measures by connecting her granddaughter securely to the rope. To further enhance the safety protocols in place, Lissa skilfully attached a French prusik knot onto each rope beneath the abseil device, clipping it securely onto the designated leg loop of her harness. In a masterful display of expertise and precision, Jorja deftly coiled the remaining length of rope in her hands before confidently tossing it over the edge, ready for her descent.

With patience and care, Lissa demonstrated to Jorja the essential mechanics of the safety apparatus, emphasising that the prusik served as a reliable failsafe in case of any mishap during the descent. Step by step, she showcased the proper technique for leaning back over the edge, ensuring a controlled and secure descent down the rugged face of the cliff. Jorja, captivated by the thrill and excitement of the descent, eagerly followed Lissa's instructions with determination and exhilaration. In no time, she descended gracefully and swiftly down the face of the rocky cliff, savouring every moment of the exhilarating adventure.

Jorja approached her grandmother, beaming with pride as she shared her preference for the gradual descent. Lissa, her face lit up with amusement, let out a soft chuckle in response, acknowledging Jorja's statement with a knowing smile. Jorja then went for a thrilling swim. Observing Jorja's increased appetite over the past few days, Lissa recognised a positive sign of her granddaughter's exertion, indicating a need to rebuild her energy reserves. This change was vital for replenishing her strength and hinted at the subtle muscle growth on Jorja's otherwise slender frame.

As they both prepared for a swim in the lake, exchanging their clothes for swimsuits, a sense of shared excitement filled the air.

Playfully splashing water at each other, Jorja and Lissa revelled in the moment's joy before the young girl embarked on a challenging goal. Striving to conquer the length of the lake and back,

Jorja displayed determination and resilience, even though she had not yet achieved her desired objective. Witnessing Jorja's swift progress as she effortlessly reached the opposite shore, Lissa admired her granddaughter's improving fitness levels, silently applauding her efforts.

Upon her return journey, Jorja adopted a slower pace, gracefully mastering the breaststroke technique. Eager and enthusiastic, she eagerly sought her beloved grandmother's approval as she proudly announced her accomplishment of reaching the lake's opposite end. Lissa's heart filled with pride, and she praised Jorja's achievement, acknowledging her physical progress. In gentle reassurance, she commended Jorja's increased strength, hinting at the positive impact of building muscle on her wellbeing. With a tender smile, Lissa lovingly embraced her growing granddaughter, acknowledging her perseverance and determination on this journey of self-improvement.

After spending two intensive hours at Telm Training, Jorja and her grandmother gracefully transitioned to Royal Training, where Lissa, with her gentle guidance, imparted a valuable lesson to her granddaughter on transitioning smoothly from sitting to standing in one fluid movement. However, Royal Training was not Jorja's preferred task; she approached it with unwavering enthusiasm, recognising the immense growth she had experienced throughout the week.

Lissa announced an end to the day's lessons before dinner, insisting that Jorja, the young girl from a quaint village in Cornwall, continue her training with the elegance and sophistication befitting a member of the royal family of Enrac. Every action and movement were to reflect grace and poise, embodying the refinement of royalty in every gesture.

Post-dinner, the duo delved into the enchanting realm of Magic Training, where Jorja's progress from moving a mere saucepan to effortlessly handling a rock showcased her rapid advancement. Witnessing Jorja's evolution, Lissa marvelled at the swift pace of her granddaughter's development, recognising the remarkable potential within her.

CHAPTER SEVEN

Friday began just like the day before, with the challenging ascent up the crag; however, this time, they managed to reach the top much faster, a clear indication of their improvements and physical stamina. Lissa could not help but marvel at her granddaughter's progress, her physical endurance and her overall perspective on the unexpected events they found themselves in. Whilst at the top, Lissa showed Jorja a cave, and they explored it for a time. It had a damp, musty smell but went deep into the rockface.

Before their departure, Lissa took a moment to check her mobile phone for any missed calls or messages, eventually dialling the school's number to leave a carefully crafted explanation for Jorja's extended absence. The narrative she chose to stick with was that of a lottery win, suggesting that she was now in a better financial position to provide Jorja with the highest quality education available. Deep down, Lissa experienced a pang of guilt, fully aware that Jorja had already received an exceptional education at Launceston College. After expressing her gratitude to the school's principal, Mr. Bradley, through the voicemail, Lissa couldn't shake off the shame within her for resorting to such deceptive measures.

Using her mobile phone, she placed a food order for the day after their return, which included a variety of dishes to cater to all their tastes and preferences. She was amazed to get a phone signal whilst in the Brecon's stunning landscape, surrounded by the rugged beauty of nature. She glanced at her surroundings and realised she needed to enlist someone's help with Jorja's training, feeling slightly uncertain about who to approach.

'What about Megan or Millie?' she thought before dismissing it. She pondered that perhaps the girls would probably have more fun than concentrating on training.

When they descended the steep crag and reached the refreshing waters below, they swam again, relishing the cool water's tranquillity. Today marked a milestone as Jorja managed to execute the front crawl all the way to the other end and back again, showcasing her growing strength and endurance. With every stroke, she could feel herself getting fitter and holding herself with more confidence and grace.

As they dried off in the warm sun's rays and returned to the yurt, they immediately dove into the Telm Training, the routine that had become a comforting anchor during their days. This was followed by the Royal Training, a regimen that demanded consistency and discipline, pushing Jorja to maintain her focus and dedication throughout the day.

Preparing dinner of jacket potatoes with cheese and beans, the aroma filled the air as they ate heartily, savouring each bite. Reflecting on past meals, Jorja recalled how she would have settled for just that dish, but now she had a pork chop and a plateful of fresh salad and thought she must be getting fitter to require more food.

Magic Training beckoned next, bringing a new challenge for Jorja to conquer. "OK, now I want you to lift something trickier. When you lift this, you have to be careful not to hurt it," her grandmother instructed with a twinkle in her eye, knowing the apprehension that lingered within Jorja's heart.

"What am I lifting, Nanny?" Jorja inquired politely, her curiosity piqued as she tried to anticipate the task ahead. Lissa chuckled softly, revealing the surprising challenge – "I want you to lift me," she announced with humour and encouragement.

"Oh⋯ my gosh, nanny, I do not think I can lift you. What would happen if I accidentally dropped you?" Jorja expressed her doubts, her voice tinged with a worrying blend of uncertainty.

"Jorja, listen to me; your power is growing rapidly, and I believe in you. What you need is a little faith in yourself. Remember, I have magic powers, too, and I trust you can succeed. If anything goes wrong, we'll manage it together," Lissa reassured, her belief in Jorja unwavering.

Despite her initial hesitations, Jorja knew, deep down inside her, that her grandmother was right. With trembling hands and a determined spirit, she mustered all her courage and focused intently on the task. As she attempted to lift her grandmother, an unexpected distraction momentarily broke her concentration, causing her to lose her grip and let Lissa slip from her grasp. However, with her seasoned skills, Lissa adeptly avoided a mishap and landed gracefully on her feet, her concern for her granddaughter mirroring her disappointment.

Observing the flicker of realisation in Jorja's eyes and sensing a wave of foreboding, Lissa's light purple crystal pulsated against her chest - a silent warning that danger loomed ahead, signalling a shift in the peacefulness of their training session.

Lissa looked closer, leaning in to examine the figure with a mix of apprehension and determination in her eyes. As she focused her mind's eye, willing it with all her might to magnify the details before her, the woman's features slowly became more evident - it was the same woman she had seen at the beach with Barney, the dog. Jorja felt unease creep up her spine, sending a shiver down her back. With her heart pounding in her chest, Lissa's thoughts raced at an unprecedented speed, the situation's urgency becoming glaringly apparent. Panic gripped her for the first time in her life, but amidst the chaos of her thoughts, one resolute determination emerged: Jorja had to be kept safe at all costs.

Acknowledging that Jorja was ill-equipped for any potential confrontation and that her magical skills had dulled due to a lack of recent practice, Lissa swiftly decided to prioritise retreat. Urgency infused every movement as she turned to Jorja, her voice firm and resolved as she instructed her granddaughter to change into her climbing gear. The sense of urgency only grew as the woman drew nearer.

"I need you to remember the cave on the top on, the other side of the crag, Jorja," Lissa directed, her gaze locking onto her granddaughter's.

"Yes, Nanny, I remember," Jorja replied swiftly, her eyes reflecting concern, yet she trusted her grandmother completely.

"Good. Quickly now, head there and hide until I come for you. No matter what, keep moving forward and don't look back. I'll be with you soon," Lissa urged, her words laced with urgency and determination.

As Jorja hastened away, oblivious to the protective spell her grandmother had cast around her, Lissa's focus shifted back to the approaching woman, her resolve unwavering. With each step the woman took, bringing her closer to their precarious position, Lissa realised the gravity of the situation. Instinctively, she reached out to Jorja's mind, a mental nudge to hasten her retreat.

Jorja, caught off guard by the unexpected communication, stumbled slightly before regaining her footing and sprinting towards the looming rock face. With trembling hands, she hastily adjusted her climbing gear, the unfamiliar weight of the harness a stark reminder of her inexperience. Though fear threatened to overwhelm her, Jorja's determination to follow her grandmother's instructions steeled her resolve as she prepared to embark on her first solo climb, each movement deliberate yet tinged with apprehension.

As Jorja sat on the driest stone at the back of the cave, her tears flowed freely, creating a small puddle beneath her. The damp, musty scent of the cave filled her nostrils, clinging to her like a reminder of the unknown dangers lurking in the shadows. She closed her eyes momentarily, feeling the weight of worry pressing down on her chest.

Slowly, she turned off her head torch as if obeying an invisible command from her grandmother. In the darkness, she felt fear and curiosity wash over her. Her eyes strained to see through the blackness, seeking any sign of life or movement. At first, she could only make out vague shapes and shadows, the cave seeming to hold its secrets close.

But as her eyes adjusted, a faint glimmer caught her attention. A speck of light danced in the distance, drawing her gaze like a beacon. Was it a glint of something artificial, like a forgotten piece of equipment, or something more mysterious and ancient, hidden within the cave? Jorja felt a surge of determination, fuelled by the need to uncover the truth and protect her grandmother.

As she focused her gaze, the scene before her shifted unexpectedly. The cave walls faded into the background, replaced by the familiar campsite bathed in the soft setting of the sun. Confusion clouded Jorja's mind as she tried to make sense of this surreal transition. Was she dreaming, or had reality become twisted into a new form, challenging her perceptions?

Amid her uncertainty, a sudden commotion erupted in the campsite. Jorja's eyes widened as she witnessed her grandmother, the figure of authority and strength, facing off against the dogwalker with fierce determination. Their words echoed faintly in Jorja's ears, a cryptic dialogue that hinted at hidden truths and unspoken alliances.

"Helgi wants the child. Hand her over, Morwenna," the stranger's voice rang out, filled with ominous intent. But her grandmother's response was an explicit declaration of power and identity: "That is Queen Morwenna to you, servant, know your place." The tension between them crackled in the air, a clash of wills that threatened to spill over into chaos.

Jorja strained to catch every word, her heart pounding heavily in her chest as she tried to piece together the puzzle before her. The cryptic mention of "Morwenna" sparked a flicker of recognition in her mind, a name that held more significance than she could grasp. As the confrontation intensified, she steadied herself, knowing the true test of her strength and courage was still ahead in the depths of uncertainty.

Lissa tossed the woman aside with little force, and she lay slumped on the ground. She felt like she was waiting forever for the woman to get up and start again, clinging to the hope that her opponent would find the strength to carry on. But the woman just stayed there, frozen as if held down by something invisible. Lissa's frustration and impatience bubbled over as she shouted, "Come on, get up, fight like a woman, and face me!" But no matter how much she called out, the woman remained unresponsive, lying there without a move.

Summoning her courage, Lissa slowly approached the unmoving figure, the tension thick in the air as she teetered between anticipation and dread. Jorja observed the unfolding scene, her mind struggling to keep pace with the rapid events transpiring before her eyes. She attempted to calm her racing thoughts, realising that the reality unfolding before her was far beyond anything she had ever experienced. The speed of the unfolding events left her reeling, unable to fully comprehend the supernatural spectacle that played out before her.

Suddenly, a swift and decisive force swept Lissa off her feet, hurling her several meters away, her head contacting a jagged rock before she crumpled in a heap on the ground. The shock written across Lissa's features spoke volumes, a silent testament to the unforeseen events that had befallen her instantly. Witnessing her grandmother's sudden incapacitation, Jorja felt a surge of panic and apprehension grip her heart, compelling her to ensure her grandmother's well-being even as chaos unfolded around them.

As Jorja anxiously monitored Lissa's condition, her gaze lingered on the enigmatic woman who had caused such chaos. Casting a glance towards the distant crag, the woman embarked on a determined ascent, scaling the treacherous terrain with inexplicable ease, unaided by any conventional climbing gear. Feeling a sense of unease that crept over her, Jorja wrapped her arms protectively around her knees, bracing herself for the unknown.

Recognising the urgency of the situation, Jorja reached out to her unconscious grandmother through the mysterious connection they shared, her voice infused with desperation and longing, "Nan, please wake up. You are my protector. I implore you to awaken and come to my aid." The weight of her words echoed in the cavernous silence, a plea for help in the face of imminent danger.

With each passing moment, the woman drew closer to her destination, her determination unwavering as she ascended the rugged cliffside with ease and resolve. Sensing the looming threat that only her grandmother could confront, Jorja beseeched her grandmother again, "Nan, I cannot fend off this woman alone. You are the queen, our beacon of hope. Please, wake up and stand with me for the fate of Enrac; I need you" Her words resonated in the stillness, a desperate call for salvation in a realm teetering on the brink of chaos.

A response came back: "Silence, child; the woman can track your abilities as they are not trained. Stop watching, stop now. I am coming for you, my child; I am coming." Lissa's response was laced with concern for the most important child ever to have been born. The urgency in her tone reflected the gravity of the situation, conveying a sense of impending danger that lurked around every corner.

Immediately, Jorja tried to release the power she was using, but she could not stop it, as she did not know how to release it. How could she let go of it? She asked herself, but she did not even know how she managed to do it in the first place. The mystical force seemed to have a hold over her, refusing to be relinquished despite her best efforts to command it otherwise. It was like an invisible barrier had formed, trapping her within its potent grip, leaving her bewildered and helpless.

Suddenly, she heard a noise that sounded like someone had kicked a stone or small rock, and she stood to see. Her mind was still attached to the woman, and Jorja watched her every step. The woman was treading cautiously, but she was getting ever closer. The woman was in the cave now, treading lightly so as not to be heard. The ominous presence of the woman grew more palpable with each passing moment, sending a shiver down Jorja's spine as she braced herself for the impending confrontation that loomed ahead.

"Come to me, child; I know you are in here. It will all be over soon; I can track you, child; wherever you go, I can track your magic." Jorja gasped at this thought as the woman got closer still, and Jorja released her magic; you are fearful of me; I can feel it. Jorja was a little shocked as she had not even known it herself, but the fear had set in, and she had no room for magic. She closed her eyes and prayed to whatever god was out there to help her. The overwhelming sense of dread threatened to engulf her, leaving her to rely on sheer instinct and faith to navigate the perilous path that lay ahead.

In her mind, her grandmother was saying something. "Jorja listens to me; when she gets close to you, turn your head torch on her eyes; it will temporarily blind her, giving me time to get to you. I am almost their child; I will not leave you, my darling," she said, convincing Jorja to be brave. The comforting words of her grandmother echoed in her mind, serving as a beacon of hope amidst the encroaching darkness that threatened to engulf her. Jorja clung to the whispered instructions with renewed determination, mustering the courage to face the looming danger head-on.

Jorja, steeling herself for the imminent confrontation with the mysterious woman, knew deep down that she lacked the strength to lift her adversary effortlessly. But magically, she knew she could. However, contemplating the possibility of throwing the woman, Jorja was overcome with uncertainty. The woman stood a mere three meters away, illuminated by Jorja's keen eyes that had acclimated to the dark surroundings. As the woman grabbed her, Jorja swiftly activated her head torch, its beam piercing the darkness to momentarily blind her attacker. Without hesitation, Jorja used her full force to forcefully push the woman, sending her stumbling over a protruding boulder before quickly regaining her footing.

In a surprising turn of events, Jorja, embracing her innate magical abilities, effortlessly levitated the woman off the ground before releasing her, catching her by surprise as she landed unceremoniously on the ground with a resounding thud. Shocked by Jorja's display of magical prowess, the woman realised she had underestimated her opponent's skills and resolved never to make the same mistake again.

Determined to reach her grandmother, who stood at the cave entrance in the distance, Jorja sprinted ahead as the woman pursued closely behind. However, the woman, fuelled by a surge of adrenaline, swiftly closed the gap between them, seizing Jorja in a vice-like grip around her throat and waist. Jorja felt the woman's nails digging into her windpipe, threatening to cut off her air supply, as she was forcibly carried towards the mouth of the cave, her heart pounding with a mix of fear and determination.

Lissa's eyes blazed with fierce determination as she confronted the woman. Then it dawned on her, Eswella, her former handmaiden. The tension in the cave was palpable, with Jorja's life hanging in the balance. Each word passing between the two women reverberated with a history of betrayal and allegiance long forgotten by one and twisted by the other.

As Eswella's taunting words pierced the air around them about Piran and Helgi, Lissa's composure wavered momentarily before she steeled herself. Her heart ached with the memory of the people of Enrac she had left behind, the burden of guilt weighing heavily on her. Yet, in that moment, she knew she had to protect her family, her daughter Saffran, at any cost.

The raw emotions swirling between Lissa and Eswella crackled like lightning, igniting a fierce battle of words and wills. Eswella's revelation about seeking Helgi's power shattered the fragile peace that had briefly settled in the cave. Lissa's calm façade shattered as she unleashed a storm of fury that threatened to engulf them all.

In a swift and decisive move, Lissa seized Eswella, her once loyal handmaiden, using her purple crystal and DrakÔn Magic and flung her aside with a strength by years of pent-up frustration and unresolved conflicts. The cave vibrated with the echoes of the stones cascading around Eswella, sealing her fate within its stony embrace. Jorja clung to her grandmother, her eyes wide with fear and awe at the power she had just witnessed.

As the dust settled and the echoes of the confrontation faded, Lissa stood amidst the debris, her chest heaving with relief and sorrow. The weight of her past actions and their consequences bore down on her like boulders, threatening to crush her spirit. Yet, in that moment of chaos and closure, Lissa knew that she had made a choice that would shape the destiny of not just herself but of everyone tied to the intricate tapestry of power and loyalty that bound them together.

Neither waited to see if Eswella was moving. Lissa knew that the rocks would not hold Eswella for long and grabbed Jorja and flung her over her shoulder, like a firefighter, instructing, "Hold on, child, we are going to use some serious magic here," she said to her granddaughter. She ran to the cliff's edge and jumped off, the wind rushing past them as they descended. Despite the adrenaline pounding through her veins, Lissa remained focused, steadying their descent with expert precision until they finally reached the bottom in mere seconds. Once her feet touched solid ground, she placed Jorja gently down, and together, they sprinted towards the campsite, their hearts racing in sync with the urgency of their escape.

Lissa's movements were fluid and purposeful as she waved her arms about, guiding Jorja with swift efficiency towards the campsite. Upon arrival, everything was packed up and ready to go, indicating Lissa's preparedness and quick thinking. "Grab what you can, not too heavy, as we will be running. Only carry light things, Jorja; my magic will cover the rest," she urged with a sense of urgency.

By the time they reached the car, sweat dripped down their faces, and their chests heaved with the exertion of their escape. They climbed into their seats. Lissa began to load the car using her magic, and it appeared that the car seemed to load itself. Strapping themselves in, Lissa started the car. The powerful engine roared to life, vibrating through their bones as they sped off down the road, leaving a trail of dust in their wake.

Despite the need for speed, Lissa, using her magic, kept a watchful eye on Eswella, who had just reached the bottom of the crag. Feeling a sense of relief wash over her, knowing they had successfully dodged capture, she slowed the car to the speed limit, focusing now on ensuring Eswella did not track them down.

Lissa felt a surge of guilt weighing heavily upon her shoulders as she reflected on the situation they had found themselves in. She reproached herself for not foreseeing the possibility of someone from Enrac being able to track Jorja. She had naively believed that only those with royal blood possessed such potent magic. The realisation set in that her son, Helgi, had allied with the malevolent Erlend, Amox, filled her with a deep sense of dread. Her heart ached with remorse as she confronted the consequences of her oversight, feeling immense responsibility for her granddaughter's predicament.

As she admonished Jorja for not controlling her thoughts, Lissa's voice quivered, revealing mixtures of frustration and concern. Despite her sharp words, she quickly regretted snapping at the young girl, knowing her emotions clouded her judgment. "Ignore me, child; I am stressed and angry with myself for not shielding you better," Lissa said apologetically. With a heavy heart, Lissa acknowledged the need to prioritise Jorja's safety before allowing herself the luxury of processing the complex web of events that had unfolded.

Their drive back home was fraught with tension as Lissa pushed the accelerator harder, keenly aware of Eswella's pursuit behind them. Jorja's request for a restroom break prompted a necessary stop at the A30 services, providing them with a brief respite to grab some sustenance and fuel for the rest of their journey home. Again, seated back in the car, Lissa showed Jorja how to shield herself from potential trackers, a crucial lesson in safeguarding her granddaughter's well-being in an increasingly perilous situation.

Determined to outdistance Eswella, Lissa multitasked by eating on the go while maintaining a steady speed on the road; she needed to put as many miles between them as possible.

They drove the rest of the way home in relative silence. Lissa only spoke to Jorja when necessary. The atmosphere inside the car had shifted from the tense rush of adrenaline to a heavy exhaustion that settled in as they approached home. The fatigue from the journey mixed with the eerie calmness after the stressful events they had just experienced. Lissa and Jorja were enveloped in their own contemplations, the weight of unspoken thoughts hanging in the air as they navigated towards their destination. It starkly contrasted the earlier intensity, now replaced by a solemn quiet that wrapped around them like a heavy cloak.

As the car turned onto the familiar drive and stopped, Lissa shut off the engine and glanced at Jorja sitting beside her. Jorja remained deep in thought, her expression betraying the internal turmoil she was experiencing. Without missing a beat, Lissa discreetly veiled them both in a layer of protective magic that no human on Enrac would know unless a drakÔn had trained them, a subtle gesture to shield them from prying eyes or unwanted attention. Lissa was aware that Jorja's silence was down to her shouting at her and knew that it was the first time she had ever shouted at the young girl.

"We have arrived home safely," Lissa gently informed Jorja, breaking the oppressive silence was now between them. The sudden sound of Lissa's voice pulled Jorja out of her reverie, prompting a whirlwind of questions and uncertainties that swirled in her mind during the journey back. Thoughts raced through her head, each question a heavy weight on her already burdened shoulders. Who was the mysterious woman? What connection did she have to this enigmatic figure named Piran, Eswella mentioned? Was there a sinister plot at play, and could her uncle, Helgi, be involved? As the night wore on, Jorja found herself lost in a labyrinth of doubts and suspicions, the lines between reality and dream blurring in a restless tide of visions and unanswered questions.

Upon entering their home and after silently unloading the car, the weight of their shared experiences hung heavily in the air. The dark, cold bungalow welcomed them back, its familiar embrace offering a sense of refuge amidst the lingering tension. Lissa busied herself with the familiar routines of drawing blinds, closing curtains, and allowing her magic to fill the space with warmth and comfort. The crackle of the fire and the inviting warmth of the Aga stove filled the room with a sense of cosiness, a stark contrast to the uncertain chill within Jorja.

Observing Jorja's dazed state, Lissa took it upon herself to prepare a soothing pot of tea, the comforting ritual a balm for their frayed nerves. The fragrant steam rose from the cup, carrying the familiar scent of tea leaves mingling with the sweetness of milk and sugar. Setting the cup before Jorja, Lissa's gentle gesture broke through the haze of thoughts that had consumed her granddaughter. Jorja started at the sudden presence of the steaming beverage, the warmth and aroma acting as a gentle awakening from the fog of her troubled thoughts and unanswered questions.

"Mmmm…. that smells good", she emphasised the words, holding the cup in her tiny hands. 'Hug a mug,' she thought to herself.

Lissa giggled softly and asked if Jorja was OK after today's antics. They discussed what had transpired, and Lissa felt that this could put Jorja's mind at rest, knowing all the facts. Jorja was like her mother in so many ways. Saffran had always been one for finding out all the information as well. Even though it was June, it felt cold that night or just shock, making them cold. Lissa thought this was the change of events, making her feel cold, or maybe they were destroying the planet so severely that the weather was changing, too. The thought stayed with her all night, and all the other things she was thinking, so she could not sleep. She tossed and turned until the small hours when the light from the sun rising at 04:00 in the east began to shine through her bedroom curtains. She was bone tired but eventually fell into a deep, satisfying sleep.

On the other hand, Jorja managed to sleep without any problems. Her problem was staying asleep; she kept waking up having bad dreams of Eswella chasing her. In her dream, she was much younger than 12 years old. She felt around five years old; still, Eswella was chasing her. All she could think of was, why is this woman chasing me? I am a small child. It repeated over and over all night until she gave up switching her bedside lamp on, picked up a book, and began to read.

Although her thoughts strayed from the book occasionally, she immersed herself in it much better than she had thought possible. The book was part of a school project they were doing, ready for the end-of-year celebration leavers' assembly. Fantasy was the theme, and the children who were due to leave this year to go to work or further education had all got together and decided to reenact some scenes from 'Call of the Herald' by Brian Rathbone. The book was very enthralling, and Jorja enjoyed it so much that she read until morning and got out of bed quite early.:

CHAPTER EIGHT

Jorja's excitement continued to build as she recounted anecdotes about her BFFs, who were expected to arrive promptly at 09:30. Walking into the warm and inviting kitchen, she was greeted by the comforting sight of her grandmother leisurely sipping tea at the table. With her characteristic grace and charm, Lissa sweetly requested Jorja's assistance with the impending food delivery scheduled during the early morning hours, between 08:00 and 09:00. Jorja, always eager to lend a helping hand, readily agreed. She could not help but conceal a knowing smile, having realised over the years that Lissa was, in fact, more than capable of managing such tasks effortlessly on her own.

Acknowledging Jorja's willingness to assist, Lissa playfully alluded to the importance of upholding appearances. The idea only added to the endearing dynamic between the two. As Lissa, in her element, proceeded to prepare a scrumptious breakfast for Jorja, she encouraged her granddaughter to freshen up and get ready for the day ahead. Taking a moment to enjoy her steaming cup of tea, Jorja winced ever so slightly as the hot liquid grazed her tongue, a small reminder of the simple pleasures in these cherished morning routines.

Mindful of the ticking clock and the impending arrival of her BFFs, Jorja swiftly made her way through her morning routine - showering, dressing, and indulging in a hearty breakfast - all the while relaying tales of anticipation and excitement about the much-anticipated visit. The kitchen buzzed with palpable energy as the morning unfolded, each moment filled with warmth, laughter, and the promise of cherished memories in the making. Even yesterday's event could and would not dampen Jorja's spirit.

Lissa had always been prepared for Jorja's lively gatherings, knowing that she would hear squeaks and giggling all day upon the arrival of her friends with their over-excited mannerisms. Their bond was strong, and Lissa cherished the girl's presence, always striving to create a welcoming atmosphere for Jorja to feel included and valued on Earth. This genuine care and consideration for her friend's well-being motivated Lissa to open her home generously, allowing the girls to have a memorable time whenever Jorja desired. The trio's adventures ranged from thrilling visits to Trethorne Leisure Park and Flambards to more enriching experiences at educational spots like the historically significant Lost Gardens of Heligan, where lush plant life filled the landscapes. With each outing, it was evident to Lissa that Jorja was determined to embrace the joy and companionship of the present with unwavering determination.

As the clock turned 08:45, it signalled the arrival of the anticipated delivery. Jorja sprang into action, hauling the bags into the kitchen with zeal and determination. Stan, the friendly and familiar delivery driver, recognised Lissa's physical challenges and often assisted her with the bags when Jorja was away at school. However, on this particular day, Jorja was on a mission, demonstrating her strength and independence by effortlessly carrying four heavy bags at a time, leaving Stan struggling to keep pace with her swift movements.

"Loads of provisions today, Maid," Stan remarked in his distinctive Cornish accent, his curiosity piqued by the abundance of supplies. "Expecting some family over for the holiday season, perhaps?" he inquired, intrigued by the bustling activity.

With a chuckle, Lissa light-heartedly responded, "Oh, no, just my granddaughter's friends coming over to enjoy every morsel in sight," playfully acknowledging the voracious appetites of the young visitors. Stan shared in her amusement, heading back to his van with a knowing smile, muttering good-naturedly about the habits of modern youth. Lissa's laughter filled the air as she closed the door behind him, relishing in the warmth of companionship and shared moments of light-hearted banter.

Lissa closed the kitchen blinds quietly, the soft click of the mechanisms filling the room as she straightened up with an air of purpose. With a gentle yet authoritative tone, she began to explain to Jorja the enchanting method of using magic to put away the shopping, a concept that genuinely delighted her granddaughter. Always mindful of Jorja's safety, Lissa assisted her and made sure not to entrust her with anything fragile, cognizant of the potential for accidents. As they conversed, Jorja eagerly shared her plans for the day with her grandmother, excitedly detailing the adventure she had mapped out for herself and her best friends. The itinerary was as ambitious as it was fun-filled: first, a thrilling go-karting session awaited them at Black Rock Beach, followed by a delightful lunch in the vibrant town of Bude. The day's entertainment would culminate in a cinematic treat, the choice between Moana 2 and Sonic the Hedgehog 3, sparking animated discussions. Anticipating the exhaustion post-cinema, Jorja envisioned a return home for a comforting dinner and a refreshing swim in the inviting pool, the uncharacteristic heat of the season only adding to the allure of the plan.

At long last, a knock at the door indicated to Lissa, with a fluttering heart and an excited Jorja, who couldn't contain her joy, that her dear friends had finally arrived. Jorja let out a gleeful squeak and dashed towards the door with eagerness bubbling up within her as the door swung open; Megan and her mother, Millie, and her mother stood with warm smiles gracing their faces. Despite the jovial atmosphere, a bittersweetness lingered as both Megan's and Millie's mothers expressed their regrets about declining the usual offer of staying for a cup of tea due to urgent work commitments that beckoned. It changed from their routine of dropping off the girls and engaging in pleasant conversations with Lissa over a steaming cup of tea.

Instead of bidding quick goodbyes with kisses and well wishes for a splendid day to their daughters, the parents swiftly took their leave, leaving a hint of melancholy in the air. The girls, unfazed by the abruptness of their parents' departure, enveloped Jorja in a warm, comforting group hug. This gesture symbolised their bond and excitement of being together once again.

Moving on from the poignant moment, Megan Millie and Jorja, hand in hand, strolled down the familiar hallway and made their way into the cosy kitchen. To Lissa's delight, she heard the affectionate title of "Grandma Lissa" uttered by the girls, a simple yet treasured reminder of the bond they shared since they were just four years old and this tradition that had endured through the years. Among the trio, Millie, at thirteen years old, held the position of the eldest, while Megan, although younger, stood tall as the tallest of the three, a fact she wore proudly.

Excitement and anticipation filled the air as the girls migrated towards Jorja's bedroom, gathering around her, eagerly awaiting news of the day's adventures. The unanimous decision to embark on a thrilling go-karting expedition was accepted. Then, the new agenda was to opt for a relaxing lunch in the charming town of Bude before venturing back to the house for a refreshing dip in the inviting swimming pool. Prepared for any spontaneous water escapades, both Megan and Millie had their swimsuits packed, ready for a day filled with laughter, friendship, and unforgettable memories.

With a twinkle of delight in her eyes, Lissa found herself enchanted by her granddaughter's whimsical plans, a soft chuckle escaping her lips as she marvelled at the depth of thought and creativity woven into Jorja's ideas. Well-acquainted with the picturesque path leading to Black Rock Beach, Lissa chose the ease of parking at the beach's lot, forsaking the rugged trails from Widemouth Beach - a departure from their customary adventure. This choice, guided by a wish to sidestep any possible run-ins with the enigmatic Eswella, was a deliberate one, deeply influenced by the echoes of yesterday's happenings at the Brecon Beacons.

They drove to Black Rock in Lissa's trusty car, a reliable vehicle that had been with them on many adventures. Upon arrival, Lissa expertly navigated the car into the car park, seamlessly activating a cloaking spell to hide it from prying eyes. Excitement bubbled within the group as they swiftly disembarked and made their way to the beach, their laughter echoing in the salty air.

Black Rock held a special place in Lissa's heart, especially during high tide when the ocean swallowed the shore, creating an air of mystery and allure. The retreating tide would later reveal a hidden world among the rock pools, bustling with vibrant marine life that never failed to captivate Lissa's curiosity. It starkly contrasted with the beaches back on Enrac, where the marine ecosystem boasted different species on a grander scale.

The beach teemed with energy, attracting surfers eager to catch the powerful waves the point and reef breaks generated. Lissa treated the girls to a thrilling go-karting lesson first and then free time after, a sport that Millie naturally excelled at due to her past experiences with her older brothers. Megan and Jorja, on the other hand, were novices to the activity, relying on Millie's guidance to manoeuvre the unfamiliar machinery.

Despite their varying skill levels, the girls found joy and camaraderie in the activity, bonding over shared laughter and friendly banter. Watching over them from the tearoom, Lissa basked in the warmth of their friendship, ensuring their safety with her protective magic. The familiarity of the cloaking spell she utilised brought back memories of her mentor, Sobex, who had imparted the spell's intricacies during her younger years.

Though confident in her ability to shield them from magical surveillance, Lissa remained vigilant, casting a watchful gaze over the surroundings. Strategically positioned in the tearoom, she had a clear view of the car park, the expansive beach, and the entrance. Ready to act at a moment's notice, she remained vigilant, determined to protect her companions and maintain the tranquillity of their day at Black Rock.

Lissa had been restless in her thoughts, for today seemed to be a day for thinking about her loving, wonderful husband Goran, a dashing man known for his courage and strength, who held the esteemed position of a general in the then King's forces, led by her imposing father, Carantok. Carantok was a formidable figure, commanding respect and loyalty from his generals and troops alike, instilling a sense of unwavering discipline and duty within the kingdom. Enrac, dominantly land and seaward, maintained a formidable army and navy, both serving under distinct banners, indicating their specialised roles in protecting the realm.

Young boys who had just turned twelve enthusiastically enlisted in either the land or naval forces, embarking on a journey of intense training to refine their abilities and commitment to the defence of their kingdom. From the moment Lissa laid eyes on Goran, a sense of destiny enveloped her as she realised he was destined to be the one she would stand beside as queen. Concealing her true feelings, she skilfully masked her heart's desires, masking her admiration for Goran as a closely guarded secret. When confronted by her father with inquiries regarding potential suitors, she shrewdly evaded revealing her affections, opting to bide her time under the guise of continued search.

As her thoughts meandered back to the present, a sudden piercing scream disrupted her reverie, which was then followed by contagious laughter and playful chatter among the children. Reflecting on the stark contrast between the carefree nature of the planet's youth and the solemn responsibilities she bore as part of Enrac's elite, Lissa couldn't help but wonder about the innocence and simplicity that seemed to define the children of this foreign world.

When the three girls finished their thrilling go-karting session, laughter filled the air as they zipped around the track for free before finishing and grabbing refreshing drinks to take along for the ride to Bude. Lissa, the cautious one of the group, made sure not to let her guard down, keeping the protective DrakÔn Magic intact as they bid farewell to the picturesque Black Rock Beach and embarked on the scenic coastal road leading towards Bude. As they leisurely drove past, she felt a presence that revealed to be Eswella's charming home, a man diligently tending to the vibrant garden in front of the house caught Lissa's attention, leaving her pondering about the source of Eswella's funds to afford such a splendid gardener.

Reflecting on the contrast between Enrac and Earth, where gardens were symbols of luxury rather than necessity, Lissa remembered how royal gardens, a privilege, were reserved for the elite on Enrac. The mere commoners, considered wealthy by Earth's standards, mainly focused on cultivating crop gardens to sustain themselves. However, the enchanting allure of gardens and minglegroves was not lost on the Eurasians, with Erlends and DrakÔn sharing a deep appreciation for nature. Lissa's father, driven by his love for Queen Sagira, ensured that the palace gardens were meticulously maintained to match her ethereal beauty, a tribute to her grace and elegance.

Upon reaching Bude, the cheerful group parked their car and strolled towards the inviting ambience of the 'Life's a Beach' restaurant, a perfect spot for a well-deserved lunch break with its diverse menu offerings. Opting to give the girls some space, Lissa monitored them discreetly from a distance while keeping her protective DrakÔn Magic ready. Her thoughts drifted to Goran and Saffran, fervently hoping for their safety and well-being amidst the turmoil. She couldn't help but worry about her other children – Keera, Baron, Treeve, and Elestren, envisioning Saffran's unwavering determination to ensure their security by guiding them to a place of refuge, accompanied by her stalwart husband, Tobias. A brave and devoted soul, Tobias stood by Saffran's side, embodying the essence of a true warrior with his steadfast loyalty and unwavering support.

Goran had been honoured with the prestigious title of general in training in the king's guards, a position that demanded respect and authority. Morwenna, driven by her curiosity and admiration for her father's new general, mustered the courage to request a meeting with Goran. Her father, intrigued by her interest, granted her wish, inquiring if this was genuinely her personal desire. Morwenna's affirmative response was met with a warm smile from her father, who saw how genuinely happy she appeared. When Goran, deeply moved by Morwenna's charm and sincerity, proposed marriage, she was overwhelmed with gratitude and joy. Joyfully skipping back to her room, she couldn't contain her elation, bouncing on her bed and singing with unbridled happiness. Her father, ever the cautious guardian, arranged for supervised meetings between Goran and Morwenna over the following weeks to ensure they were compatible and genuinely meant for each other. Goran's love for Morwenna was instantaneous and profound, leaving little doubt in either of their minds of their shared destiny. At the tender age of sixteen, they exchanged vows and embarked on a journey of love and commitment, with Goran dedicating himself to making Morwenna the happiest woman in the realm.

After indulging in a delicious lunch of delectable shellfish, the trio of friends decided to head back home, opting out of the cinema for a leisurely afternoon. Feeling worn out, Lissa retreated to the comfort of her living room, leaving the girls to frolic in the inviting pool. Their laughter echoed through the air as they splashed around, creating ripples of pure joy in the water. Sensing their hunger, Lissa emerged from the house, bearing a tray laden with scrumptious treats, urging the girls to take a break from their aquatic playtime.

Under the balmy sun, they savoured glasses of cool lemonade infused with fresh fruits, the condensation glistening on the sides of the pitchers as they soaked up the afternoon warmth. Lissa, always attentive to their preferences, had prepared multiple jugs of the refreshing beverage, knowing the three girls well enough by now, their penchant for nibbling on the infused fruits. As evening approached, a delightful spread awaited the friends for dinner, featuring a vibrant salad accompanied by an assortment of delectable foods such as dainty sausage rolls, miniature pork pies, savoury quiches, chicken, and barbeque ribs, ensuring their culinary delight.

The abundance of food at the table caught the eye of Jago, their neighbour, who peered over the fence with a hungry gaze reminiscent of a longing for a taste of the feast. Moved by a sense of generosity, Lissa prepared a plate brimming with delectable treats. She extended it to Jago, who hesitated momentarily, trying to maintain his pride despite the rumblings of his protesting stomach. However, the tempting aroma and sight of the spread proved too irresistible, prompting him to accept the offering from the kind, albeit quirky, old woman. With a satisfied grin, he wandered off to enjoy his unexpected treat, a silent acknowledgement of the warmth and generosity that resonated in the air between neighbours on that pleasant evening.

The three amigos walked over to Jago and said it was okay to eat more as they had so much food. 'Now those girls are caring,' thought Lissa. She knew the girls had made the right choice to be BFFs.

Feeding Jago was also the right call. When he asked for more, Jorja returned to the table and refilled his plate again, insisting that he come into the garden to sit, eat, and refresh with some lemonade. Jago complied, telling himself he would do it just this once to please the girls. Jago saw himself as a gentleman if nothing else. His fantasy levels were extremely high; in his real life, he had nothing except his thoughts.

The rest of the evening was spent with Jago laughing and joking with the girls, splashing them so they would return to the paddling pool. He wouldn't get in himself, as he had nothing to change into, even though he lived less than a hundred meters away. The girls let it slide, knowing he was fostered and thinking giving him a break might make him more likeable to them at school.

The three girls were sad when Millie's mum came to collect Megan and Millie. The girls had enjoyed their day and were all yawning but still smiling. Millie's mum thanked Lissa and took the girls home.

Jorja and Lissa said goodnight to Jago and went inside. Jorja expected washing up to be needed, but it was all done and stored back in its rightful place in the cupboards. Lissa closed all the blinds, and for the first time that day, she stood straight. Her back ached, and she needed to exercise. She moved all the furniture in the living room to one side (making it all small enough to fit into a jewellery box) and began her Telm.

The day had been full of joy and laughter, but as the twilight deepened, she felt the weariness settle in her bones. Jorja shouted a thank you to her grandmother. Lissa heard her exuberant shout of gratitude and couldn't help but smile at the genuine joy in Jorja's voice. Lissa, absorbed in her Telm, glanced over at the sleeping figure, her heart swelling with affection for her granddaughter. In a gesture of love, she carefully draped a thin blanket over Jorja, ensuring she was snug in her slumber.

As Lissa concluded her evening rituals, thoughts of Jago, her new companion, flitted through her mind. With a sense of purpose and a contented sigh, she padded into her cosy bedroom and flopped down, a beaming smile gracing her features.

The following day brought a knock at the door, and there stood Jago, eager to lend a hand and earn his keep. His offer to assist with tidying up from the previous day's activities was met with Lissa's welcoming smile, inviting him into their humble abode. Seated together, Lissa shared her plans with Jago, emphasising the importance of his role in Jorja's training and fitness regimen. Enthusiasm sparked in Jago's eyes as he eagerly embraced the opportunity to be her sparring partner, realising the significance of his contribution. Deep down, he was a kindhearted boy who was misunderstood.

In agreement, Lissa assured Jago that she would provide nourishing meals and proper attire for his training sessions, an arrangement he embraced with genuine gratitude. Their bond strengthened through mutual respect and shared goals, setting the stage for a promising partnership forged through trust and collaboration.

This day was filled with food, food, and more food. Lissa briefly took a break to order more food and opted to look at clothing for Jago, who sorely needed it. She thought sports clothing was appropriate for him as his training would be vigorous.

CHAPTER NINE

The following day, Jago arrived as planned at 08.00. Lissa made a hearty breakfast. Jago, who had heard the word 'dragon' mentioned upon his arrival, wanted more information on the subject. He was driven by a burning curiosity about dragons and held steadfast to his identity as a gentleman. He perceived his quest as requiring the noble act of slaying the mythical creature. Jorja shared their zeal, adding a layer of excitement to their knowledgeable expedition. Recognising the genuine eagerness in their eyes, Lissa settled them down whilst she washed up, ready to divulge enlightening information about the wondrous beings known as drakÔns. Lissa corrected Jago and Jorja and informed them it was drakÔn, not dragon.

She began by expounding on the intricate nature of Drakôn Magic, a mystical force that sets these creatures apart. This magic, known as Nitte, is not merely a learned skill but an innate ability that flows through their very existence, a legacy passed down through generations. It is a sublime fusion of elemental control, intricate healing techniques, and potent shielding spells seamlessly integrated into their being. Each Drakôn, upon hatching, inherits a wealth of knowledge and power gained from their forebears, creating a lineage of formidable magic wielders.

Mastering Drakôn Magic, a culmination of ancient wisdom and profound skill, is a lifelong, rigorous training and dedication journey.

Through this practice, drakÔn's hone their abilities to manipulate the elements, mend wounds with unparalleled precision, and craft impregnable shields capable of safeguarding entire realms. Legends speak of seasoned DrakÔns transcending the boundaries of reality, their command over magic allowing them to reshape the very fabric of existence to fulfil their desires, a testament to the formidable prowess bestowed upon these magnificent creatures.

The birth of Sobex's son, Sodux, was a momentous occasion that signified the unbroken continuity of a lineage characterised by formidable power and wisdom. Sodux, inheriting the profound knowledge and strength of his exceptional parents, Sobex and Kasa, emerged as a being of unparalleled potential. Their legacy, woven from the extraordinary prowess of two remarkable individuals, melded within Sodux to form a being destined for greatness. Morwenna's strategic counsel, urging safeguards against Helgi's malevolent intentions, was instrumental in thwarting the machinations seeking to exploit Sodux's innate abilities for dark purposes.

Sobex, revered as a legendary Drakôn of unparalleled skill, stood out among his kin as a master of Nitte, showcasing a level of mastery that few could ever hope to achieve. His striking purple scales served as a visual testament to the vast reserves of power and wisdom he possessed. Recognising Morwenna's crucial role in protecting his son and her innate ability to wield ancient magic, Sobex decided to teach her the secrets of Drakôn magic. This bond was unlike anything seen before in history.

The enigmatic Nitte, a mystical art steeped in the depths of time and wisdom, demanded rigorous dedication and patience to master its intricate nuances. Morwenna reminisced about the countless hours spent absorbing the ancient wisdom imparted by the magnificent being. With Sobex's singular purple hue standing as a rarity among drakÔns for centuries, the birth of Sodux, bearing the same unique colouration as Lissa's crystal, marked a momentous occurrence reflecting the heritage passed down through generations. In the realm of drakÔn's, transferring knowledge from parents to offspring was an innate process, enabling the accumulation of profound wisdom and skill with each successive generation. Sobex, renowned for his unparalleled talents and cunning intellect, and Kasa, his mate, equally gifted but graced with a compassionate and nurturing spirit, coalesced their exceptional qualities within their son Sodux, setting the stage for a being destined to redefine the boundaries of greatness.

When Sodux came into the world, he captivated all who beheld him with his remarkable beauty, radiating a mesmerising shade of purple that outshone even his illustrious father. However, amidst this joyous occasion, a harrowing conflict loomed in the background - the relentless war that had just begun between Helgi and his family. Morwenna, a wise and caring soul, went to Sobex's to offer her congratulations and gifts to the newborn drakÔn and his parents. Among the presents she brought, her most precious gift was not a tangible item but rather invaluable advice. She sternly warned Sobex of the imminent danger posed by Helgi's sinister intentions towards Sodux, emphasising the crucial need to protect and shield the young drakÔn at all costs.

It was that Sodux, blessed with inherited knowledge from both his parents, Sobex and Kasa, held a unique and coveted power that would make him a prime target for those with nefarious motives. If Helgi were to capture him, the consequences would be dire - Sodux's purity would be corrupted, and he would be twisted to serve evil. In light of this grave prophecy, Sobex understood the gravity of his duty to guard Sodux with unwavering vigilance. And in a rare moment of trust, Sobex decided to share the secrets of the ancient drakÔn language and magic with Morwenna, an act that showcased the depths of their alliance against the looming darkness.

Dwelling upon the diverse hues adorned drakÔns, Morwenna reminisced on the various colours she had encountered in these majestic creatures. Typically, drakÔns presented themselves in shades of blue, green, yellow, gold, or silver, each hue reflecting the unique traits and essence of the individual. However, an anomaly existed for Helgi's DrakÔns, particularly the corrupted soul of Oighodit, transformed by the treacherous hand of Erlend, Amox. This once-beautiful drakÔn of yellow had succumbed to the shadows, donning a menacing black cloak that forewarned the dangers lurking within the Dark Side. Reports and sightings of Helgi's DrakÔns painted a sinister picture, suggesting a preference for darker tones - hues of deep brown, charcoal grey, and obsidian black, mirroring the malevolent aura that enveloped Helgi's domain. Helgi used Amox's magic to make his drakÔn larger than the norm.

Within the drakÔns' realm existed a division that mirrored the eternal struggle between light and darkness - a dichotomy symbolised by the contrasting kingdoms of Helgi and Queen Morwenna. Helgi's dominion, aptly named "The Dark Side" or "wer whedab symba" in the melodic drakÔnic tongue, stood as a bastion of shadows and malevolence. On the opposing end of the spectrum lay the radiant domain from which Queen Morwenna hailed - "The Realm of Light," known as "wer Grikor di mitre" in the ancient tongue. Between these two conflicting realms stood the monumental landmark of Drakôn Mountain, Lanrah Grikor, a towering assembly of peaks that served as a silent witness to the eternal tug-of-war between light and shadow, good and evil, that defined the very essence of the drakÔnic world.

Lanrah Grikor, known to humans as the legendary Drakôn Mountain, stood as a treasured haven for the mystical drakÔn beings. It enchanted all allowed entrance, shrouded from prying eyes by an intricate veil of magic. Inside the mountain's majestic embrace, a sprawling crater unfurled, teeming with a kaleidoscope of vibrant ecosystems - from sun-kissed grasslands to lush jungles, serene rivers snaking through the landscape, and majestic waterfalls that cascaded in a mesmerising display of nature's artistry.

The dwellings of the drakôn denizens were nothing short of opulent; every corner oozed with luxury and splendour. The fabrics adorning their abodes boasted a myriad of hues, each one more mesmerising than the last. Ancient parchment tomes filled their libraries, repositories of knowledge spanning epochs. At the same time, the very structures themselves were crafted from a fusion of rare materials - wood, marble, precious gems, and other mystical elements from the heart of the earth. It was a realm where magic pulsed through every stone, harmony reigned supreme, and creatures of all kinds dwelled in perfect unity.

Serving as the guardians of this enchanted realm was the revered Drakôn Council, a venerable body tasked with safeguarding Lanrah Grikor's sanctity and shielding it from the prying machinations of the outside world. Invitations to enter this hallowed ground were few and far between, rigorously scrutinised to preserve the secrecy that veiled the mountain's majesty. So, when Helgi, driven by nefarious ambitions, sought to breach the mountain's defences, his efforts were in vain, for the elusive entrance remained beyond his reach. Resorting to ambush tactics outside the mountain's protective cloak, he realised the daunting challenge of gaining entrance to Lanrah Grikor's impregnable façade. Even attempts to soar over its towering zenith were thwarted as the very mountain seemed to defy his intrusion, sealing off access with an arcane barrier that defied all his attempts to penetrate it.

Meanwhile, within this realm of wonder and mystique, Princess Saffran, much like her venerable predecessor Morwenna, was honing her skills under the tutelage of the esteemed masters Sobex and Kasa. With each passing day, she absorbed her mentors' profound wisdom and formidable powers, blossoming into a force to be reckoned with in her own right. Amidst her training, Morwenna often found her thoughts drifting back to the ancient days when Sobex, the revered drakôn who had imparted so much knowledge, guided her along her path. Curious ponderings danced in her mind - if Sobex still roamed Enrac, he would have weathered the aeons, a living testament to the eternal wellspring of Kitte that flowed through the ages, shaping destinies and empowering generations yet unborn.

As Lissa watched the two children's faces light up with wonder and curiosity, she couldn't resist the urge to delve deeper into the magical world of dragons on Earth. Enthralled by the spark in their eyes, she wove a tapestry of mythical tales and fantastical adventures, each story more captivating than the last. She could feel their imaginations taking flight alongside the majestic creatures she described with each word she uttered. The children hung on her every word, their eager expressions reflecting genuine fascination and delight. Each tale she wove seemed to transport them to a world of wonder, where magic and adventure felt tangibly real.

In her mind, Lissa envisioned a world where dragons soared through the skies, their scales glinting in the sunlight as they breathed fire and performed awe-inspiring feats in the air. The joy of sharing her imaginative visions with the children filled her heart with warmth, and she knew that she was powering their sense of wonder and creativity.

As her stories unfolded, Lissa's excitement mirrored that of the children, their eyes widening in amazement at each new revelation. She revelled in the connection forged through the magic of storytelling, knowing that the bond they shared in that moment would be etched in their memories forever. The children's animated reactions only fuelled her enthusiasm further, each gasp and giggle serving as a realisation of the power of imagination and the joy of discovery.

Lost in the enchanting world of dragons and adventure, Lissa marvelled at the transformative impact of a simple tale spun with love and authenticity. As the children's faces lit up with delight, she knew that the magic of storytelling had created a lasting spark that would continue to illuminate their hearts and minds long after the stories had ended.

A Tale of Myth, Language, and Power

The Scribe's Discovery

The clay tablet felt cool beneath his fingertips, the damp scent of earth clinging to its surface. The young scribe, barely out of his apprenticeship, traced the intricate symbols carved into the wet clay.

Among them was a word that had long fascinated him - ušum-gal. It was older than any temples he had seen, yet it held power. It whispered of serpents coiled in the deep, kings who dared challenge the heavens, and a beast that could only be spoken of in hushed tones.

He once more dipped his stylus into the soft clay, deepening the etchings. His master had told him of these creatures, how they were neither lion nor snake but something more significant - a being of shifting forms, part god, part monster. The gods feared them, and only the strongest kings could claim dominion over them.

The Akkadians had called them ušumgallu, the great lion dragon, while the Babylonians wove their likeness into their sacred gates. Each culture that followed added a new layer, a new whisper of truth and fear. But where did the first story come from? And more importantly, what if the stories were real?

The Dragon Emperor

Thousands of miles away, a different kind of dragon soared beneath a sky thick with storm clouds. Its sinuous body coiled through the heavens, weaving between bursts of thunder. The emperor stood on his palace steps, his golden robes reflecting the flickering lanterns that lined the courtyard. To his people, he was the Son of the Dragon, the earthly manifestation of celestial power.

Legends spoke of China's long, sacred dragon, a creature without wings yet capable of flight, unlike Western dragons, who hoarded gold and fire; this being carried the power of rain, fortune, and change. It symbolised dynasty and divinity, shaping history as much as it shaped rivers and storms.

As the emperor watched the rolling clouds, he could almost hear the whispers of his ancestors. Were the dragons real? Had they once swum through rivers, their glistening scales flashing beneath the surface? Or were they merely stories crafted by those who longed for order in a world of chaos?

The Guardian of Gold

In the heart of the mist-laden hills, a cave yawned open, its darkness impenetrable to all but the bravest. Here, deep within, lay the creature known as the wyrm. It had slithered through English folklore for centuries, its massive coils hidden beneath the soil, only emerging when the world forgot to fear it.

The villagers whispered of the Lambton Worm, a vast serpent that could encircle a hill. They spoke of the hero who had found its weakness and watched it writhe and wail as steel bit into its flesh.

And yet, the legend endured. It was not just a story; it was a warning.

For where one dragon fell, another would rise.

And so, the stories continued - woven into the stars, carved into stone, whispered in the halls of power. The dragon remained from the ancient deserts of Mesopotamia to the storm-laden peaks of China. It was more than a creature; it symbolised fear, power, and the unknown.

The Last Dragon

As the modern world grew, the creatures of legend retreated into the shadows. The Asian lions, once great predators of the Middle East, dwindled into near extinction. The Chinese alligator, perhaps once mistaken for the dragons of old, became a rare sight. And in England, the adders, the remnants of the wyrm's legacy, vanished into the depths of forgotten woodlands. But the dragons had never indeed left.

They lingered in words, in names whispered at dusk. They danced in the flickering light of festival lanterns, curled in the delicate brushstrokes of ancient manuscripts. They lived in the stories passed from parent to child, changing and adapting as they always had. Dragons were never meant to be caged in time. They were creatures of transformation, shifting as the world did, their forms evolving but their essence eternal.

Perhaps they still waited somewhere in the untouched corners of the earth. Or maybe they had become part of us, woven into the very fabric of our fears and dreams. And if we listened carefully, in the hush of twilight, we might still hear the echo of their wings.

When she finished, both Jorja and Jago were in awe. Jorja thought, 'Boy, that woman can spin a tale.' She giggled as she offered Jago tea and cake.

Jago had the biggest piece; when offered more, he took more.

Lissa thought he would put on weight in no time.

CHAPTER TEN

Lissa, a wise and experienced woman of magic, meticulously maintained a potent cloaking spell that enveloped her and her beloved granddaughter, shielding them from prying eyes or eavesdropping ears, whether mundane or mystical. Fuming with frustration at her momentary lapse in vigilance, she felt the pressing urgency to safeguard her granddaughter more than ever before.

Determining to escalate Jorja's magical tutelage exponentially, the weight of responsibility bore heavily on her conscience as she chided inwardly, questioning her judgment with a tinge of self-reproach. Amidst the internal turmoil, a sense of duty propelled her to act, prioritising the need to bridge any rifts and foster clarity between herself and Jorja, ensuring a harmonious journey ahead. As the pivotal moment loomed, an internal debate raged within her, contemplating the opportunity to bestow Jorja with the coveted crystal, a potent artefact teeming with unparalleled power and protection. Deep-seated concerns gnawed at her, apprehensive that Jorja might falter under the weight of such formidable energy. Opting for prudence, Lissa postponed the momentous bestowal, channelling her efforts into nurturing Jorja's proficiency in vital defensive spells, fortifying her granddaughter for the trials ahead.

"Jorja, I want you to imagine a bubble in your hand. Can you see it?" she asked. "Yes, Nanny, I can see it," Jorja replied quietly, not wanting to anger her grandmother again like she had done in the car on the way back from Wales. She had tried to protect herself in the car, but had failed as she had no clue how to do it.

"Good. Now, make the bubble bigger. Yes, that is it; now, move yourself inside the bubble. Keep it around you at all times when using magic outside the bungalow. This is your protection bubble. Should anything ever happen to me, you will be safe. I will not let anyone get close to you again, my angel."

"I have got it, Nanny! Ha, I am inside my bubble. This is so cool. Nanny, will this protect me against Eswella?" she asked. "I sure hope so, but just in case, I will add a little extra help," she said. "I am so sorry I shouted at you the other day, darling; I did not mean it. I was so scared I could hardly breathe at the thought of losing you to that horrid woman." She began weeping, and Jorja moved towards her and cuddled her. Lissa smiled even though she still felt dreadful.

"This bubble will also protect your thoughts and magic from being detected, but not from someone using magic on you if they are close enough. Until you are strong enough to use magic, you must use protection; use this." Lissa did not want to scare Jorja, but needed her to understand the severity of the situation. "Today, we'll learn all the protection magic there is to learn. I want you to be so protected that not even an ant could find its way in," she said, trying her hardest to lighten the mood.

Lissa clapped her hands. "Well done, honey. You are doing well. Keeping the bubble up will drain your energy at first, but as you get stronger, so will your bubble. But let us see if you can maintain it for ten minutes."

Upon realising the extent of Jorja's abilities, Lissa felt a surge of both pride and concern. She knew that her granddaughter's potential might exceed that of even the drakÔn and Erlend, the most formidable beings on Enrac. With this newfound awareness, Lissa was more determined than ever to safeguard Jorja.

Having safeguarded the village with a protection spell years ago, Lissa decided to bolster its defences that night with the potent magic of the drakÔn. Surveying their surroundings using her magic, she discovered Eswella at Widemouth Bay and, reassured that their location remained unknown to her, dismissed the notion of relocating, as it would leave their neighbours vulnerable to potential threats.

Observing Jorja's fatigue following the taxing bubble spell and rigorous morning training, Lissa instructed her to freshen up with a quick shower and change clothes. As Jorja attended to herself, Lissa diligently reinforced the protective enchantments guarding the bungalow and the village, focusing on fortifying their defences against possible adversaries.

Once clean, Lissa told Jorja, "Today, we must engage in extensive Magic Protection Training. Are you able to maintain your protective bubble during our practice?" she questioned. "I will try, Nan. I'll do my best," Jorja replied, hoping not to upset her grandmother again. "You need to do better than try. Protecting yourself is crucial. We do not know Eswella's capabilities now that Amox and Helgi have given her powers. She may be very powerful, so you must keep your protection bubble up outside the bungalow. Am I making myself clear, Jorja?" "Nanny, do I have a crystal, and does Eswella know of my crystal? Does Uncle Helgi know where I am?" Jorja asked, concerned.

Lissa tensed, thinking before relaxing. "Yes, you do have a crystal of your own, and when you are ready, I will give it to you. Regarding Eswella, you were in the dark cave when you met

Eswella. I do not believe she saw into your eyes, so I do not think she would know that you even have a crystal, suspecting that we left Enrac in a rush, forgetting to take it with us." She saw Jorja relax, having worried about it all night. Jorja's neck throbbed from Eswella's grip two days before, and the bruising started to go purple.

"Come here, child, let me take care of that." Lissa hovered her hands over Jorja's bruised throat, concentrating. Jorja felt warmth and heat, like a hot water bottle. Even though nothing touched her skin, the bruising faded to a slight yellowish tinge. "How's that?" she asked. "Thank you, Nanny. It feels much better now," Jorja said, relieved.

Lissa was keenly aware of Jorja's lingering wariness toward her, compounded by their tension. Despite this, Lissa remained hopeful that her clear and heartfelt explanation, coupled with the dedicated training she had initiated, would act as a soothing balm to soothe Jorja's lingering doubt and unease. Ultimately, Lissa's deepest desire was for Jorja to understand the depth of love and concern she held for her granddaughter, which had been the sole motivation behind her emotional outburst. By showcasing her unwavering commitment and patience through her actions, Lissa aimed to foster a renewed sense of trust and connection between herself and Jorja, setting the foundation for a more harmonious and understanding relationship to blossom between them.

As they embarked on Telm Training, Lissa temporarily set aside Royal Training. Their commitment to mastering the complexities of Magic Training indeed took centre stage. Prioritising the intricate art of magic, they ventured out into the lush garden to hone their skills and delve into its mysteries. Amidst the vivid blooms and rustling leaves, Jorja's keen eyes caught a glimpse of Jago discreetly observing them from the window of his bedroom, his expression a mix of intrigue and admiration for their diligent efforts in unlocking the secrets of Telm. Jago was unsure whether he was meant to knock, just come in or peer over the fence. He looked over the fence to see if they were there first.

"Nanny, is there magic to stop Jago from watching us during training? He is watching us!" she asked. "No, child, there is not. We could ask him over and swear him to secrecy," Lissa sighed. "But he is so nasty and mean; look at his dirty clothes," Jorja retorted.

"Jorja, remember your Royal Training. Although we may think negatively, we must never speak of it. He may be poor or neglected," she stated. Jorja felt ashamed for thinking ill of Jago. She realised he looked thin, and she felt sorry for him.

"Let us invite him over and feed him; that should ensure his silence." Jorja giggled, and Lissa joined in. They waved Jago over, and he joined them at the garden table with fruit cake and tea.

Jago brushed off his clothes, clearly embarrassed, and sat down. Jorja poured tea and asked, "Do you take milk and sugar, Jago?" "I don't know, never had it before," he replied in a thick Cornish accent. "Well, let's try with milk, and you can add sugar if you like," Jorja said, adding a dash of milk.

Lissa cut the fruit cake and served Jago a slice before Jorja.

"Jago, how do you fancy being my helper?" Lissa asked. "I'd do anything for another bit of that cake, Mrs," he said, mouth full. "You shall have your fill, but do not overeat. We still have lunch and dinner," Lissa said, seeing Jago's eyes bulge at the thought of more food. She felt sorry for him but kept her thoughts to herself. "That would be nice of you, Mrs," he said, stuffing more cake into his mouth. "Good, but Jago, you must never repeat anything you see or hear. Is that all right?" "It is OK. I already know you are witches. I saw you lifting plants last week. Did not know I was watching. Plus, I don't got no one to tell," he said, slurping his tea. "Think I'll have some of that sugar, please, maid," he said, glancing at Jorja. She added two spoons of sugar to his tea. Jago enjoyed the tea much better with sugar.

Lissa and Jorja used cake forks, while Jago used his fingers. "First, you need to clean up to be my helper," Lissa said, pulling out new clothes. She had bought them online yesterday and had arrived early this morning. "Thank you, Mrs," he said.

"Right, a shower and haircut, then you will be fit to dine with the Queen," she joked, not revealing their true identities and never mentioning which queen. Jago went indoors, and Lissa gave him towels, a face cloth, and a new toothbrush. "Everything you need is on the side. See you on the other side, dear," she smiled. Jago sheepishly went to the bathroom.

As he stood beneath the soothing spray of the shower, feeling the warmth against his skin, he couldn't help but reflect on the neglect he had endured. He realised it had been far too long since he last experienced such a simple pleasure as a proper wash. With each gentle rub of the soap, he felt the weight of his past discontent wash away, leaving him longing for more moments like this, even though he knew his foster parents might not permit it regularly.

He meticulously dried himself off post-shower before slipping into a fresh set of clothes, marvelling at the unusual luxury of owning new attire. It was a novel experience for him that brought a sense of dignity and self-respect he had never experienced before. His dripping hair hinted at his recent shower as he emerged from the bathroom, where Lissa stood waiting, armed with a comb and scissors, ready to help him with his grooming needs.

The ringing phone interrupted the unfolding scene, prompting Lissa to answer swiftly. Megan's concerned mother was on the line, seeking assurance that Jorja, too, had not succumbed to the illness that had befallen her daughter. Lissa graciously conveyed her gratitude for the care shown and reassured that Jorja remained in good health, putting Megan's mother's worries to rest.

During Jago's absence in the refreshing ritual of his shower, Lissa busied herself making further provisions for him, investing £300 in acquiring additional clothes to cater to his newfound needs. Additionally, she prepared the spare bedroom, ensuring it was welcoming and ready for him to utilise whenever he desired, acknowledging and honouring his newfound sense of belonging and comfort in her home.

"My word, you look so much better," Lissa said, cutting his matted hair. She gave him a nice cut and passed him a mirror. 'I don't look arf bad,' he thought.

"Fit for purpose," Lissa smiled. They went to the garden, and Jorja exclaimed, "OMG Jago, you look amazing." She could not believe it was the same boy.

They stopped for tea at 11 am, and Jago sat next to Jorja, enjoying the tea more and more.

"Tell me about your family, Jago?" Lissa urged. He hesitated but began. "Well, my mother started using drugs when my father left. I was taken into foster care and placed with Demelza and Keverne. Those two are always drunk; the only food is chips and occasionally ham. I don't talk to them much," he said miserably.

Jorja's heart melted, and tears rolled down her cheeks. She decided to care for Jago as she would a brother. "Nan, can we help him? I feel so sorry for him," she sent a message to her grandmother using her mind. "Yes, child, we can; I will visit his family later," Lissa responded in her mind.

"Jago, we are from another world. I'm Queen Morwenna, and Jorja is a princess. I left our realm to protect Jorja," she started. Jago sat with his mouth open. "I knew there was something weird when I saw you lift those plants," he responded. Lissa chuckled. "So, what do I call you?" Jago asked. "Lissa is fine. We do not want special treatment, but we need your help," Jorja said, smiling.

"What help?" Jago asked nervously, his dubious nature kicking in. He sure did not trust people much. "Training Jorja, we have decided we would like you to be her training partner," Lissa said. "Training for what? Like a marathon?" He knew sports were not his strong point, but the food was enticing. "No, dear boy, we will return to our home planet, Enrac. A battle is raging, and Jorja needs to take the throne and protect it from her Uncle Helgi. He wants to take the kingdom by force, and we must protect it," Lissa explained. Jago could not believe what he heard. He pinched himself, but it hurt, so he knew it was real.

"What do you need me to do?" he asked. "First, learn Telm Training. Then, spar with Jorja to help her train. You will have all the food you need, together with new clothes, and I have made up the spare room just in case you wish to stay over," Lissa stated. Jago had never heard anything like it and repeated the word "food." "Yes, there is plenty of food. I've ordered more clothes for you, which will arrive tomorrow. You can stay with us if you want," Lissa again said.

Though already content with the arrangements in place, Jago was particularly pleased with the substantial amount of food provided. The delivery was right on time, arriving precisely at noon, prompting Jorja and Jago to immediately start unpacking the abundance of crates filled with various goodies. As he assisted in the unpacking, Jago couldn't help but be struck by the sheer volume of food before him, far more than he had ever seen catered to a single household.

Lissa's practical mind was already devising a plan to ensure everything would run smoothly with the additional help. However, Jago's reaction took everyone by surprise when he was overwhelmed by the generosity and abundance of food he had encountered since arriving, and he finally let his emotions show. With tears welling up in his eyes, he hung his head, emotions brimming over. Concerned by his sudden emotional outburst, Lissa gently inquired about his well-being, worried she might have overlooked something important. In response, Jago mustered the courage to express his simple yet profound realisation that he had never experienced such an outpouring of kindness and generosity. Sheepishly admitting that this unexpected act of kindness had deeply touched him, Jago couldn't help but entertain the thought of staying indefinitely in this new, welcoming environment.

"Jago, you do not have to feel ashamed. We are all friends here," Lissa replied. "Put everything away, Jorja. Please show Jago where things go. I am off to see Keverne and Demelza. I expect you to be teaching Jago Telm on my return," Lissa said, heading for the front door.

Lissa crossed the road and was taken aback by Jago's dilapidated house. As she crossed the road to knock on the door, she could not help but cringe at the sight of the tattered door and the peeling paint that adorned the entrance. It contrasted the careful attention she bestowed upon her subjects on Enrac, ensuring their well-being and care.

Upon hearing the unfamiliar voice inviting her in, Lissa hesitated momentarily before knocking again, this time more firmly. The voice insisted the entrance was open, prompting her to push the door ajar and step inside. Her unfamiliarity with entering neighbours' homes was evident in her hesitant movements.

As she entered the dimly lit house, a man abruptly stood up and approached her, his demeanour defensive and wary. The house smelt of cigarettes and stale beer. He was most definitely Keverne as Lissa surveyed the chaotic scene surrounding her - a clutter of beer cans, alcohol bottles, and grime that seemed to cover every surface. The overpowering stench of sweat, alcohol, and stale cigarettes hung in the air, assaulting her senses.

Maintaining her composure, Lissa addressed the man, informing him that Jago would no longer stay in such neglectful conditions. She explained that she had reported the situation to Social Services, who had a comprehensive file on the neglect in the household. With a sense of authority, she declared that Jago would now reside with her, receiving the proper care and education he deserved.

In response, Demelza, a woman with a dishevelled and angry appearance, erupted in a fit of rage at Lissa's words, accusing her of wrongdoing and demanding the return of Jago. Despite the woman's harsh words, Lissa remained resolute in her decision, determined to provide a better future for Jago, even as she perceived that Demelza could benefit from some self-care and cleanliness.

Taking a stand against the neglect and dismal living conditions, Lissa confronted Demelza in the dingy hallway. Her voice rang with authority. She pointed out the severe state of Demelza, Kevern, and the boy, underscoring the deplorable lack of hygiene and nourishment permeating the air. With a sense of urgency, Lissa emphasised the need for intervention, highlighting the dire need for help for the boy. In response, Demelza, in a defensive and defiant tone, tried to downplay the severity of the situation, suggesting that the boy should know better at his age. Undeterred, Lissa remained resolute and firm in her decision to involve Social Services and provide a safer environment for the boy. As tension escalated, Demelza's verbal threats only fuelled Lissa's determination to ensure the boy's well-being. Demelza went for Lissa, too, leading her to take swift action and lift Demelza off her feet, a reaction born out of frustration and disbelief at the neglect she had witnessed. Before parting ways, Lissa reiterated her commitment to aiding the boy, showing compassion despite the challenging circumstances.

Stepping away from the chaos and stench of the house, Lissa focused on seeking help for Jago, making the necessary call to Social Services to secure a better future for him. Demelza grabbed Lissa by the arm, but without thinking, Lissa lifted the drunken woman off her feet again, with her mind, and flung her to the ground on the other side of the hallway. Lissa did not object to using her magic on these people, mainly because no one would ever believe two drunken specimens like them. "I said good day to you," she repeated, stepping outside again into the clean, fresh air, thankful to be away from the eyesore and the smell of that wretched home.

She walked home with more determination than ever before and immediately made for the house phone, calling social services. "Hello, good day to you. My name is Mellissa Jayne Rosewall. I reside at Number 1 Trelawne Close, Whitstone, Cornwall, and I want to report child neglect. I have taken the boy away from the foster parents you entrusted him to. They are constantly drunk, and they do not feed him. They beat him and made him work. The boy's name is Jago, and he is now under my protection. He has been washed and fed and is currently being educated. I have employed a tutor for both him and my granddaughter. He will receive the highest education and be well-fed and clothed under my roof. Do you have anything to say on this matter?" Lissa informed the gentleman on the other end of the phone.

The gentleman was at a loss for words. "I will call up the information on my computer. Please wait a moment, Ms Rosewell," he said, putting her on hold.

Another voice came on the phone, this time a woman. "Hello, Mrs. Rosewall. I understand that Jago is at your house. We have had complaints this week about him. We do know about the foster parents, but unless Jago tells us what is happening, we are powerless to do anything. I saw him last week at school when I visited, and he was too scared to say anything about them. I thank you for caring for him and ask you to impress upon your kindness for a while longer until we can sort out suitable alternative accommodation," the woman asked.

Lissa was taken aback by this, "Who am I speaking with? I do not believe I heard your name," Lissa asked in her most regal voice.

"I'm sorry. In my haste, I forgot to introduce myself. My name is Tressa Penhale. I am Jago's Social Services advisor," she replied, somewhat embarrassed. "Firstly, Ms. Penhale, may I return to your statement about more suitable accommodation? I wish to adopt the boy so that no other suitable accommodation will be required. In the meantime, I think it would be a good idea for you to visit us. Secondly, how do I obtain legal guardianship of Jago until I can adopt him?" Lissa politely asked.

"Yes, Mrs Rosewall, I think a visit would be marvellous. I have some free time on June 28. Is that suitable for you?" Tressa asked. "That is more than a month away. So, you are entrusting me with the boy until then? I expect you here Monday at 10:00 sharp," the queen said. Showing her royal status and unwillingness to be brushed off, she did not wait for a response and continued, "Good day to you, Ms. Penhale. I shall see you on Monday."

She hung up the phone, feeling a deep sense of satisfaction radiating through her being. Her morning had been filled with grand and minor achievements, and this sense of accomplishment now filled her with contentment. Utilising her innate magical abilities, she created a wholesome and delectable lunch for herself and those around her. In a burst of creativity, she conjured a large jug filled with a delightful concoction of freshly cut fruits mingled with the zesty essence of oranges and pineapples. Preparing this vibrant medley took mere minutes showing her skill and efficiency.

As she deftly arranged the spread upon a tray, a flicker of magic enveloped her, causing the tray to float effortlessly behind her as she exited the bungalow. Placing the tray gently upon the waiting table, she let out a soft sigh of contentment, feeling the warmth of a job well done spreading through her.

Turning her attention to the children, she gently commanded them to tidy up before indulging in the feast. Jago, in particular, couldn't help but be awestruck by the delicacies before him: sandwiches, sausage rolls, miniature Cornish pasties, and salads brimming with vibrant colours. The table seemed to groan under the weight of its delicious offerings.

Taking a seat, Jago eagerly reached for a glass of the refreshing juice before him, savouring its incredible sweetness. Uncertain of the proper etiquette, he hesitated, wondering if he should wait to be served or help himself. Eventually, he decided on the former.

Noticing his decorum, Lissa smiled warmly at him and placed a plate before him, a silent invitation to partake in the culinary delights. Meanwhile, Jorja, ever the gracious hostess, busied herself refilling the glasses with more invigorating juice, ensuring their guests' glasses were constantly refreshed.

As Jorja extended a plate of sandwiches towards Jago, he hesitated momentarily before taking only a quarter, his actions a blend of courtesy and restraint. In this simple gesture, he unwittingly reflected the values of politeness and modesty, a reminder of the importance of manners even amidst the most tempting feasts.

"You may take as many as you wish. There is only one rule in this house: if you put it on your plate, you must eat it," she said with a cheeky smile. It was not a rule; it was to stop people from taking more food than necessary. He thought it was not a rule but a challenge to see if he could eat everything; of course, he could. Jago was starving, and his stomach had grumbled at him since the cake.

He took two more quarters and waited for everything else to be served.

"You may offer something around, Jago, if you wish," Jorja stated. "You are part of this family now, and as such, you are allowed to serve as well," she said, handing around the salad with a huge smile. Jago returned her smile, feeling happier than he had in years.

"Family," he whispered so no one heard. "Yes, dear boy, family," Lissa responded.

After devouring a filling and satisfying lunch, Jago's heart brimmed with contentment, and a sense of happiness flooded over him, washing away any lingering doubts or worries. At that moment, profound gratitude enveloped him, prompting him to utter a silent prayer deep within his soul. He basked in the warmth of the fleeting moment, wishing fervently that the joy and peace he felt would be a constant presence in his life. As he looked towards the future with newfound hope, he whispered a heartfelt plea to the universe, expressing his desire never to cross paths with his foster parents again, yearning for a life free from the shadows of the past and filled with the promise of brighter tomorrows.

"Jago, can you show me what you have learned in your Telm Training?" Lissa asked. Jago's face suddenly turned bright red. "I'm not sure I can remember it all, but can Jorja go through it with me?" he asked shyly. "Of course, she can, dear boy, and Jago, you do not have to fear me; I shall never lay a finger on you or make you work for food. As a child living in this house, I ask that you help Jorja with her training by training alongside her. For this, you will receive food, clothing, and shelter. You are not some animal on display. I am interested in knowing that you have learned some things and are happy here," Lissa said, trying to calm the boy's embarrassment and reassure him that he was safe living with her and Jorja.

"I just don't want to disappoint you," he responded. "Nothing you could do would let me down. You need to realise that we are your friends, your family. Jago, how would you feel if I legally adopted you?" Lissa asked. "You mean live here with you forever? I could not think of anything nicer, to be honest," he responded.

"Then it is settled. Tressa Penhale, your social worker, will arrive at 10:00 on Monday, and we will start all the paperwork; for now, you can call me Lissa," she stated. "Oh, Jago, that's wonderful news!" Jorja squealed with excitement. She had grown fond of him. He had worked hard on his training, and she was impressed. He was courteous with her, not the nasty boy he was at school.

The two children got up and happily showed Lissa their Telm Training. Lissa was very impressed with what Jago had learned. She liked the boy and thought he would make a good companion for Jorja. "Very good. You are both doing so well. Jago, I had no idea you were such a quick study. Well done, young man," she complimented.

"Think it could be time for some Magic Training! What do you think, Jago?" Lissa asked, with Jago looking like one of those

'Nodding Dogs' you find in the back of a car. She sent Jorja a mind message, reminding her to keep her protection bubble up in case someone was tracking her magic. Lissa decided to leave Jorja to manage her magic bubble and take Jago inside to show him his room. Jago was amazed. He had a bed, wardrobe, chest of drawers, and bedside cabinet. He had never had anything like this before. It was so overwhelming that he sat on his bed and cried. "It's alright, Jago," Lissa said. He was unable to speak through the emotional tears.

When he recovered, he began telling Lissa about his mother.

"When I was a baby, and I cried for food, you know, like a baby does, Mum used to inject me with heroin to quieten me down. When Tressa eventually got me away from her, they put her in prison and me with Demelza and Keverne. I was content at first, but as I got older, the beatings started. When I was about five or six years old, I had to go out in the garden in winter and chop wood for the fire. I had sandals, shorts, and a T-shirt and was out there for about five hours until Keverne deemed he had enough wood. It never stopped. It felt like I only had to breathe, and I would be hit. I have never had such nice things. My bed at home is a blanket on the floor," he said through his tear-stained face.

"It is time for a little fun in your life, Jago. Come on, follow me," she said, gently pulling at his arm and leading him to the garden. Jorja was practising lifting the table and chairs with her mind when they walked back into the garden. Jago gasped, and upon hearing him, she gently placed them on the ground again. He slumped into one of the chairs, unable to believe what he had just seen.

"Would you like to be able to do that?" Lissa asked. "OMG, would I ever?" his eager little face beamed up at her, making her heart swell even more for this boy. He was not a bad boy; he had just had a rough start in life, and she hoped to change that for him.

"Since I will adopt you, you will officially be a royal. Royals of Enrac are allowed to give other people powers. But, Jago, you must not abuse these powers. You must only use them for good. I have looked into your heart and seen that you are a good boy who has had a horrid life until now. Your heart is pure, good, and kind." With that, Lissa entered a trance and reached out with her arms towards Jago.

She wobbled on the spot, and after some time, she put her hands on his shoulders. Jago flinched away from her.

"If you wish to be able to do magic, you must allow me to put my hands on your shoulder," she stated. He agreed, and she returned to her trance, connecting to the Kitte. When she finished, she pulled out a small pouch from her pocket. She opened it and showed Jago what it contained. It contained gems of different colours and sizes, yet only one glowing, a deep red gem almost like the colour of a good Beaudoux wine. Jago gasped and covered his mouth with his hands; Lissa nodded so he could pick out the glowing crystal, informing him that she could not touch it herself. He lowered his hands, reached for the glowing crystal, and pulled it out. His eyes began to glow lightly, the same colour as his crystal. When the glow had stopped, his eyes took on a red tinge. "Jago, you can now do magic if you wish, but you must learn alongside Jorja and work hard. Learning magic will not be easy for a non-royal, but you will do well with the correct guidance and willpower. Jago, you must always keep this crystal with you, no matter what." Jago was dumbstruck and unable to say a word. He just stood open mouthed, looking at Lissa, to which she giggled and led him outside. "I will have your crystal made into a necklace, I think so that you wear it always," she said confidently.

"I have to warn you about one thing, though, Jago, you must only use your powers for good, or they will be taken away from you," she warned. Lissa instructed him to use his magic, and he began practising. By the end of the day, both Jago and Jorja were moving objects with their minds. Jago was quick to learn and had caught up with Jorja's training. They ate dinner and washed, ready for bed.

Lissa visited Jorja first and kissed her goodnight. Then she knocked on Jago's door and entered. "Is everything alright, dear?" she asked. "This bed is so comfortable. I really cannot thank you enough, Lissa," he said. Lissa sat beside him on the bed and told him he did not need to thank her. "How would you like to go camping after Tressa's visit on Monday? We could go to the moors and have some fun. We can train more and swim in the lakes," Lissa suggested. "Jago, can you swim?" she asked politely. "No, but I love the water, and I'm not scared of it," he informed her. "Would you like to learn? I can teach you!" she offered. "You have done so much for me, Lissa. I really could not ask for anything else," he objected. "Nonsense, child. It is a good skill; it may save your life one day, plus it was fantastic training," she chuckled. "Do you need anything else, dear?" she yawned.

Lissa got into bed that night, very satisfied with all they had accomplished that day.

Sunday was as eventful as Saturday, with everyone preparing the camping gear and packing food and drinks. The children fit in their Telm and Magic Training, which Jago liked best. He had fallen into a routine of helping when things needed doing and seemed content, not moaning or grumbling. He enjoyed being around Jorja, and together they made a great team.

The delivery came, and it made Jago cry again. He had never seen such nice clothes, certainly not for him. He decided to shower and change his clothes daily, even though he had never had more than one outfit. He felt guilty for having evil thoughts about his previous life but knew he was safe with Lissa and Jorja.

They ate, and Lissa could hardly believe how much food Jago consumed. 'Poor soul, he has not eaten properly for so long. It is no wonder he is so thin. Well, we will soon change that,' she giggled to herself. She liked having him here, and so did Jorja. Jorja had been walking around with a permanent smile on her face. She thought Jago was a good influence on her, but she dreaded their first disagreement. 'You know what children are like when they disagree; OMG, the world has ended,' she chuckled again.

Lissa magically caught up on all the washing and ironing with another person in the house; more washing was needed. Jago enjoyed his showers each morning and the feeling of wearing fresh clothes. Maybe she could place a more significant order when they return from camping. Jorja could do with some new clothes. It would be good if the children helped pick some clothes out.

CHAPTER ELEVEN

The household was busy getting the house cleaned for Tressa's visit. Lissa showed the children how to use their magic for household chores. It was fun and exciting, and the children loved it. There were accidents, like Jorja accidentally knocking over a plant pot, but Lissa was on hand to show her how to clean it up.

At 10:00, there was a knock at the door, and Lissa calmed herself enough to open it. "Hello, I'm Tressa Penhale from Social Services," the woman announced, showing Lissa her ID badge.

Tressa had long, straight black hair and deep, soulful brown eyes. She was pretty and wore just a hint of makeup. She wore a smart trouser suit, which was practical for visiting clients. Tressa had no idea why she was there. These meetings usually took months to set up, but here she was, standing at the front door, checking her watch to ensure she was on time. She could not shake her strange feeling when she spoke to this woman on the telephone.

"Please come in. My granddaughter and Jago are in the lounge," Lissa said. Tressa was guided to the lounge and sat next to the children. "Jago?" she asked quizzically, her eyes widening in surprise at the unexpected reunion. "Yes, it's me," he responded shyly, his voice barely above a whisper as he nervously shifted in his seat. "You look very well, Jago," she remarked, her words laced with genuine warmth.

"You're not going to make me go back to Demelza and Keverne, are you?" he asked, concerned, the worry evident in his furrowed brow. "No, I think not. You look much happier here," she reassured him, her tone gentle and understanding. "Can I offer you some tea?" Lissa interrupted, her kind gesture breaking the tension in the room. "Yes, please. Thank you. Mrs. Rosewall, you have a lovely home," she complimented, her gaze wandering around the cosy living space. "Thank you, dear," Lissa said, tottering off to make the drinks, her steps slow and deliberate as she disappeared into the kitchen.

In the kitchen, she called Jorja to help her, the clinking of teacups and saucers mingling with their hushed conversation as they prepared the beverages using a touch of magic, allowing Tressa and Jago a moment of solitude to reconnect.

Jorja returned with a plate of freshly made cake slices, the sweet aroma wafting through the air as she settled the plate down quietly. Her presence added a newfound sense of comfort to the room.

"Tell me about your education, Jorja, is it?" Tressa inquired, her curiosity piqued by the young girl's poised demeanour. "Jago and I attended the same school, but my nan won the lottery, and starting tomorrow, we will have a home tutor," Jorja stated matter-of-factly, her words tinged with a hint of secrecy. "Oh, I see. Private education is rather good fun," Tressa remarked, nodding in acknowledgment as she took a sip of the fragrant tea.

"Will you be visiting Demelza and Keverne on this visit?" Lissa asked, her voice filled with genuine interest in their upcoming plans. "No, I have an appointment with them on June 28," she retorted, a flicker of resolve in her eyes as she mentioned the scheduled meeting. "I think it would be a good idea to turn up unannounced so you can see their true colours," Lissa suggested.

Tressa just smiled, but Lissa knew she would have to intervene.

She offered tea and thought for a moment. She decided to use her magic to persuade Tressa, thinking long and hard before sending the subtle magic to Tressa, who shuddered softly.

"Are you cold, dear?" Lissa asked. "No, but on reflection, I think I may just pop in and visit Demelza," Tressa suggested. "What an excellent idea. Come back afterwards. We have much to discuss," Lissa stated, smiling. Tressa had asked Lissa for her assistance, and she had gone along to help in any way she could.

Tressa and Lissa walked quickly to Jago's foster parents' house. There was a lot of shouting, banging, and crashing, and then a window broke. Tressa grabbed her phone in case the police were needed. The front door was ajar, so Tressa and Lissa entered the property. Demelza and Keverne were drunk and fighting.

Jago wondered what was going on. They rarely argued, only ever shouted at him to do more work. It was irregular.

"Enough of this foolishness," Tressa ordered. Lissa removed the spell, thinking she might have gone overboard. Demelza and Keverne immediately stopped fighting and sat down, unable to understand what had happened. They looked at Tressa, standing over them with her hands on her hips and shaking her head.

"You got all that money for fostering Jago, and this is how I find you! Beer bottles, cigarette stubs, dirt, and grime. I am happy that you will lose Jago. You are a disgrace and will be charged with child neglect and banned from fostering again," Tressa said and stormed out of the house, with Lissa following.

Tressa was steaming mad. She knew what was happening but was powerless unless Jago had spoken up. They probably made him clean up before one of her visits. She could not believe she had lost her temper like that. It was most unusual, but she loved children and did not want them hurt.

She marched back to where Jago was living with her fists clenched, needing to know what had happened to him while he was with those two degenerates.

Inside, Jorja and Jago were drinking tea. Jago was concerned, and Jorja tried to calm him down. She decided to perform a magic trick, carrying a cake using magic while walking. It was not as easy as her grandmother made it look. She almost dropped them before gently setting them down on the coffee table. Jago laughed, and she sneered at him jokingly.

Jago liked Jorja but was not sure she felt the same. He had the impression she pitied him. He would bide his time, but he already knew his feelings.

The door opened, and Tressa stormed in, followed by Lissa. Tressa asked Jago to tell her everything, which he did. Knowing he was safe from Demelza and Keverne, he found it less constraining to speak out.

"Right then, now that's sorted, shall we discuss what will happen with Jago and how I go about adopting him?" Lissa asked. "Well, we need to slow down. Firstly, it will take years to adopt Jago. Secondly, I cannot leave Jago in your care until that happens. There are formalities in place," Tressa explained. Lissa was having none of it.

She used her powers to persuade Tressa.

"I tell you what, let us complete the paperwork, and in the meantime, Jago can stay here with you until the adoption goes through. You can foster him in the meantime," Tressa commented.

Lissa smiled, thankful her magic had not let her down.

Tressa was confused, unable to understand why she was agreeing. Her boss would be mad, but she could not stick to her guns.

"I need you to fill in one more form to cover us while the adoption goes through," Tressa informed her, handing Lissa the form. Lissa returned it with a completed foster carer's form.

Tressa informed them that a court case would be brought against Demelza and Keverne, which Jago would need to attend and give his statement. She then left. Lissa sighed with relief, knowing she could relax for a while. The court case might prove problematic, but she now pushed the thoughts from her mind.

CHAPTER TWELVE

On Tuesday, Lissa decided that it was finally time to infuse their routine with additional excitement and adventure. She completed the perpetual task of washing the never-ending stack of clothes before rounding up the children and instructing them to prepare for their upcoming journey to the moors.

After loading the vehicle, the trio brought all the essentials for a successful expedition. Jago ensured that the food supplies were safely secured, eliciting chuckles from Jorja and Lissa. The atmosphere inside the car was vibrant and cheerful as they embarked on their road trip towards the moors.

Questions swirled in Jago's mind as the vehicle travelled towards the moors, prompting him to gather his thoughts and prepare for a heart-to-heart conversation about his uncertainties and fears with Lissa.

Upon reaching their destination, Lissa meticulously selected a secluded spot strategically away from potential disturbances to set up their camp. While aware of the legal issues concerning camping on Bodmin Moor, they prioritised their need for seclusion and tranquillity.

They efficiently began establishing their temporary home in the wilderness, laughter intermingling with their efforts. Jago faced challenges assembling the yurt and used his magical abilities for assistance. Realising the importance of safeguarding their actions,

Lissa maintained a vigilant lookout, contemplating the potential detection of Jago's magic.

With a growing concern for their safety, Lissa swiftly moved to protect Jago with her magical prowess, imparting him the knowledge of creating a defensive shield. Despite Jago's swift grasp of the technique, the drain on his energy reserves mirrored Jorja's initial struggles, underscoring the complexities of magical applications in their adventure.

Lissa's instructions were evident as she emphasised the importance of maintaining a protective bubble outside the bungalow or yurt, particularly when utilising magic to prevent unwanted visitors from intruding upon their space. She knew the shield bubble was impenetrable to all but royal magic, granting them security while on Enrac. However, with this knowledge in mind, Lissa realised the necessity of devising alternative methods to ensure their safety amidst the new environment.

Given the circumstances, they consciously decided to avoid taking an extensive walk that day instead of taking a brief stroll from the conveniently located car park to their designated spot. As they traversed the picturesque landscape, crossing a quaint clapper bridge, their gazes were drawn to the impressive sight of Rough Tor, pronounced Row Tor to locals, majestically towering in the distance. Catching a glimpse of a sombre stone memorial near their campsite bearing an inscription recounting a tragic past event. Jago took it upon himself to read aloud the poignant words etched into the stone: "This monument erected by Public Subscription in memory of Charlotte Dymond who Matthew Weekes murdered on Sunday 14th

April 1844."

Amidst the tranquil setting, they also observed the numerous ponies roaming freely in the vicinity, accompanied by a few majestic buzzards gracefully circling above, scouting for their next meal. The scene before them was enchanting, encapsulating a blend of natural beauty and historical significance, intertwining the past with the present in a harmonious symphony of elements.

Back at camp, Telm and magic training were the order of the day. As a skilled magic wielder, Lissa created a protective cloak of invisibility around their camp, shielding it from prying eyes and casting a powerful barrier to ward off any potential threats, whether mundane or magical, that dared approach. The diligent Telm training sessions progressed smoothly under Lissa's guidance, as the young learners honed their abilities to execute precise and formidable movements with grace. Daily dedication to training became a vital routine. This fostered their physical strength and nimbleness, with both children making commendable progress.

As the day ended, a sumptuous meal awaited the trio. To replenish their energies, Lissa skilfully prepared a hearty feast of sausage, creamy mashed potatoes, and baked beans. The satisfying meal concluded with a shared sense of contentment and gratitude despite the lingering exhaustion from their magical exertions. Lissa, reflecting on her past reluctance to use magic, wrestled with self-reproach for underestimating her magical prowess, perceiving it as a sign of weakness; a realisation dawned upon her, understanding that her conscious restraint was, in reality, a manifestation of her steadfast resolve to shield her grandchild from harm, a noble sacrifice that underscored her unwavering dedication to their protection.

Slumber beckoned the weary trio, the peaceful quiet of the night enveloping the camp. Though physically and emotionally taxing, their restful repose brought a sense of solace, a temporary respite from the demands of their magical pursuits. Anticipation lingered in the air for the forthcoming day, where the prospect of engaging in friendly sparring with sticks loomed on the horizon, promising a blend of challenge and camaraderie that awaited them in their magical journey.

The morning began with a sense of freshness and vitality at exactly 07:00, as the harmonious symphony of birds and various wildlife greeted the day, stirring everyone from their slumber under the serene backdrop of a beautiful blue sky. Lissa, basking in the splendour of the fine morning, couldn't help but smile, feeling truly fortunate to call Cornwall her home rather than a bustling and cramped town. As they readied for the day's adventures, they diligently packed their backpacks with essentials before leisurely driving towards the renowned Minions.

The scenic journey to the Minions was a delightful experience, albeit slow-moving due to how the road twisted and was extremely narrow, extending the drive time to roughly twenty minutes. Upon arriving at the quaint village of Minions, they were greeted by the timeless sight of locals tending to their sheep, cattle, and ponies - a practice steeped in centuries-old tradition. Observing the amusing spectacle of sheep leisurely positioning themselves in the middle of the road, seemingly indifferent to passing vehicles, highlighting the charming rural lifestyle unique to the area. The lush hedgerows adorned with a myriad of wildflowers in full bloom during early summer imparted a fairy-tale essence to the landscape, with lush trees and undergrowth enveloped in moss and lichen. Intrigued by the folklore surrounding Bodmin Moor, Lissa eagerly purchased a book detailing the region's rich myths and legends, intending to regale the children with enchanting tales later that evening, further enriching their visit.

Immersed in an atmosphere teeming with romance and historical significance, remnants of ancient civilisations dotted the landscape, evoking a profound connection to the past. The presence of The Hurlers, a trio of stone circles dating back to approximately 1800 BC, served as poignant reminders of the pagan rituals once practised within their sacred confines. Motivated to share the intriguing local legends with the children, Lissa recounted the captivating tale of St. Cleer, who, as the story goes, petrified men for engaging in Sunday hurling matches instead of attending church, illustrating the region's rich tapestry of folklore and tradition.

Delving deeper into the lore of the land, Lissa narrated the myth surrounding the Cheesewring, a grouping of colossal granite boulders perched prominently on the landscape. According to Cornish folklore, these imposing structures were attributed to the giants of old. Legend has it that the Cheesewring originated from a legendary contest between a man and a giant during the initial introduction of Christianity to the British Isles. The giant, Uther, challenged Saint Tue to a rock-throwing contest, wherein the outcome would determine the fate of the giants. Unyielding in his resolve, Saint Tue, aided by a divine angel, prevailed as the rocks flung by Uther tumbled. At the same time, his own remained steadfast, signifying the giants' eventual conversion to Christianity.

The children thoroughly enjoyed Lissa's fascinating history lessons, immersing themselves in the captivating stories she shared.

Little did they know that the tales they assumed were made up turned out to be deeply rooted in the rich tapestry of myths and legends woven throughout Cornwall's history.

After a delightful lunch stop at the quaint Cheesewring Hotel, the children were so enamoured with the cosy atmosphere that they decided to extend their stay for a dinner treat. Relishing in the warm ambience, they leisurely returned to camp for a soothing cup of tea.

Anticipation bubbled within them as they enthusiastically crafted their plans for the following day. They excitedly discussed their upcoming adventure of climbing Rough Tor and exploring the other mystical tors that dotted the landscape, with their final destination being the majestic Brown Willy.

Their day was peppered with joyous moments as they ogled at the array of wildlife, joyfully spotting various animals and birds while skilfully navigating past grazing sheep and peaceful cattle. Jorja's heart was captivated by the adorable sight of the ponies that crossed their path, her repeated exclamations of their cuteness adding an extra layer of delight to the already magical day.

When they returned to their cosy yurt nestled in the serene wilderness, a gentle breeze filled the air with the sweet scent of wildflowers. Feeling a chill after their long hike, Lissa turned to Jorja and kindly asked her to prepare a pot of soothing tea. As Jorja busied herself with the task, Lissa reached into her backpack and pulled out a brand-new book she had picked up from the quaint local store in the nearby village of the Minions the day before. Nestling into a plush cushion near the crackling fire, she eagerly opened the cover, immersing herself in the world of a captivating tale. Lissa read aloud.

The soft flicker of the flames danced in her eyes as she lost herself in the written words, enjoying the quiet companionship of the children's friend and the cosy shelter of their temporary home. Outside, the sounds of nature provided a soothing symphony that only enhanced the peaceful atmosphere of the moment. Time seemed to stand still as Lissa delved deeper into the story, each page offering a new adventure within the familiar walls of their yurt.

"Make no mistake in thinking all these legends are ancient and irrelevant to the modern day. In the late 1970s, an unusual excursion of reports of mutilated livestock on Bodmin Moor stirred local headlines, asking questions of how and why this could have happened. Locals reported sightings of a large black cat, similar to that of a leopard, which stirred rumour and gossip around the area as people grasped to come to terms with the strange chain of slaughtered animals. Since then, over sixty police reports have been filed claiming to have sighted the mythical beast."

"These reports ranged from being chased to spotting an eerily and unnaturally large animal in the distance. Some photo and video evidence exists, too, but this legitimacy has not been confirmed. The legend of the beast has been integral to the local culture of Bodmin Moor. Many believe that the beast has since bred and that more exist. In the 1990s, rumours became so serious that an official government investigation concluded that this type of beast, compared to a panther, could not survive in the UK. Alas, the myth continued as this was still not concrete enough to declare it did not exist."

"Theories of how the beast could have surfaced include the illegal importing of three pumas by a circus entertainer in 1978, which were eventually freed but never declared due to their illicit nature. Perhaps they bred and found a haven in the vast expanses of

Bodmin Moor. Perhaps these vast expanses are responsible for explaining why they are rarely sighted and not officially documented. Perhaps this legend will invite you to search for it yourself."

She enjoyed telling stories and carried on eagerly. "The Legends of King Arthur are possibly the most famous and recognisable tales in history. The complex interpolations of events of his life include many locations across Cornwall and, in this case, entails Dozmary pool in Bodmin Moor."

"King Arthur's sword, Excalibur, has many various sources of mythical enquiry! The contradicting stories of his legend by many authors in history all locate the origins of his sword as somewhere different, but one of the core and most believable sources detail that Arthur obtained the sword (which in Cornish is called <u>Calesvol)</u> from the lady of the lake who guided him through the mist of Dozmary where he could take the sword out of the stone."

"The sword was carried throughout his lifetime, but in his final moments, he ordered it to be taken back to the lake, where a knight threw it into the water. According to myth, an arm reached up and captured the sword, burying it under the water ever since."

"Many believe the sword may still be in Dozmary today, as the legend is so believable due to Bodmin Moor's mystique matching the description of the texts. Furthermore, its proximity to Glastonbury, Tintagel, and other key locations of Arthur's story furthers this theory over others that try to match the lake to those in Normandy, France. Whatever you believe, a trip to the lake is vital in visiting the Moorlands, so be sure to watch for a glistening under the water." The following story was short, so Lissa decided it would be the last one for the night. "St Cuby's Well is another legend. Holy

Wells are abundant in Cornwall, hidden in many beautiful hideaways and secret woodlands. Many are a source of great fortune to religious people, blessed by God to bring luck and healing. For this reason, so many are ornately crafted and carefully preserved."

"However, not all these Holy Wells have maintained their mythical status for positive reasons. A well-constructed by St. Cuby in 480AD has a story that makes the area feel more cursed than blessed. St Cuby created a chapel to feature a hand-crafted bowl with dolphins and griffins (gryphons) to celebrate and remember his time travelling. He was immensely proud of his creation but anxious of thieves looking to take from his sight and so cursed the bowl for anyone who may remove it."

"For many decades, the locals were aware of this curse and frightened enough to respect the well's status. However, one day, a spiteful farmer decided to test the curse, bringing all four of his strongest oxen to transport the well for himself. On arriving at the well, every oxen pulled as hard as they could, but all collapsed and died one by one. In complete shock, the farmer returned home empty-handed with neither the well nor his strongest oxen."

"Today, the bowl has been moved to the local parish church. To some, the curse is said to have passed itself onto whoever decided to move it. To others, its movement into a new place of worship meant the curse was not triggered. Please, however, do not try and test this curse, for you may suffer ill fate for the rest of your life!"

"The folklore and mythology circulating Cornwall brings the land to life. The stories like those above are only a small cut from centuries of tales told by the residents here. The connection of Cornish people to the land and the stories embedded within the land sets the Cornish identity apart from other cultures in the UK.

Bodmin Moor is usually suffocated in fog or sea mist. Thus, you will find yourself unlucky to stay in the area and not experience the eerie but enchanting nature of the environment it has to offer when the fog sweeps in."

As the night fell upon them, the group wearily went to their respective beds, still filled with laughter and playful banter over the mysterious Beast of Bodmin Moor. The cosy warmth of their blankets and sleeping bags enveloped them, providing peace and security despite the eerie tales that sparked earlier conversations. For most, slumber came effortlessly, their minds drifting into the realm of dreams.

Yet, amidst the stillness of the night, Jago found himself unable to find solace in sleep. His thoughts wandered to his birth mother, a woman shrouded in mystery and lingering questions. Each time he closed his eyes, vivid images of her flashed before him, stirring up a whirlwind of emotions that left him restless. The moon's ethereal glow cast shadows upon his troubled face, the yurt having a clear plastic top enabling one to look out through it as he tossed and turned, the weight of his subconscious thoughts pressing down upon him.

Amid the night, Jago's peaceful façade shattered, replaced by a visage of vulnerability. Beads of sweat formed on his forehead, cold and clammy against his skin, while his chest rose and fell rapidly, consumed by the chaos within his dreams. Whispers of the past intertwined with the present, blurring the lines between reality and the subconscious realm, leaving Jago in disarray.

The silence of the sleeping yurt was punctuated by the occasional creature scuttling past as Jago's internal turmoil played out in the depths of the night. The gentle rustling of the trees outside seemed to echo the restlessness within him, a symphony of unease that reverberated through the darkness. Despite his best efforts to find peace, Jago remained ensnared in the grips of his turbulent thoughts, grappling with emotions buried beneath the surface.

As dawn approached, casting a soft golden hue upon the horizon, Jago finally succumbed to the exhaustion that weighed heavily upon him. His dreams, though tumultuous, gradually subsided, allowing a fleeting moment of respite to wash over him. With the first light of morning creeping through the yurt, he awoke, the remnants of his turbulent night clinging to him like a shadow, a lingering reminder of the inner turmoil that had plagued his slumber.

The day commenced again with the delightful symphony of the dawn chorus filling the tranquil air, creating a serene beginning to their adventure. Excitedly anticipating the day ahead, they gathered together to enjoy a hearty breakfast before carefully packing their backpacks with nourishing food and essential provisions. With their supplies secured, they eagerly began their walk on the trail path in high spirits.

The well-marked path guided them effortlessly as they ventured forward, revealing the intriguing remnants of ancient stone settlements dating back to the illustrious Bronze Age. These archaeological treasures added a sense of wonder and historical depth to their journey, vividly depicting the region's rich past. As they ascended, the landscape unfolded before them, treating their eyes to a stunning panorama from the summit. To the west, a glistening lake sparkled beneath the sun's golden rays while sweeping vistas extended beyond Davidstow Airfield, captivating their senses with natural beauty and vastness.

Their route led them to the enchanting Little Rough Tor, where they paused to take in the rugged scenery before continuing to the imposing Rough Tor. From this vantage point, they saw the distant Brown Willy to the south, a majestic sight that inspired awe and admiration. Crossing the babbling De Lank River, they proceeded through a gate and over a stile, embarking on the challenging ascent towards Brown Willy's lofty peak.

Upon reaching the summit, they were greeted by a breathtaking land stretching endlessly before them, offering sweeping views from the historic Tintagel in the north to the picturesque Fowey in the south. As they luxuriated in the scenic grandeur before them, they observed a mesmerising display of wildlife unfolding in the skies above. Buzzards soared gracefully overhead, their keen eyes scanning the earth below until one abruptly dived, skilfully snatching a tiny vole in a swift, impressive display of hunting prowess.

Taking a well-deserved break, they relished a leisurely lunch at the summit, engaging in lively conversations about the mesmerising views and sharing stories on various topics. Eventually, the time came to bid farewell to the summit and begin their journey back to camp, their hearts filled with a sense of contentment and gratitude for the unforgettable experiences and cherished memories created throughout the day.

Feeling fatigued from their journey, they wearily arrived at the campsite, greeted by the picturesque scene of people leisurely absorbing the surrounding views. With a sense of responsibility, Lissa took charge as she engaged with the children, cautioning them against entering the yurt to avoid drawing unwanted attention that could result in their mysterious disappearances as the yurt was concealed in magic. Making sure that protective bubbles shielded both Jorja and Jago, Lissa meticulously scanned the crowd in search of anyone wielding magical abilities, a challenging task due to the influx of a whole coachload of new arrivals.

Relief flooded over Lissa once she confirmed that none of the individuals present possessed magical powers, allowing her to relax her guard temporarily. Witnessing her granddaughter's mastery of their magical bubbles, Lissa heaped praises on Jorja, wrapping her in a warm embrace. Curiosity piqued, Jago probed into the concept of the magical bubble, prompting Jorja to provide an intricate explanation about Eswella's magical tracking and the ongoing war in Enrac, carefully omitting details about the crystal.

As the sky opened up and rain began to fall, prompting the other visitors to depart, Lissa led the children into the expansive yurt, revelling in the thrill of a hidden sanctuary shielded from prying eyes. Inside the yurt, amidst shared laughter and merriment, they indulged in a scrumptious feast of sandwiches, pieces of chicken, scotch eggs, and quiche. With an insatiable appetite, Jago salivated at each bite, engrossed in animated conversations. At the same time, Lissa regaled them with enchanting tales of Enrac, fostering a sense of unity and joy among the small group gathered in their secret haven.

The following day started with a lovely blue sky, but fog and clouds quickly gathered on the horizon, casting a veil over the promising morning. Despite the impending rain, Jorja and Jago seized the opportunity to squeeze in some Telm and magic training before the deluge arrived. Their determination to hone their skills was palpable as they exerted themselves within the confines of the yurt, eager to absorb every ounce of knowledge and power they could grasp.

With hiking out of the question and the heavy rain forecast, Lissa resorted to checking her reliable weather app, a modern tool in an ancient land. The fateful decision to curtail their expedition loomed like a storm cloud on the brink of unleashing its heavy burden. The realisation hit hard that their adventure in the lush environs of the moors would be cut short by the relentless downpour prophesied for the week.

Amidst Jorja and Jago's disappointment, the unwelcome news rained down on Lissa like an unpleasant surprise. The call rattling the day's calm bore the weight of unexpected responsibility as Tressa Penhale brought news of the impending court appearance for Jago's adoption. Lissa's mind raced as she deliberated over the conflicting commitments, torn between the progress of Jorja's training and the looming deadline of the court summons.

The gravity of the situation deepened as Tressa revealed further details about the impending court date, setting the stage for a critical juncture in Jago's fate. Lissa grappled with conflicting emotions, torn between the desire to return to Enrac and the uncertainty of Jago's future. The looming courtroom battle painted a picture of tough choices ahead with no clear path.

Lissa made a decisive stand in a moment of clarity amidst the murky waters of uncertainty. The decision to opt for an affidavit instead of Jago's physical presence at the court hearing added a layer of complexity to the already intricate web of events. The tug-of-war between duty and affection played out in Lissa's mind as she navigated the delicate balance between loyalty to Jago and the demands of the legal system.

As Lissa wrapped up the call with a mix of resolve and apprehension, the realisation dawned that the unforeseen events would truncate their idyllic retreat on Bodmin Moor's. The children's disappointment echoed in the sombre mood that enveloped the makeshift dwelling, a stark contrast to the cheerful anticipation that had marked the start of their adventure.

Eager to shield the children from the impending storm, Lissa sought solace in explaining the peculiar meteorological phenomenon, the Brown-Willy effect, in which heavy rainfall develops over high ground and then travels downwind for a long distance. The effect produces heavy localised rain, which can cause disastrous flash flooding. The intricate dance of wind and rain painted a vivid picture of nature's power, unfolding like a mystery in the moody landscape of Cornwall. The children, now enlightened by Lissa's impromptu lesson, absorbed the knowledge like sponges, eager to unravel the mysteries of the natural world around them.

With a sense of urgency hanging in the air, the hurried packing and the hushed whispers of preparation underscored the gravity of the impending departure. The looming threat of the thunderstorm added a sense of urgency to their movements as they hastened to leave. The tangible tension in the air mirrored the charged atmosphere of the impending storm, a symphony of nature's might and fury set to unfold.

Just as the car became their sanctuary from the impending tempest, the rain descended in a tumultuous cascade, drumming against the metal shell like a relentless drumbeat. The crackling of lightning and the rumble of thunder above only heightened the children's unease, prompting Lissa to drown out the cacophony of the storm with the soothing strains of music on the radio.

Upon returning home from their exciting outing in the late afternoon, where they had left the rumbling thunderstorm in the distance, the atmosphere inside was serene. The soft light filtering through the windows illuminated the living room, casting a cosy glow over the scene. Despite the chill that seemed uncharacteristic for the time of year, a warmth enveloped the family as they settled in. With her culinary skills in full swing, Lissa began preparing her signature dish of Cornish Hen Pie infused with the enticing aromas of garlic and rosemary, accompanied by perfectly crisp roast potatoes and an assortment of vibrant veggies.

As the heavenly scents filled the room, Jago's anticipation grew, and his satisfaction was palpable as he indulged in each delectable bite. With contented smiles exchanged around the table, their shared meal became a moment of joy and connection. However, the evening's surprises did not end there. Ever the charmer, Jago managed to elicit giggles from the group with a cheeky request for dessert, showcasing his endearing personality that never failed to lighten the mood.

Looking ahead to the future, Lissa's thoughtful gesture of ordering a sleek suit and a stylish dress online for Jago and Jorja was evidence of her caring nature. With Jago's upcoming court appearance on Friday, she envisioned them exuding confidence and style in their new attire. To ensure a perfect fit, she took note of Jago's probable shoe size, opting for a size five to cover all bases and guarantee their impeccable presentation at the courthouse in ten days.

Amid their everyday routines and gestures of love and consideration, this family's bond grew stronger, reinforced by shared laughter, delicious meals, and thoughtful gestures that spoke volumes of their deep connection and mutual care.

Before going to bed, Jago sorted Lissa and asked if he could visit with his mother in Durham Prison. Lissa spoke with Jorja, and they agreed to set out the following day.

CHAPTER THIRTEEN

Jago, Lissa, and Jorja embarked on a significant journey to HMP Low Newton Prison in County Durham, marking the beginning of a life-altering experience that would test the limits of their relationships and resilience. Jago and Jorja had both expressed their interest in other creatures on Enrac, so Lissa decided to tell the children everything she knew.

Lissa captivated the children with additional stories and initiated an enchanting exploration into the mystical world of Undines, immersing herself in the rich lore that has fascinated countless generations with accounts of these extraordinary beings that challenge traditional understanding. Distinctive and remarkable, Undines can soar through the skies without wings, setting them apart from the typical image of Fairies and establishing a mysterious and singular presence within the expansive realm of myth and legend. Their origins, veiled in the mists of ancient tales handed down through history, continue to ignite intrigue and wonder, leaving a lasting impression on the human imagination with their breathtaking narratives.

As Lissa unravelled the intricate tapestry of Undine lore, she skilfully revealed the interconnectedness of these supernatural entities with diverse cultures worldwide, highlighting the profound ties that bind them to the natural world in which they dwell. Whether revered as benevolent nature spirits on Earth or revered as divine ancestors and deities on the mythical realm of Enrac, Undines embody a timeless symbolism of magic and mystery that transcends geographical boundaries and cultural divides, casting a spell of wonder upon all who dare to explore their enchanting stories.

In a mesmerising conclusion to her narrative, Lissa eloquently traced the etymology of the term 'fairy' back to its Latin roots, shedding light on the profound significance of 'fata' and its association with the intricate interplay between fate and existence. Through her words, Jorja and Jago found themselves spellbound by Undine folklore's enduring charm and timeless allure, opening their minds to a world brimming with fantastical possibilities and untold wonders.

The Evolution of Their Appearances: Through the annals of Enrac's rich history, the transformation of Undines has been profound and captivating. Initially characterised in ancient lore as ethereal and wise entities with an aura of unpredictability, they gradually underwent a romanticised metamorphosis, evolving into the endearing, diminutive beings we recognise today. This evolution of Undines intricately mirrors the ever-shifting societal perspectives. It plays a pivotal role in shaping our collective understanding of these mystical figures as they navigate the tapestry of time. In essence, their evolution serves as a testament to the dynamic nature of folklore and storytelling across generations, showcasing the adaptability of mythical beings to the changing needs and desires of the human imagination.

Erlends in Various Cultures: Across diverse mythologies and cultural tapestries, the manifestations of Erlends are a kaleidoscope of perceptions and beliefs. Some mythologies paint a picture of Erlends as revered and formidable beings, while others depict them with an air of grace, intelligence, and profound wisdom. This kaleidoscopic portrayal is an acknowledgement of the enduring allure of Undine-like entities. It underscores their versatile and multifaceted significance across different cultural landscapes, weaving a rich tapestry of beliefs and legends that transcend geographical boundaries and epochal shifts. Furthermore, the diverse interpretations of Undines in various cultures highlight the universal human fascination with the mystical and otherworldly, showing how these beings continue to captivate and inspire imagination across civilisations and ages.

Undines, the enigmatic guardians of the natural world, play a vital role in preserving the delicate balance of Inorac's ecosystem. Through their ethereal presence, they nurture the land, ensuring the vibrant growth of flora, the pristine purity of water bodies, and the overall well-being of the surrounding environments. The essence of nature itself seems to reside within these mystical beings, some of whom possess unique dominion over specific elements like lush woodlands or meandering rivers, further solidifying their connection to the earth they protect and uphold. Their symbiotic relationship with the environment emphasises their importance as protectors. It highlights the interconnectedness of all living things, illustrating a profound harmony that transcends physical existence and delves into the intricate web of life that sustains the world.

Lissa took a deep, calming breath, giving her body and mind a brief moment of respite. With a gentle smile adorning her features, she lovingly addressed the children, her words imbued with compassion and understanding. It was evident in her demeanour that she was not merely a caretaker but a nurturer, fostering a sense of belonging and comfort within the hearts of those under her care.

Slowly and deliberately, she glided towards the welcoming embrace of the kitchen, a place suffused with the warmth of familiarity and the tantalising aroma of culinary delights waiting to be born.

As the minutes stretched into moments, the children's anticipation mounted, their eyes shining with unbridled excitement at the prospect of what awaited them. When Lissa finally reappeared, her arms cradling a veritable cornucopia of culinary delights, their gasps of pleasure filled the room like a chorus of joyous melodies. On the tray she bore with grace and finesse lay a mouth-watering assortment of hot, flaky sausage rolls, their golden exteriors glistening in the soft light; succulent pork pies, their Savory aromas wafting through the air like a siren's call; freshly baked bread, its crusty exterior giving way to pillowy softness within; a colourful mosaic of cheeses, each offering a different delight to the palate; and slices of succulent ham, their richness promising a journey of gastronomic bliss.

The tableau that unfolded before the delighted children was nothing short of a feast fit for royalty, a banquet that transcended mere sustenance to become a celebration of the senses. Lissa's eyes sparkled with mirth and contentment as she witnessed the sheer delight etched on the faces of her young charges, their gratitude and joy a reflection of the love and care she poured into every morsel prepared.

They stopped for a quick toilet and tea break at the first motorway services on the M5. Jago and Jorja's faces lit up with sheer delight, their eyes sparkling with excitement as they eagerly indulged in the delectable treats Lissa had purchased, savouring each mouthful with unabashed gusto. And as they settled around the table, laughter and chatter filling the air, it was not just a meal they shared but a moment of connection and communion, a brief respite from the cares of the world grounded in the simple pleasures of good food and loving company. The sheer joy radiating from the children was palpable, creating an atmosphere of pure contentment that enveloped them all like a warm embrace. Lissa, their caring guardian, couldn't help but chuckle playfully as she gently teased the youngsters to take their time and pace themselves, a mischievous glint in her eyes hinting at the possibility of having to replenish the rapidly disappearing treats. With a fond smile, she excused herself, disappearing briefly into the toilets.

Back in the car, Lissa regaled them with enchanting tales of the mystical Erlands, ethereal beings reminiscent of elves that played a profound role in the lives of the Erlends. She also had ulterior motives for the storytelling: to keep Jago occupied and his mind of the visit with his mother.

With animated gestures and vivid descriptions, she painted a captivating picture of the whimsical nature of the Undines - beings of delicate beauty with wings akin to those found in ancient fairy tales, capturing the vivid imaginations of the young listeners.

Delving further into the intricate lore of the Erlend society, Lissa skillfully wove a tapestry of words, illustrating a vibrant community steeped in rich traditions and elaborate customs where music and dance were revered as sacred arts. The graceful movements of the Undines in their ethereal dances stood in stark contrast to the lively steps of the Erlends as they engaged in intricate rituals designed to open portals, bridging their world with others. She eloquently described the complicated web of trade and barter that formed the backbone of the Erlend economy. Emphasising the interconnected relationships, she highlighted how each thread of interaction contributed to the intricate fabric of their community, lending a sense of depth and richness to their society.

With fervour and enthusiasm, Lissa recounted the complexities of the Erlend languages, each intimately tied to elemental forces that governed their world. As she delved deeper into the intricacies of their communication, she vividly painted a picture of the seamless interactions between Erlends and Undines, highlighting how their bond transcended linguistic barriers, rooted in a deep connection to earth, air, fire, and water, resonating through the melodic cadence of their spoken words. This beautiful symphony of language served as a testament to the harmonious coexistence of these mystical beings, enveloping them in a shared aura of ancient wisdom and profound understanding - a harmony that echoed in the very essence of their existence.

Moreover, Lissa shared the profound healing powers that Erlends possessed, a unique gift bestowed upon them by nature itself. Their unparalleled knowledge of herbs, spells, and enchantments surpassed that of any other beings in their realm, including humans, DrakÔn, and Undines. She unveiled the sacred art of their healing practices, describing how they skillfully wielded the forces of nature to mend wounds and cure ailments with unparalleled precision and compassion. This innate ability served as a poignant reminder of their role as the benevolent guardians of all living things, their symbiotic relationship with the natural world reflected in every act of restoration and rejuvenation.

As Lissa concluded her captivating narrative, she couldn't help but smile warmly at the children's enraptured expressions, their eyes brimming with awe and fascination. She took solace in the knowledge that the enchanting tales she shared planted seeds of wonder and curiosity in their young hearts, sparking dreams of embarking on their magical quests and encountering legendary beings like the revered Erlends.

Expanding on the portrayal of Erlands, Lissa's voice carried a tinge of enchantment as she shed light on these whimsical tricksters within the realm of mystical creatures. Despite their diminutive size and ethereal wings that defied earthly logic, Erlands radiated a surprising aura of majesty, their playful nature tempered by a strong work ethic that underscored their diligent nature. Nestled within the enchanted Dees Ygrene, known as Dees in our earthly realm but revered as mystical abodes in Enrac, Undines found refuge and playground, seamlessly integrating their playful spirit with their responsibilities. The unique ecosystem of Enrac, boasting the magnificent minglegroves alongside the intimate Dees Delisforte near Lanrah Grikor, offered a glimpse into the profound connection between the inhabitants and their enchanted surroundings, where every leaf whispered ancient secrets and every branch hummed with mystical energies, creating a tapestry of enchantment that blanketed the land in an aura of timeless wonder.

In the waning light of the day, as the sun gracefully dipped below the horizon, a soft golden glow enveloped the enchanting minglegrove where the ethereal dees made their home. It was a moment of quiet reverence and deep connection as the mystical witches, whose robes billowed gently in the evening breeze and whose pointed hats added to their mysterious aura, approached the sacred realm with hearts filled with awe and respect. Their heads bowed in a gesture of solemn acknowledgement, not just to pay homage to the vast power and profound wisdom of the majestic Dees but also to signify their humility and unwavering admiration for the benevolent beings who infused magic into the realms of the Undines, Erlends, and their fellow witches.

The bond between the dees and the magical creatures dwelling in the mystical minglegrove was an intricate symbiosis. It was a delicate dance of harmonious interactions where each entity held a crucial role in upholding the delicate balance of the natural world. While the magnificent drakÔns drew their mystical powers from a different source, the Erlends and Undines depended on the benevolent guidance and magic bestowed upon them by the Dees to ensure that the cyclical rhythms of the seasons flowed seamlessly, the rivers pulsed with vibrant life, the fields yielded bountiful harvests, and the very air hummed with the sweet perfume of blossoms.

Among the enchanting Undines who graced the mystical minglegrove, there resided a Queen whose presence shimmered like a beacon of otherworldly beauty, commanding both awe and admiration from all fortunate enough to gaze upon her radiant form. With cascading locks that glistened like liquid gold, gracefully descending to meet the minglegrove floor, and eyes that sparkled with an intensity reminiscent of the purest sapphires, the Queen exuded an aura of timeless grace and unparalleled wisdom. The Undines were known for their remarkable longevity, with an average lifespan extending to an impressive three centuries. The Queen, however, stood as a paragon of her kind, carrying the weight of countless years and embodying the wisdom of her people's enduring legacy.

As the eager children hungrily absorbed Lissa's mesmerising tales with wide-eyed wonder and undivided attention, the gentle fading of daylight reminded them that dinnertime had arrived, and they suggested another break to have dinner with Lissa. The echoes of fantastical lore still lingering in the air like a half-remembered dream, they drove into Durham, where Lissa already had a spot in mind. She went to a restaurant and stopped the car, stretching as she got out. Bone-tired and weary, they ate a relatively quick dinner before driving off to the hotel Lissa had diligently booked the night before. It was not far from the prison itself, and they all could see it looming ahead as they gathered their belongings and went to the rooms for much-needed rest.

Jago lay quietly, pretending to be asleep, trying to process the whirlwind of events that had taken place so rapidly. The overwhelming flood of kindness, the promise of being part of a new family, and the prospect of facing his foster parents in court left him conflicted. Lissa and Jorja had been incredibly generous and caring, offering him a life filled with warmth and opportunities he had never imagined. However, replacing his mother with Lissa felt like an impossible hurdle to overcome. Would his incarcerated mother approve of the adoption, and did she have any say in the matter?

CHAPTER FOURTEEN

The prison, 464 miles and 8 hours of driving without stops from Cornwall, loomed ahead as a formidable destination—the closest women's high-security facility that would reveal its dark secrets and challenges. Lissa had meticulously planned and prepared for this trip, recognising the importance of booking a hotel for a week to provide Jago with the time needed to process his emotions and thoughts, especially regarding his mother, Freya, who was held within the confines of the prison.

Upon their arrival at the prison, the trio was met by a stern woman whose no-nonsense demeanour set the tone for the stringent security measures enforced within the facility. Each step they took towards the warden's office was a solemn reminder of the environment they were entering, where rules, restrictions, and surveillance dictated every action. As Lissa, Jago, and Jorja made their way through the controlled surroundings, a palpable mix of anxiety and anticipation hung in the air, each breath laden with the weight of the unknown that awaited them behind those imposing walls.

As Lissa was led into the warden's office, a sense of unease settled upon Jago and Jorja, who remained in the stark, sterile waiting area. Warden Hope, a commanding figure with a face etched by the trials of overseeing such a complex institution, greeted Lissa with a firm nod, gesturing to begin a conversation that revealed the harsh realities of Jago's mother, Freya's situation. The warden spoke of Freya's tumultuous past and the events that had led her to HMP Low Newton with a tone that bore the weight of countless similar discussions. As the details unfolded, it became clear that Freya's presence within the prison was not merely a result of her past crimes but a testament to the chaos and danger she continued to incite within its confines.

The warden's words painted a grim picture of Freya's actions - from her previous offences that had warranted her relocation to HMP Low Newton to the disturbing incidents that had transpired since her arrival. Freya's involvement in riots, her alleged role in a fellow inmate's tragic demise, and her continued access to contraband despite stringent measures were chilling reminders of the darkness that lurked within the seemingly impenetrable walls of the prison. With each new revelation, the gravity of the situation grew heavier, weighing on Lissa as she grappled with the harsh reality of Freya's circumstances and the challenges ahead in their quest for understanding and resolution.

Lissa felt a deep sense of shock and disbelief as she tried to process the full scope of Freya's actions and her persistent drug use within the supposedly secure confines of the facility. Considering Freya's current condition, the warden raised concerns about the appropriateness of allowing a visit. Struggling with conflicting emotions, Lissa was overwhelmed by dismay and discomfort. She decided to heed the warden's advice to gather more information about Freya's well-being before committing to any visitation plans.

Upon the warden's and Lissa's return, Jago, driven by a steely determination to confront the unfolding situation head-on, insists on a private conversation despite the warden's suggestion to involve Lissa. Unfazed, Jago composedly approached the warden's office, exuding a palpable sense of resolve. Within the confines of that office, Jago embarked on a series of probing inquiries aimed at getting the intricate tapestry of his mother's circumstances.

Emerging from this intense exchange, Jago found Lissa anxiously pacing in the waiting room. With a sombre determination in his eyes, he expressed his firm resolve to see his mother, seeking closure amidst a journey fraught with emotional turbulence and unexpected revelations. Despite the stark realities painted by Warden Holme, Jago was unwavering in his determination to confront his past and gain a deeper understanding of his mother's choices. For Jago, the visit represented a pivotal moment that underscored the intricate dynamics of familial relationships and the profound challenges inherent in confronting a painful history.

The stern woman arrived again, her purpose clear as she ushered them toward the designated visiting area. Freya was already stationed there, her dishevelled appearance starkly contrasting the scene. Covered in grime, she presented a pitiful sight, yet Jago sat before her without flinching in a display of remarkable composure. "Hello, mother," he acknowledged, his voice tinged with determination and vulnerability.

As Freya stirred, her gaze met the young boy seated before her. Struggling to place him, she knew she had a son, but the image she held in her memory was of a mere infant. The passage of time within the confines of the prison seemed to distort her perception, leaving her uncertain of the current year or the boy's identity.

Jago's following words pierced the air, laden with longing and frustration. "Do you wish to reconcile with me, Mother, or shall you remain inert?" The gravity of his question lingered in the air, plunging Freya into a brief moment of panic as she struggled to grasp the full meaning of his words, much less summon a coherent response. "Who... are you?" she articulated slowly, the effort producing a scarcely intelligible query.

"I am Jago, your son," came his curt reply, a hint of disappointment lacing his tone. Sensing the tension, Lissa intervened with a mind meld, urging Jago to grant his mother the time to process the unfolding situation. "You seek another fix, don't you, mother?" he challenged, prompting Freya to offer a muted nod in response, the unspoken truth hanging heavy in the air.

Lissa watched intently as tears welled in Jago's eyes, seeing the turmoil within him as he stood there, poised to exit. However, something held him back - a glimmer of concern, perhaps, for the woman seated opposite him. With a tense pause, he leaned forward, hands firmly planted on the worn wooden table that separated them. He issued a stern yet caring ultimatum in a voice laced with a mixture of frustration and love. "I will return in two days, but you must promise to take care of yourself and be drug-free for my visit. Remember, mother, you have two days," he implored, his words tinged with desperation. The air seemed to thicken with emotion as Jago continued, his tone increasingly forceful. "I need you to understand, mother," he insisted, his gaze boring into her unwaveringly.

As the tension in the room peaked, Jorja wisely stepped in, gently guiding Jago out, the weight of his conflicting emotions palpable in the air. Once outside, Jago's appearance was a stormy mixture of anger and embarrassment, his feelings swirling beneath the surface like a turbulent sea. Sensing his need for space, Lissa allowed him to lead the way, a silent companion to his tumultuous thoughts.

At the car, Jago waited with a heavy, brooding silence between them, his inner turmoil casting a shadow over their lunch plans. The trio made their way to 'The Picnic Basket,' the cosy atmosphere offering a brief respite from the whirlwind of emotions that engulfed them. Ordering their meals in subdued tones, they settled into a tense calm, punctuated only by the clink of cutlery against plates.

Menu 5A (min 5 people)

Assorted cocktail sandwiches

Indian canapés with raitha dip

Chicken skewers with sweet chili dip

Homemade quiche

Crisps

£8.50/person

Add homemade cake or chocolate, brownie £1.70

Even though the menu said it was for five people, the manager of this quaint establishment agreed that they could order five portions. Lissa knew that Jago would quite comfortably polish off the rest of the food. They also ordered five desserts, knowing Jago would eat three portions comfortably.

When Jago expressed his wish to take a walk, a wave of unease washed over Lissa, caught between honouring his autonomy and her innate urge to safeguard him. After a moment of quiet deliberation, she proposed they follow him unobtrusively, striking a balance between protecting him and preserving his independence.

Agreeing to their plan, Jago embarked on a solitary journey, his footsteps echoing through the cobblestone streets as he navigated the familiar paths of the city. His destination, the majestic Durham Cathedral, loomed ahead, a beacon of quiet contemplation amidst the chaos of his emotions. Finding solace on a weathered bench nestled among the cathedral grounds, he sat in silence, the weight of his thoughts mirrored by the ancient stones surrounding him.

Lissa, captivated by the remarkable architecture and intricate carvings adorning the splendid cathedral, marvelled at the expenses incurred for such a grand place of worship. She pondered the source of the vast funds that must have been poured into its construction. The detailed sculptures, like the elm carving of Saint Cuthbert and the representation of the Dun Cow with Milkmaids, reflected a rich historical and religious significance that left her in awe.

As they stood outside the cathedral, Lissa lost track of time, admiring the structure's elaborate details and sheer magnificence. Each passing moment revealed new nuances and hidden beauty, making her realise the depth of craftsmanship and dedication that went into creating such a masterpiece.

When Jago returned and expressed his desire to revisit the prison in two days, seeking her assistance in arranging a meeting with Warden Holme, Lissa readily obliged. She promptly contacted the prison authorities, her eagerness palpable as she inquired about the possibility of Jago's additional visit.

Upon being connected with Warden Holme, Lissa articulated Jago's request earnestly and clearly, mentioning his urgency to meet his mother, Freya, for a significant discussion. The warden, taken aback by Jago's unexpected request, eventually granted permission for the visit, appreciating Lissa's dedication to facilitating the meeting.

Grateful for the warden's cooperation, Lissa conveyed her thanks before ending the call, knowing that she had played a part in reuniting a son with his mother. This gesture held immeasurable significance for both of them.

"I will not be wanting you at the prison; this is something I need to deal with myself," Jago firmly stated, his tone leaving no room for negotiation. With genuine concern, Lissa immediately countered, "Jago, darling, are you sure? We can be there just for moral support." She was met with a resolute response, "No, thank you, I have to do this on my own. You can wait in the car or at the prison visitor's café. That will be fine." With those words, Jago retreated into his room, leaving Jorja and Lissa perplexed by his solitary resolve, questioning his seeming lack of concern for their emotional support. They decided to give him space, allowing him to gather his thoughts in the quiet confines of the hotel room. After a while, they gently tapped on his door, offering comfort and normalcy, "Jago, would you like to join us for a cup of tea in the hotel tea room?" Their well-intentioned invitation hung in the air, a glimmer of hope for connection amidst the looming shadows of solitude and isolation.

The trio joyfully immersed themselves in Durham's rich historical tapestry the next day. As they delved into the city's past, they discovered that Durham exuded an ancient charm, with its roots deeply intertwined in history. With her insatiable appetite for knowledge, Lissa was particularly captivated by the historical narratives that unfolded before her. Together, the three companions eagerly devoted their entire day to exploring every nook and cranny of the region in search of more intriguing stories and hidden gems.

One fascinating aspect of Durham is its geographical layout. Situated on a meander of the River Wear, the city is enveloped by the gentle embrace of the river on three sides, creating a natural barrier that accentuates its beauty. The surrounding landscape, characterised by rolling hills, offers a picturesque backdrop to the cityscape, punctuated only by the flat floodplain of the Wear stretching north and southeast, adding a touch of serenity to the vibrant city life.

Durham's origins date back to the year 995 when Anglo-Saxon monks, desperate to safeguard the relics of St Cuthbert from Viking invasions, established a sanctuary in this peaceful haven. The history of Durham unfolds like a well-worn parchment, each chapter revealing tales of resilience and fortitude. The original church erected by the monks stood proudly for a mere century before being replaced by the magnificent Durham Cathedral following the Norman Conquest. This architectural marvel and the imposing Durham Castle have earned the prestigious title of a UNESCO World Heritage Site, a testament to its enduring legacy.

From the 1070s until 1836, Durham thrived as a sovereign stronghold within the County Palatine, ruled by the revered Prince

Bishops whose authority bestowed a distinct and unparalleled autonomy upon the region. This unique semi-autonomous jurisdiction served as a strategic buffer zone between the rival kingdoms of England and Scotland, shaping the city's political landscape for centuries to come. The echoes of history reverberate through the ages, with significant events like the Battle of Neville's

Cross in 1346, where English valour triumphed only a stone's throw away from the city.

The annals of time also record the cathedral's noble duty as a sanctuary for Scottish captives following their defeat at the Battle of Dunbar in 1650, a poignant reminder of the city's humanitarian spirit amid tumultuous times. The Industrial Revolution heralded a new era for Durham, fuelled by the abundant coal reserves beneath its soil. Once dotted with collieries and bustling with industrial fervour, the landscape now bears the marks of transformation as the city has embraced a new chapter of growth and renewal.

Historically renowned for its diverse industries, including hosiery, carpets, and mustard production, Durham's legacy as a hub of innovation and craftsmanship continues to thrive. The community spirit echoes through the ages, embodied by the enduring tradition of the annual Durham Miners' Gala. This vibrant celebration unites the city and its residents in a shared heritage.

In education, Durham stands proudly as the home of Durham University, a prestigious institution founded in 1832. This venerable establishment claims to be the third-oldest university in England, a beacon of knowledge and learning that illuminates the region. Alongside the university, the city thrives as a hub of employment, with institutions like the local council, national government agencies, and the University Hospital of North Durham offering diverse opportunities for its citizens.

As the trio embarked on their historical odyssey through Durham, they uncovered the city's past and forged enduring memories that would linger in their hearts for years. The intricacies of heritage, culture, and innovation blended seamlessly in Durham, creating a timeless tapestry of experiences that transcended mere sightseeing, immersing them in a journey of discovery and wonder.

The harsh reality of the challenging circumstances surrounding him had inflicted a heavy emotional toll on Jago, weighing heavily on his heart and mind. Despite the resilience he portrayed, a mixture of resolve and acceptance coloured his demeanour as they braced themselves for the impending visit. Jago's internal turmoil was evident, a blend of determination driving him forward while a lingering sense of resignation anchored him in the present moment. He recognised the imminent encounter as crucial for his healing and growth, yet the gravity loomed large, casting a shadow over his usually composed facade.

On the morning set for the visit, a cloak of silence enveloped Jago as he grappled with the impending reunion. Lissa and Jorja, ever attuned to his unspoken emotions, granted him the solitary reflection time he sought, offering silent support in the face of the emotional storm brewing within him. The journey to the prison was shrouded in tense stillness, each mile echoing the unspoken anticipation that gripped the car's occupants. As they arrived, Lissa and Jorja held back as Jago had requested, respecting his need for emotional space and readiness as he braced himself for the encounter ahead.

Upon stepping into the stark visiting area, Jago's gaze met Freya's transformed appearance, a subtle effort on her part to conform to his unspoken wishes. Though her physical presentation held a semblance of tidiness, the emptiness in her eyes mirrored the depths of unresolved emotions between them. With a deep inhale, Jago settled into the chair opposite her, his heart heavy with the weight of unspoken words and unreconciled feelings, poised to navigate the turbulent waters of their shared past in search of closure and clarity.

As they delved deeper into the heart-wrenching conversation, Jago grappled with many conflicting emotions. The room seemed to grow heavy with the weight of their shared history, every word echoing like a reverberation of past anguish and unspoken dreams. Freya's tears glistened as a poignant reminder of the shattered bond between mother and son, her vulnerability tugging at Jago's hardened facade.

In a moment of raw honesty, Freya's voice quivered with remorse as she confessed the harrowing grip that heroin had on her, unravelling the layers of pain and regret that had consumed her life. Jago, despite his palpable anger, couldn't ultimately stifle the flicker of empathy that blossomed within him, recognising the complexity of her struggle and the profound toll that the addiction had taken on their family.

Their interaction, fraught with unspoken apologies and unshed tears, became a poignant dance of vulnerability and resilience. Jago's unwavering demand for accountability mingled with Freya's fragile promises of change, creating an intricate tapestry of hope and scepticism woven with the threads of their shared past. As they navigated the turbulent waters of forgiveness and redemption, each word spoken became a stepping stone towards a new chapter of healing and reconciliation.

Before parting ways, a bittersweet resolve lingered, a fragile promise of an uncertain future. Jago's determination to support his mother's journey to recovery was tempered with a haunting awareness of the arduous road ahead; each visit was a poignant reminder of the fragile balance between love, loyalty, and the inexorable pull of addiction.

The prison gates loomed ominously in the distance, a stark reminder of the barriers that separated them physically yet did little to contain the intangible bond that persisted between them. He knew that their journey was far from over, that the road to redemption was fraught with uncertainty and setbacks. Yet, in that moment of shared vulnerability and unspoken truths, a glimmer of hope existed—a tentative member of reconciliation flickering in the darkness of their shared past.

After the visit, Jago left the prison with a heavy heart but a clearer mind. He rejoined Lissa and Jorja in the café, where they offered him quiet support. After the intense morning, they spent the afternoon exploring Durham, trying to find some peace and distraction. The trio wandered through the town's winding streets, each step echoing with uncertainty and determination. They stumbled upon quaint shops and bustling markets, the city's vibrant energy providing a welcome respite from the weight of their thoughts.

They revisited the tranquil and historic Durham Cathedral, a place where Jago found a deep sense of peace amidst its timeless beauty. As they sat quietly on the cathedral grounds, Jago reflected thoughtfully on the day's events, feeling the stillness of the surroundings bring clarity to their mind. He knew the path ahead with his mother would be challenging, but he felt a glimmer of hope that maybe, just maybe, things could improve. The old stones of the cathedral whispered stories of resilience and redemption, their ancient walls offering a silent yet reassuring presence to Jago's troubled mind.

The trio returned to their hotel that evening, exhausted but hopeful. Jago had taken the first steps toward confronting his past and healing the wounds it had inflicted. He knew it wouldn't be easy, but with the support of Lissa and Jorja, he felt stronger and more determined to face whatever came next. The soft glow of the hotel lobby welcomed them back, casting a warm light on their weary faces. Each carried a piece of the day's emotional journey, a shared burden that bonded them closer.

Once again, Jago returned to the prison to see his mother the next day. This time, his resolve was fortified by a clear purpose. He would tell Freya that a family wanted to adopt him and that he did not want her to contest it. The weight of this decision bore down on him, but he knew it was necessary for his future. The drive to the prison was filled with unspoken tension, the air heavy with unvoiced fears and hopes. Lissa and Jorja sat in the car, their quiet presence a comforting reminder of the solidarity that anchored them through this turbulent time.

Upon arrival, they again waited in the visitor's café as Jago prepared himself for the difficult conversation ahead. The familiar routine of the café provided a sense of grounding amidst the looming uncertainty of their meeting with Freya. Jago's fingers curled around his cup, the warmth seeping into his palms, offering a brief moment of solace before the storm of emotions awaited them in the prison's visiting room.

As Jago entered the visiting area, he saw Freya sitting at the table, looking slightly less composed than the day before. She had tried to clean herself up again, but heroin had taken its hold on her once more. Jago observed the soft contours of Freya's face, noting the lines etched with worry and the faint hint of fatigue in her eyes.

Despite his own conflicting emotions, a sense of compassion stirred within him as he acknowledged the complexity of their relationship, weighted with years of shared history and unspoken sentiments.

"Hello, mother," Jago began, his voice steady but filled with a sombre determination. He took his seat across from her, locking eyes with Freya, who seemed to sense the gravity of the situation. The atmosphere hung heavy with unspoken words, a poignant silence enveloping the space between them as they navigated the emotional territory ahead. Each breath they took seemed to echo the weight of their shared past, lingering in the tense air like an unspoken plea for understanding and closure.

"Jago," she greeted him softly, her voice tinged with regret and longing. The syllables of his name carried a world of emotions – love, guilt, and a yearning for reconciliation that had long remained unaddressed. The vulnerability in her voice mirrored the rawness of her feelings, laid bare in the quiet confession of maternal love tinged with remorse.

He took a deep breath, steeling himself for what he needed to say. "Mother, there is something important I need to tell you. A family wants to adopt me." The words hung heavy in the air, their implications casting a shadow over the already sombre scene. Though steady, Jago's voice bared the conflict within him, torn between loyalty to his past and the desperate hope for a future free from the tangled web of his upbringing.

Freya's eyes widened, and she looked both shocked and pained. "Adopt you? But... I'm your mother." The disbelief in her words rang clear, a heartbreaking realisation that echoed the depths of her maternal love and the shortcomings that had brought them to this moment of reckoning. The bond between mother and son quivered under the weight of unspoken truths, fragile like a thread stretched taut to its breaking point.

Jago nodded, his expression resolute. "Yes, you are. But I need stability, a chance at a normal life, and this family can give me that." The stark contrast between his words and the tumult of emotions swirling within him laid bare the complexity of his decision - seeking solace in the embrace of strangers rather than holding fast to the shattered remnants of his past.

Freya's eyes filled with tears. "Jago, I I don't want to lose you.

You're all I have left." The vulnerability in her voice cracked like fissures in a fragile façade, revealing the depths of her fear and the tendrils of loss that gripped her maternal heart. Her words, laden with desperation and love, bore witness to the ache of a mother facing the prospect of losing the only remaining connection to a past marred by regrets.

He reached out, taking her hand gently but firmly. "Mother, you lost me a long time ago. This isn't about you anymore; it's about me and my future. I need you to understand that and not contest the adoption." The touch of his hand against hers conveyed a sense of finality, a silent plea for acceptance that resonated with the weight of unspoken truths. Jago's words, though tinged with sorrow, echoed a resolve born of a longing for autonomy and a desperate bid for a new beginning.

Freya looked down, tears streaming down her face. "I've made so many mistakes. I don't want to lose you, too." The tears that trickled down her cheeks mirrored the silent lament of a mother haunted by the spectre of her past failures, a whispered reminder of the fractures that had irrevocably scarred their relationship. Her words, a poignant soliloquy of regret and yearning, sought absolution in the face of impending loss.

Jago's grip tightened slightly on Freya's hand, his voice softening but remaining firm. "You've already lost me, Mother. This is my chance to start over. Please, don't take that away from me." The tension in his words carried the weight of a son's unspoken pain, a plea for understanding that reverberated with the ache of a soul seeking emancipation. Though tinged with compassion, his gaze bore a man's resolve on the brink of self-discovery, poised to embrace a future untethered from the shadows of his past.

The room fell silent, enveloped in a heavy cloak of stillness that seemed to magnify the weight of Jago's words as they lingered in the air, sinking into the very fabric of the walls. Overwhelmed by the stark revelation of her son's words, Freya felt her composure crack, tears welling as the full impact of his confession settled deep within her heart. A moment of poignant silence passed before she mustered the strength to lift her gaze, her eyes now rimmed with redness and swollen from the weight of unshed tears.

"If this is truly your desire, Jago," Freya's voice trembled with a mixture of resignation and unconditional love, "I will not stand in your way. Your happiness means a lot to me, even if I must release you."

Fraught with a complex blend of relief and sorrow, Jago met his mother's gaze with gratitude etched in his every feature. "Thank you, mother. I only wish for your path to be one of self-discovery and transformation."

A sombre nod from Freya followed this exchange, her slender fingers reaching up to brush away the evidence of her silent weeping. "I will try to change, Jago. I give you my word - I shall try with every fibre of my being."

The conversation drew to a close with an unspoken understanding lingering in the air, a palpable sense of resolution permeating the space between mother and son. With a steady resolve, Jago rose from his seat, casting a final gaze of love and forgiveness upon his mother before leaving the room. As he crossed the threshold and exited the visitors' chamber, a profound sense of surrender washed over him, shedding the weight of unresolved emotions like a heavy cloak lifted from his weary shoulders.

Rejoining Lissa and Jorja in the quaint café, a sense of togetherness enveloped the trio as Jago earnestly divulged the intricacies of his recent conversation. Their tender embrace, filled with understanding and unwavering support, served as a comforting balm to Jago's weary soul. Subsequently, the atmosphere transformed into one of serene reflection, with the trio spending the remainder of the day in quiet contemplation, each processing the emotional expedition upon which they had collectively embarked.

Later that evening, as the hotel room enveloped Jago in its warm embrace, a newfound hope and possibility gradually illuminated his path. While cognizant of the inevitable challenges ahead, Jago found solace in the unwavering support of Lissa, Jorja, and the soon-to-be embraced adoptive family. With this newfound sense of purpose and belonging, Jago stood resolute, ready to confront the unknown journey that awaited him.

The decision to forge ahead, to embrace this new familial bond and the uncharted future it promised, acted as a pivotal turning point in the tapestry of Jago's life. As they embarked on the return journey to Cornwall, their joy was palpable, laughter and light-hearted banter echoing through the air. Despite the fatigue from their earlier walk, the trio's spirits remained high as they eagerly anticipated their forthcoming camping trip to Bodmin, the giddy chatter of the children adding an infectious excitement to the air. In the brief moments of respite within the hotel room, they found time to engage in their Telm Training, their shared dedication reaffirming the unity and strength of their bond. The promise of the upcoming adventure infused their hearts with anticipation and a renewed sense of familial love and interconnectedness.

CHAPTER FIFTEEN

The morning sunlight gently filtered into the room, casting a warm glow on the freshly arrived attire - the pristine suit, polished shoes, and elegant dress. Excitement filled the air as the children eagerly rushed to their rooms, their hearts beating with anticipation as they slipped into their carefully chosen outfits.

With pride shining in her eyes, Lissa couldn't help but praise the children. "What a stunning pair you make! You both are a sight to behold, and tomorrow at court, you will dazzle everyone," she beamed, her voice filled with confidence in the children's abilities.

With a renewed sense of purpose, the day's training commenced under the bright blue sky. Lissa had ingeniously repurposed some sturdy branches, transforming them into makeshift swords for the Telm training session. The children embraced the challenge, their eager spirits driving them to perfect their moves and techniques.

After a satisfying lunch, Lissa gathered the children with a twinkle in her eye, instructing them to spar with the improvised swords. The clashing of branches filled the air, punctuated by laughter and determination as the children engaged in friendly combat, each strike bringing them closer to mastering the art of Telm.

Throughout the afternoon, the sound of playful banter and the rustle of leaves filled the outdoor training area, a mix of fun and focused dedication emanating from the young warriors. As the sun began its descent, painting the sky with hues of orange and pink,

Lissa watched with pride, knowing that her young charges were on the path to becoming skilled fighters, ready to face the challenges ahead.

Jorja and Jago were far stronger in their muscular tone, especially Jorja, whose physical prowess outshone even her expectations. It became evident to Lissa that Jago would soon close the gap in strength with his renewed access to food. Although shorter than his peers, Lissa couldn't help but attribute this stature to his prior malnourishment.

Their progress in sparring brought a sense of accomplishment to Lissa as she watched them execute light-contact training with ease. The makeshift swords they wielded stood the test of their movements, prompting Lissa to ponder how they would fare when engaging in full-contact sparring.

With the impending journey to Enrac looming on the horizon, Lissa began to see Jago as a vital asset, realising the sharpness of his instincts and his vigilant nature towards potential threats. As she envisioned his growth in strength and magical abilities, she considered how he might navigate the challenges ahead, particularly the upcoming court appearance. She speculated how he would handle articulating his thoughts, noting his lack of eloquence juxtaposed against his pure-hearted nature.

Despite Jago's tendency to be easily frightened by seemingly inconsequential matters, Lissa pondered the thought of him facing someone as formidable as Eswella. She anticipated observing his reactions and contemplated the support he might need in such encounters, all while acknowledging his unique blend of strengths and vulnerabilities.

That evening, while Jorja was enjoying a relaxing shower, Lissa approached Jago to discuss the impending adoption court case.

"Jago, my dear, is there anything on your mind regarding the court proceedings scheduled for tomorrow?" Lissa inquired, her expression reflecting her concern for her son and nephew.

Upon hearing Lissa's question, Jago smiled gently, "Just one thing. If all goes as planned, I will officially be considered Jorja's uncle, correct?"

Lissa nodded affirmatively, taking a moment to clarify, "Indeed, in the eyes of this world, you would hold the title of Jorja's uncle. However, when we transition to Enrac, our roles will slightly alter, not our bond. You will still be regarded as my son, residing under my care and protection in the grand palace. Your role will evolve slightly to be the guardian of Jorja and me. As the protector of the reigning and forthcoming queens, this role requires the utmost trust, which I wholeheartedly place in you. Jago, your qualities and abilities align perfectly with the responsibilities of a guardian," she expressed proudly.

Excited by the prospect, Jago pondered aloud, "This sounds incredibly exciting, but I cannot help but wonder - what exactly will my duties entail on Enrac? I feel a bit youthful to take on the bodyguard title."

Having sensed Jago's budding connection with Jorja, Lissa wished to show her admiration for them without unveiling her awareness of Jago's affection for her. Understanding the mutual fondness growing between Jorja and Jago filled Lissa with utmost joy and anticipation for their future together.

As Jago rested and allowed his weary body to relax, he turned his thoughts inward, seeking solace in the visions that danced through his mind. Among them was a striking image of Jorja bravely facing off against a frightening, headless figure, with him valiantly springing forth to protect her. Although he found comfort in these daydreams, he couldn't shake the nagging awareness that Jorja was more advanced in many ways. Full of determination, he resolved to bridge the gap and elevate himself to a level where he could be taken seriously on Enrac. The realisation dawned on him that impeccable speech was a vital asset in his quest - a crucial skill that could pave the way for him to become a trusted bodyguard to the revered Queen and her Princess. Considering this significance, the idea of seeking out Lissa for speech training occurred to him. Still, he hesitated, not wanting to impose any additional burdens on her already full plate.

The following day, Jago found Lissa in the lounge, engrossed in the daily news as she sat comfortably on the plush sofa. The soft rustling of the newspaper echoed lightly in the room. "Can I ask you a question, please?" Jago's voice enquired, a hint of eagerness apparent in his tone.

Lissa gently set the newspaper aside with her usual warm smile and turned her attention to Jago. "Yes, of course, dear," she replied, her voice laced with kindness and understanding, a reassuring tone that instantly put Jago at ease.

Upon hearing his request for speech training, Lissa's eyes lit up with a sense of purpose and determination. "Can you give me some speech training? I do not want to look stupid on Enrac," Jago's voice reflected a mix of vulnerability and determination, clearly showing his desire to improve himself.

"Of course, dear boy. I will do everything I can to help you," Lissa responded, her voice filled with encouragement and support. "Do not worry, I will get you ready." Her words carried a sense of conviction, symbolising her commitment to aiding Jago in his quest to enhance his public speaking skills. This journey was of significant importance to both Jago and Jorja.

Understanding the gravity of the situation and the vital role Jago's ability to speak publicly played in safeguarding Jorja, Lissa's determination only grew stronger. She knew that ensuring Jago's proficiency in speech was crucial for their shared mission's success.

With a gentle yet firm tone, Lissa gave Jago clear instructions, considering the steps needed to prepare him for the challenges ahead. She instructed him to shower, and when he returned, they would begin. Lissa's guidance was practical and caring, reflecting her dedication to helping Jago overcome his insecurities and sharpening his skills for the tasks ahead.

Jago took his time in the shower, relishing the sensation of the hot water cascading over him. The warmth enveloped him, coaxing a sense of peace he wanted to linger in. Though he longed to linger in the soothing embrace of the rejuvenating steam, a quiet reminder of duty urged him to quicken his washing routine, mindful not to squander water needlessly. With efficiency, he cleansed himself swiftly and emerged from the shower, invigorated, ready to tackle the day ahead. As he hurriedly went about his post-shower routine, Jago's enthusiasm was palpable, almost leading him straight into a chance encounter with Jorja. Their unexpected meeting prompted a warm exchange of smiles, reflecting a mutual acknowledgement that their journey together had brought about positive changes.

As they embarked on this journey together, Lissa's mentorship provided valuable lessons in speech training and a sense of unwavering support and encouragement that would fortify Jago's confidence and preparedness for the demanding scenarios that awaited him on Enrac.

Jorja observed Jago with awe and admiration, noting his strides in just a few weeks. She could not help but marvel at his newfound grooming habits, which highlighted his natural good looks. The tousled charm of his shaggy hair complemented his carefree look, adding to his overall appeal. Beyond the physical transformations, Jorja admired his optimistic outlook, a quality that resonated with her deeply. His remarkable ability to navigate the complexities of magic, coupled with his unwavering determination to master its nuances, captivated and inspired her deeply. In a defining moment, she strove to embody his indomitable spirit, embracing challenges with the same fortitude and resilience that he so effortlessly displayed.

Under Lissa's patient guidance, Jago delved into the nuances of speech, building upon the foundational skills he had already mastered. His training regime, encompassing etiquette ranging from sitting to dining like a royal, provided a solid groundwork for his linguistic development. While Jorja, endowed with the advantage of early and continuous tutelage from Lissa, surpassed him in speech, Jago's dedication and progress were unmistakable. Encouraged by his commitment and quick learning pace, Lissa expressed her satisfaction with his advancements, offering encouragement for the ongoing journey of self-improvement.

The arrival of Friday morning heralded a day of anticipation and activity, compelling Jago and his companions to rise early and prepare for their commitment at Truro Court. With each group member attending to their morning routines, Jago indulged in a leisurely shower, enjoying the quiet introspection that the early hours afforded him. As he emerged, refreshed and ready to tackle the day's agenda, the group gathered for a communal breakfast, sharing anecdotes and exchanging words in a convivial atmosphere. Clad in their newly acquired attire, they brimmed with purpose and anticipation for the day's events.

"Don't we all look fine," Lissa said excitedly as she glanced over at the children, a warm smile on her lips. "Did you bring something to occupy you in the car?" she asked, her voice filled with anticipation for the journey ahead. "Come on, let us get in the car," she urged them gently, a hint of eagerness in her tone. "We have a long drive ahead of us, full of adventures waiting to unfold and memories to be made."

The children, thrilled by the unknown road ahead, scrambled to find something to entertain themselves during the trip. Jago found himself empty-handed, a touch of disappointment flickering across his face until Jorja, ever the thoughtful one, offered him a book to enjoy, her gesture filled with kindness and camaraderie. With their chosen diversions in tow, they all settled into the car, the day's promise stretching out before them like an open book waiting to be written.

"Let's go then," Lissa exclaimed jubilantly, her fingers poised over the ignition, ready to set their journey in motion. As the engine hummed to life, she steered them onto the familiar path that stretched approximately fifty-nine miles from Whitstone to Truro Family Court, a well-travelled route in Lissa's memory. She knew all too well the quirks and challenges that the roadworks on the A30 presented, mentally calculating the time it would take, just under two hours, a calculated dance of timing and precision that would see them arrive right on schedule.

Throughout the drive, Jago's inquisitive nature shone through as he bombarded Lissa with questions about court etiquette and protocol, his eagerness palpable in the confined space of the car. Sensing his nerves and desire to be prepared, Lissa offered wise counsel, advising him to seek guidance from the Clerk to discern the nature of the presiding judge - a Magistrate or a High Court Judge. "Let's speak with the Clerk at the Court and find out," she suggested, her tone reassuring and supportive, a steady hand guiding Jago through the labyrinthine World of legal proceedings.

As the weight of the impending court appearance loomed larger in Jago's mind, Jorja, ever the pillar of strength, reached out and clasped his hand in a gesture of solidarity and comfort, her touch a grounding presence amidst the whirlwind of emotions. "It is okay, Jago. I'm here with you. And so is my Nan," she reassured him with unwavering certainty, her words a beacon of assurance cutting through the uncertainty like a guiding light.

A moment of levity danced between the siblings as Jago, attempting to quell his nerves, quipped with a light-hearted smile, "You do realise that if this goes through, I'm going to be your uncle!" Jorja, caught off guard by the thought, mirrored his surprise with a perfect 'O' shape in her mouth, her eyes widening with the realisation of the new familial dynamic unfolding before her. Jago's infectious giggle rippled through the car, dispelling some of the tension that hung in the air, a moment of shared laughter serving as a balm for their jangled nerves and uncertainties.

The car pulled into the bay with fifteen minutes to spare, offering a brief respite before the impending legal proceedings. It was only five hundred meters to the Court House, and they had time to ask the Clerk which Court they would be in and how to address the Judge. With a mix of nerves and determination, Lissa told Jago to address the Judge as "Your Honour," a formality that carried weight in the solemn halls of justice. Jago, eager to comply with Lissa's guidance, earnestly practices the title in preparation for the moments ahead.

As the day's session commenced, Judge Isaac, a figure of authority and scrutiny, presided over the Court, his discerning gaze scanning the room. Feeling the weight of her mission, Lissa was the first to be called to the stand, stepping forward with a measured pace that belied the turmoil within. Placing one hand on the Bible, a symbol of truth and solemnity, she raised her other hand, pledging her oath with a firm voice and unwavering gaze. "I promise before God that the evidence I shall give shall be the truth, the whole truth, and nothing but the truth," she affirmed, her words echoing in the hallowed courtroom.

The Judge, known for his no-nonsense attitude, wasted no time seeking clarity. "Are you Mellissa Jayne Rosewall, residing at Number 1 Trelawne Close, Whitstone, Cornwall" he inquired sharply, his tone cutting through the air expectantly. "Yes, Your Honour," Lissa replied, her voice steady even as her heartbeat quickened with anticipation. "And you wish to adopt the boy known to the Court as Jago?" the Judge pressed, his scrutiny unwavering. "Yes, Your Honour, I do," Lissa affirmed, a quiet determination resonating in her response as she fixed her gaze on the Judge.

However, the Judge, bound by protocol and legal ethics, raised a pointed concern. "Ms Rosewall, you do realise it is highly irregular to adopt a child after only a few weeks, don't you?" he questioned sternly, his brow furrowed with a mix of confusion and disapproval. "I do, Your Honour, but I have known Jago for many years and could no longer watch the abuse he received at the hands of his foster parents, Mr and Mrs Treloggan," she retorted, her voice tinged with unwavering conviction rooted in years of witnessing Jago's struggles.

The Judge, grappling with the complexities of the case before him, acknowledged Lissa's concerns. "I am aware of this, Ms. Rosewall. However, it would be highly unethical of me to allow this adoption after such a short time," he stated firmly, his resolve unwavering even in the face of her impassioned plea.

Judge Isaac, a seasoned arbiter of justice, could not shake off his disbelief at the extraordinary circumstances that led to this moment. 'Ridiculous,' he thought, trying to reconcile the urgency of Lissa's plea with the formalities and procedures that governed the courtroom, a clash of emotion and protocol unfolding before his discerning eyes.

She glanced at a very nervous Jago, his whole being a whirlwind of emotions as he sat sandwiched between Jorja and Tressa, their supportive presence a calming beacon in the maelstrom of uncertainty. She sought out the reservoir of her magic with a gentle smile, reaching out to offer Judge Isaac the quiet nudge of persuasion he needed, a subtle touch of influence akin to the one she had recently bestowed upon Tressa. "But upon reflection, your efforts with the lad over the past weeks have been remarkable. I shall carefully consider your application. You may step down, Mrs.

Rosewall," he declared, and Lissa settled back between Jago and Jorja, her presence a silent embrace of encouragement.

Turning his attention towards the still apprehensive Jago, the Judge's tone softened as he made his subsequent request, "Jago, would you kindly take the stand?" Following a solemn oath on the Bible, Judge Isaac prompts Jago to vocalise his identity. "Now, Jago, please express to me in your own words the reason behind your desire to proceed with this adoption," inquired Judge Isaac with genuine curiosity.

Jago trembled uncontrollably, his voice betraying him as it quivered, unable to break free from the tight grip of anxiety that knotted around his throat. Sensing his distress, Lissa unfurled the tendrils of her mind, offering reassurance and support directly to Jago's innermost thoughts. 'Jago, fear not. You are capable of this.

Have faith in yourself. Both Jorja and I stand by you, my dear,' she whispered into the recesses of his mind.

Upon hearing the soothing cadence of Lissa's voice inwardly, a sense of tranquillity enveloped Jago, allowing him to gather his composure. "Lissa has bestowed upon me a warm bed, nourishment, new garments, and the guidance of a private tutor to nurture my education. Never before have such comforts graced my days. She tends to me with profound care, as if I were her flesh and blood, instilling a yearning for her to exist as my mother. I hold her in the highest regard, Sir, Your Honour, Sir," he articulated with nervous reverence.

'Well done, dear Jago. You have conveyed your sentiments beautifully,' Lissa echoed encouragingly within his mind, her words a quiet, affirming echo amidst the courtroom's dignified solemnity.

"Ago, do you understand that Lissa, as you call her, may be a kind woman, but do you know enough about her to want to be adopted by her?" the Judge asked, his voice gentle yet probing, intent on getting to the depths of Jago's feelings.

Jago thought long and hard, the weight of his past experiences bearing down on him, but Lissa's presence offered a glimmer of hope in the darkness that clouded his heart.

Sensing Jago's inner turmoil, Lissa opened her mind to reassure him, her words a comforting embrace that enveloped his uncertainty. 'Whatever you choose, it is your decision, Jago, she whispered, her voice, in his mind, a beacon of warmth amidst the uncertainty that lingered in the courtroom.

"Yes, Your Honour, I do. She has given me more love in two weeks than anyone else in my whole life" Jago's words resonated with a sincerity that tugged at the Judge's heartstrings. "She is a very nice lady, Your Honour, and I want to call her mum," he stated calmly, his resolve unwavering despite the tumult of emotions swirling within him.

"Jago, you may step down now. Thank you for being honest with us today." The judge's approval was evident in his tone, and he was impressed by the young boy's candidness and courage in facing his past.

As Jago scooted next to Lissa, a sense of belonging washed over him. His arms found solace in the reassuring embrace of his newfound mother. Lissa, in turn, held him close, a silent promise of unwavering support and love etched in her touch.

"Ms Rosewall, please return to the stand. Remember, you are still under oath." The judge's words brought the focus back to the pivotal decision, urging Lissa to elaborate on the provisions she had to mend the broken pieces of Jago's shattered past.

"Your Honour, I have a child therapist on hand should I need one." Lissa's voice held a steely determination laced with tenderness, a testament to her unwavering commitment to Jago's healing journey. "Jago has never known kindness, fun, or love. I intend to give him all of these and more." Her words carried the weight of a solemn vow, a promise to shower Jago with the nurturing care he had long been deprived of.

Seeing the Judge's unwavering resolve and discerning gaze, Lissa mustered her inner strength, her steadfast determination shining through as she reached for her inner reserves of resilience.

"Alright, I will grant the adoption. Jago, it gives me great pleasure to introduce you to your mother," the Judge's proclamation echoed through the courtroom, culminating in a journey marked by resilience, love, and newfound hope. "From now on, you will be known as Jago Rosewall," he said, handing Lissa a slip of paper that symbolised the dawn of a new chapter in Jago's life, a chapter filled with the promise of love, belonging, and unwavering support.

For the life of him, he had no idea why he was granted the adoption. He hoped the boy would be happy, as he seemed so far, a flicker of optimism igniting within the Judge's heart at the sight of Jago's radiant smile, a beacon of hope in the darkness that once clouded his world.

Judge Isaac was puzzled by his decision to grant the adoption, finding it to be a departure from his usual stance. The thought that external influences may have swayed him lingered in his mind, a notion that seemed straight out of a storybook rather than reality. His disquiet was palpable, evident in the curious glances between the Stenographer, the Court Usher, and Judge Isaac. The sense of unease intensified as they left the courtroom and made their way to the office, where the Judge's handwritten note and the adoption documents were submitted. The group, now comprising Jago, Jorja and Lissa, proceeded back to the car, sharing a moment of camaraderie and satisfaction over their successful task completion. Lissa observed Jago and Jorja's expressions, noting Jorja's furrowed brows, which sparked a sudden realisation - she had forgotten to seek Jorja's consent for the adoption. Alarmed by this oversight, she giggled to herself.

Lissa anxiously inquired about Jorja's feelings toward the adoption, prompting a quizzical response from her granddaughter. Jorja's question about calling Jago "Uncle" elicited laughter from Lissa and Jago, the tension dissipating as they collectively found humour in the situation. Their laughter continued as they drove home, with Lissa reassuring Jorja that she need not address Jago as "Uncle," a declaration that brought a sigh of relief from Jorja, further cementing the bonds within their newly forged family dynamic.

After enjoying every bite of their scrumptious meal at The Wilsey Downs Hotel, Jorja, Lissa, and Jago shared delightful conversations filled with warmth and joy. It was a special moment when Jago, touched by the blossoming sense of family, affectionately called Lissa "Mum" for the first time. This endearing gesture not only melted Lissa's heart but also filled Jago with newfound happiness of finally having a mother figure in his life.

Surprising everyone, Jago managed to finish every last morsel on his plate, even surpassing everyone's expectations by devouring the entire 8 oz steak, much to Lissa's amazement. As they awaited the arrival of their decadent dessert, Jago expressed his heartfelt gratitude to Lissa, acknowledging the unbelievable experiences and love she had brought into his life. "Thank you, Mum, for everything you have given me. I never imagined I could feel such happiness and love. I am grateful beyond words," Jago said, his eyes reflecting his genuine appreciation. Overwhelmed with emotion, Lissa struggled to hold back tears as she contemplated the deep bond growing between them. Knowing that Jago was feeling content in their presence, she replied with a warm smile. "You know, Jago, if calling me 'Mum' brings you joy, it brings me joy too. But you are free to call me Lissa if that feels right for you," she said, playfully winking at him. In response, Jago returned the wink, silently conveying that he would cherish this moment and the special bond they were forming.

CHAPTER SIXTEEN

Week after week, the two children's training intensity continued to rise at an impressive pace. As the days unfolded, Jorja and Jago found themselves fully engrossed in their rigorous Telm Training sessions every morning, where they delved deeper into mastering the ancient arts and honing their skills. The afternoons were devoted to Magic Training, where they explored the mystical realms of spellcasting and enchantments before engaging in exhilarating sparring sessions that tested their newfound abilities.

Evenings marked the commencement of the Royal Training, a period devoted to enhancing their manners, strategic acumen, and martial skills. Jago is having his much-needed speech training. Both Jorja and Jago exhibited notable commitment, endeavouring to excel in all facets of their training. During these education and development sessions, Jago, in particular, began to experience a significant transformation in stature and strength. Outpacing Jorja in these areas, he became a formidable presence, making a lasting impression on their shared journey.

Observing Jago's rapid progress with awe and pride, Lissa could not help but envision a bright future for the young boy. Her maternal instincts intertwined with her role as a trainer, leading her to believe that Jago would be a worthy match for Jorja and a firm companion in their quest ahead. As she pondered the possibility of taking him through the portal, a wave of conflicting emotions swept her. Despite her initial reservations, she had grown deeply attached to Jago, forging a bond she found hard to sever.

The dilemma lingered in her mind, torn between her duty to guide the children and her burgeoning affection for Jago. The thought of leaving him behind weighed heavily on her heart, as the young boy had proven himself to be a skilled trainee and a dear friend. Their intertwined fates had created a tapestry of loyalty and camaraderie, and deciding to part ways was increasingly arduous. Amidst the trials of training and the bonds of friendship, Lissa found herself at a crossroads, her choice poised to shape the destinies of those under her tutelage.

Sitting comfortably under the cool shade provided by a large umbrella, Lissa contentedly observed the playful interaction of the children as they sparred and learned together in the serene ambience of the garden. She leisurely sipped on a refreshing glass of fruit juice, taking in the sight of Jago's growing fondness for fruits, a small but significant detail that warmed her heart. Witnessing the blossoming bond and increasing strength between the two children, a profound sense of contentment and gratitude washed over Lissa, reinforcing her feelings of joy for the beautiful family they had become.

Engrossed in the careful observation of the children during their Royal Training session, she detected a glimmer of magic in Jago that seemed to be awakening, a spark she had not noticed before. His mastery over the elements advanced remarkably, hinting at his immense potential and promising future. With this realisation dawning upon her, Lissa decided it was time to discuss his destiny with Jago, contemplating the possibility of guiding him through the mystical portal to the Enrac.

Upon the conclusion of their training session, Lissa warmly beckoned Jago into the study, a place where they could converse privately and openly. She seated him comfortably, taking a deep breath before diving into an earnest conversation about the significance of his burgeoning powers and the pivotal role he could potentially play in the revered Kingdom. Jago's eyes sparkled with excitement at venturing into a new world and harnessing his magical abilities to aid and protect others, showcasing his unwavering eagerness and determination to embrace this extraordinary journey.

Offering heartfelt reassurances, Lissa pledged to stand by Jago's side every step, serving as his unwavering guide and protector as he embarked on this remarkable and transformative path.

Understanding the importance of gaining Jorja's full support for this pivotal decision, Lissa ensured that her granddaughter was included in the conversation, recognising the deep bond between the siblings. To her relief, Jorja showed remarkable understanding and encouragement, acknowledging and embracing that this journey was essential to Jago's destiny, showcasing her unconditional love and support for Jago's ambitions.

Amidst the unfolding events of familial unity and magical discoveries, prospective buyers were interested in purchasing Lissa's charming bungalow. This development could provide the means to retrieve her precious jewellery previously sold in Australia. Amid negotiations for a private cash sale of the two properties, one in Whitstone, Cornwall and the other in Abridge, Essex, the involvement of solicitors to facilitate the transfer of title deeds stood as the next step in the intricate process, marking the progression towards fulfilling both practical and emotional aspirations in Lissa's journey.

Late afternoon, a gentle knock on the door roused Lissa from her thoughts, prompting her to open it and find herself face-to-face with Tressa, who had earnestly wished to see Jago following his court appearance, was pleasantly surprised by the transformation she encountered. Standing before her was a Jago who seemed to have grown taller, exuding a newfound confidence reflected in his impeccable dressing and overall healthier appearance. Tressa could not help but feel a wave of contentment washing over her as she took in the visible changes in Jago.

In awe of Jago's remarkable progress, Tressa nodded in agreement as Lissa attributed these positive changes to the power of love. Despite any potential professional repercussions she might face, Tressa departed from their encounter with a sense of quiet vindication, assured that her belief in Jago had not been misplaced.

Anticipation filled the air as the next day dawned, with Jorja eagerly counting down to her birthday. With excitement bubbling over, she reached out to Lissa, expressing her desire to spend the day at the beach in the company of her dear friends Millie, Megan, and Jago. Recognising the joy such a gathering would bring, Lissa quickly endorsed the plan, encouraging Jorja to finalise the details with her friends.

As the day progressed, Lissa gave the children the task of gathering vegetables for dinner. Little did they know that this routine chore would lead to a discovery of extraordinary proportions. Much to everyone's surprise, Jago stumbled upon a magnificent sight: a massive, vibrant blue crystal gleaming in many colours, its ethereal beauty casting a spell on all who beheld it.

Lissa had carefully warned Jago of the dangers of touching a crystal meant for someone else, emphasising its potential for unexpected consequences. Despite her caution, a moment of inadvertence led to a jarring collision that triggered a cascade of dazzling blue lights, casting a mesmerising display across the tranquil garden and propelling her through the air with an unexpected force that left her bewildered and disoriented. Sensing the sudden disturbance, Lissa sprang into action, racing towards the source of the commotion with a sense of urgency sharpened by a deep-seated intuition of imminent peril.

Rapidly assessing the situation, Lissa moved to contain the unfolding chaos, deftly enveloping the glowing crystal in a protective blanket to stifle its luminous exhibition. Yet her efforts were in vain - the radiant glow endured, casting an eerie lustre that deepened Jorja's unease and underscored the weight of the mysterious threat looming near.

Intrigued by the unanticipated spectacle, a curious neighbour approached Lissa, inquiring about the mesmerising lights that danced in the twilight. Thinking on her feet, Lissa skilfully deflected the inquiry, attributing the captivating phenomenon to a mundane accident involving toy lightsabres. All the while, she concealed the true nature of the inexplicable events that continued to unfold with alarming intensity.

As unease gnawed at her resolve, a semblance of foreboding crept into Lissa's heart as the persistent glow emanating from the crystal served as an ominous harbinger, signalling Jorja's tenuous predicament at the hands of the looming threat personified by Eswella's malevolent intentions. Faced with the escalating danger that encroached upon their sanctuary, Lissa resorted to ancient drakÔn incantations, weaving spells of concealment and deception to erase the memory of the peculiar lights from the villagers' minds, safeguarding their fragile peace amidst the encroaching shadows that threatened to engulf them.

After he carried Jorja inside, Jago, a stalwart defender and loyal companion, heeded Lissa's call to arms. He ensured the protective bubble was in place and embarked on a perilous mission to scout the surrounding environs for any signs of intrusion. His senses honed to a keen edge as he navigated the labyrinthine alleys and dimly lit corners of Whitstone, alert for any whisper of impending danger.

Minds intertwined in a harmonious symphony of shared purpose and silent communication, Jago relayed his findings to Lissa. His mental report painted a chilling picture of unidentified figures lurking on the periphery, their intentions shrouded in mystery and menace. Unwavering in her resolve, Lissa instructed Jago to maintain a facade of normalcy, masking the lurking dread that gripped her heart as the sinister presence drew ever closer, casting a pall of uncertainty over their fragile bastion of tranquillity.

Meanwhile, Eswella, a figure of shadow and malice, consumed by a maelstrom of dark emotions and festering grievances, embarked on a frenzied quest through the village's twisting paths. Her eyes glittered with a mad fervour fuelled by a thirst for retribution and vengeance that brooked no restraint. Driven by an all-consuming obsession, she scoured the cobblestone streets and shadowed alcoves, driven by a relentless pursuit of her elusive quarry. This pursuit threatened to unravel the fragile tapestry of peace that Lissa and her companions sought to preserve.

Before Eswella and Piran were sent to Earth, Amox had a deep-rooted knowledge of a mystical way to open a portal that could potentially lead them to the realm where Morwenna had disappeared. However, the key to pinpointing the specific location within that vast realm eluded him. Amox sensed that something of Morwenna's would serve as the missing link. Eswella stealthily infiltrated Morwenna's opulent bed chamber within the palace walls and purloined the queen's possession - her treasured hairbrush. This seemingly inconsequential item, imbued with the essence of Morwenna, proved to be the pivotal component that ultimately enabled Amox to accurately home in on the elusive realm where Morwenna resided.

Grateful for Eswella's unwavering dedication and loyalty, Helgi successfully interceded with Amox, persuading him to grant both Piran and Eswella extraordinary magical abilities. These newfound powers bestowed upon them by Amox were not only to assist in their quest to locate Morwenna and Helgi's missing niece but also as a token of appreciation for their steadfast commitment.

Driven by desperation and longing, Eswella fervently persuaded Piran to join her on this perilous journey through the mysterious portal. As they tentatively traversed the ethereal passage, apprehension flickered in Piran's eyes while Eswella exuded unchecked enthusiasm at the prospect of reuniting with Morwenna. Their emergence from the portal found them in the picturesque town of Lattes, nestled near the serene city of Montpellier in the sun kissed region of Southern France.

With neither of them comprehending the unfamiliar local dialect, they discreetly found passage on a vessel bound for the shores of England. While Eswella grappled with the unpredictable nature of her newfound magical prowess, Piran exhibited remarkable adaptability and poise in harnessing his innate abilities. Only when Morwenna's latent magic briefly shimmered into view could Piran detect her presence in the quaint coastal village of

Widemouth in Cornwall. Morwenna's erratic use of her magical powers presented a formidable obstacle for Eswella and Piran, hindering their relentless efforts to pinpoint her precise location.

Meanwhile, in the secluded hamlet of Whitstone, Lissa maintained a powerful protective enchantment. This mystic shield meticulously cloaked their magical signature, rendering her virtually untraceable by those seeking her. This invisible barrier proved a formidable obstacle for Eswella, exacerbating her growing fixation on finding Morwenna. As time dragged on, Eswella's manic declarations of having pinpointed Morwenna's location led to destructive outbursts, leaving Piran emotionally distressed and disheartened. Witnessing the havoc her actions wreaked, Piran yearned for the peace of his former life, free from the chaos and tumult that now seemed to define their quest.

Despite his wife's madness, Piran tended to his garden, which became Widemouth's envy. Eswella, failing to understand his passion, often ridiculed him. However, Piran's love for Eswella remained unwavering, a beacon of steadfast devotion amidst the turmoil. This stark contrast in their emotional landscapes deepened the chasm between Piran and Eswella, fuelling his resentment toward her chosen path.

A familiar light flickered through the air one fateful day, igniting a mixture of hope and dread within Piran's soul. Battling the temptation to heed its call, he tried to shield this moment of significance from Eswella's inquisitive gaze, wary of the storm that would follow. Alas, his attempts were in vain, for their shared curiosity drew them irresistibly toward the source of the enigmatic glow, leading them to a secluded village hidden deep within the countryside.

As they ventured deeper into the village, Piran's keen eyes caught sight of a young boy, who appeared for all intents and purposes to be cloaked in a shroud of secrecy that piqued Piran's interest. A sense of foreboding crept over him as he realised the boy's watchful gaze followed their every move, a silent guardian in the shadows. Determined to unravel the enigma surrounding this elusive figure, Piran chose to shadow him discreetly, each step leading them closer to a revelation shrouded in uncertainty and intrigue.

Finally, as the boy's clandestine path led them to a humble bungalow nestled amidst the verdant landscape, Piran's instincts sharpened, sensing that the key to unlocking this unfolding mystery lay within the walls of this unassuming abode. Concealed from view, he held his breath, poised on the edge of discovery, ready to confront the secrets that awaited him in the bungalow's heart.

Realising the dire situation unfolding before her eyes, Lissa could not help but feel a deep sense of urgency creeping into her every thought. It seemed as if the essence of her magic waned as her worry for Jorja's well-being grew, causing an overwhelming sense of shock to grip her heart at the sheer power emanating from the crystal that Jorja held. The all-consuming force that seemed to flow from the crystal was unlike anything she had ever encountered. With resolve in her heart, Lissa silently vowed to seek guidance upon her return to Enrac, considering seeking counsel from Sodux or his father, Sobex, if the ancient drakÔn was alive and willing to impart his wisdom.

The unexpected events unfolded swiftly as Eswella's initial suspicion of her husband's peculiar behaviour culminated in a dramatic confrontation inside the grand bungalow. After impulsively using her magic to force the bungalow's door open, Eswella found herself injured by the door she had pushed, her nose bearing the brunt of the impact. Intrigued by the luminous glow from within, Eswella pressed on despite her injury, her curiosity leading her to the room where Jorja stood, clutching the radiant crystal with an intensity that seemed to defy logic. With Jago's valiant attempts to shield Jorja proving futile against the overwhelming power, Eswella attempted to intervene, only to find herself forcefully accosted by Lissa, who unceremoniously dragged her out by her hair, informing her of her authority as a commanding presence.

The chaotic scene escalated as Eswella's rage flared upon encountering Piran outside, resulting in a physical altercation that left her with a broken leg caused by Piran's defensive actions. Amidst the tense stand-off, Piran, seeking to clarify his position and gain Lissa's trust, offered a respectful bow, acknowledging her as his queen. Still grappling with suspicions that lingered after the unfolding events, Lissa instructed Piran to stand guard over Jorja. At the same time, she dealt with the fallout of Eswella's escape through a mysterious portal.

With the dawn of a new day came a shifting of roles as Jorja, weakened and pallid, was tenderly guided to rest by Piran, who endeavoured to ensure her safety under Lissa's watchful eye. The ensuing daybreak saw Lissa preparing Piran for the tasks ahead, entrusting him with gathering essential provisions and weapons for their impending journey. Grateful for the responsibility bestowed upon him, Piran accepted the duties with a sense of duty and hope, eager to prove his fidelity to Lissa and the cause they now shared.

As discussions between Lissa and Piran delved into logistics and strategy, the weight of their circumstances became increasingly apparent. Recognising the looming threat posed by Helgi's tracking abilities, Lissa decided to relocate swiftly, keen on keeping Jorja safe from harm while navigating the intricate web of dangers surrounding them. With Jorja's fragile state necessitating careful handling, Piran's unwavering loyalty shone through as he pledged to carry her, a symbolic gesture of his commitment to standing by Lissa's side through the trials ahead.

Lissa meticulously prepared their car with essential supplies and belongings, ensuring every necessary item was securely stowed. Alongside Jorja, Jago and Piran, Lissa embarked on a journey towards a safer destination amidst the looming dangers. Arriving in the quaint town of Abridge, situated in Essex, brought a sense of familiarity to Lissa, who had sought refuge in a house she had purchased. This residence, shielded by potent spells that protected it, became their temporary sanctuary from the threats that loomed outside.

With an air of gratitude, Piran, whose loyalty had gained their trust, played a pivotal role in helping the family settle into their newfound abode. Lissa's watchful eyes remained ever alert, scanning their surroundings for any signs of danger that could jeopardise their safety. As the household protector, Lissa imparted instructions to Piran, tasking him with collecting essential weapons and supplies from the garden shed while she guarded the premises with unwavering determination.

Understanding the gravity of their precarious situation, Piran dutifully executed each directive with precision and diligence, firmly committed to fostering trust with Lissa through his actions. As the foursome readied themselves for the subsequent leg of their arduous journey, Lissa maintained a steadfast vigilance, aware of the relentless pursuit. The unwavering loyalty exhibited by Piran and the resilient strength demonstrated by the Jago would be a pivotal asset in the inevitable confrontations ahead, forging a bond that could withstand the trials.

In the face of mounting peril, their unity became their greatest strength, a bond forged in trust and necessity. Together, they stood ready, prepared to confront whatever darkness lay ahead, knowing that survival depended on their unwavering resolve.

CHAPTER SEVENTEEN

In a twist of fate, the news of Eden's pregnancy, which should have been a cause for celebration, had unleashed a torrent of curses from Eswella. The bitter truth weighed heavily on her sister's heart, for she was cursed with barrenness, a wound that had festered deep within her soul, leaving no room for joy. Just two days after Eden cradled her newborn son, Cador, in her arms, Eswella had dragged her husband, Piran, through the shimmering portal, her anger palpable.

Cador, a delightful child, grew up with a spirited nature that brought joy and mischief. He inherited his father's raven-black hair, yet his curls and delicate features were a mirror of his mother. His striking grey eyes, reminiscent of stormy skies, sparkled with the same hue as his crystal, a curious contrast to the vibrant gems of the Royal Family. Now, at eleven, Cador had blossomed into a dashing young lad, his charm capable of ensnaring the hearts of all who beheld him.

Eden's heart had not initially warmed to Helgi, her husband, yet he proved to be a steadfast companion, always kind and attentive. He respected her wishes to raise Cador, provided she instilled the proper Royal Training in him and dutifully complied. Whenever tensions flared between Helgi and his subordinates, he would ensure Eden was shielded from the storm, treating her as a fragile blossom rather than a warrior. In time, she found herself growing fond of him.

As Eden sat in the lush gardens of the Palace, her gaze fixed on Cador as he practised his Telm Training, a portal suddenly burst open, and Eswella tumbled through. Instinctively, Eden rushed to her sister's side, only to be met with a fierce command to stay away. Eswella limped forward, her leg broken, but after a moment of stubbornness, she relented and accepted Eden's aid. Eswella recounted the tale of betrayal with a heavy heart, revealing how Piran had allied himself with Morwenna, igniting a fire of fury within Eden.

Determined to protect her sister, Eden, and Cador, now a strong boy of twelve, helped Eswella to her feet and entrusted her to Amox for healing. With resolve, they stormed into the throne room, where Helgi was engaged in a meeting with his military advisors, unaware of the tempest brewing just beyond the doors.

Eden and Cador had swiftly roused Eswella and entrusted her to Amox for healing before storming into the grand throne room where Helgi convened with his chief military advisors. As she burst through the ornate doors, all eyes turned upon her, for they had never witnessed the gentle wallflower in such a tempest of fury. With a fierce determination, she advanced toward Helgi, who sat frozen in shock, his mouth agape at her approach. Typically, she would honour him with a graceful curtsy. Today was different; her anger surged like a storm, and Helgi felt a flicker of concern for the first time. With a piercing glare, Eden dismissed the assembled officials, then fixed her intense gaze upon her husband.

"Dearest, what could trouble you so that you would dare to disturb your King and husband amid his duties?" Helgi inquired, a teasing lilt in his voice. "Do not jest with me, Helgi! I am not in the mood for your games," she retorted, her eyes flashing with fury.

"Very well, my love. Pray, enlighten me as to what has cast such a shadow upon your spirit," he implored, striving to maintain his composure even as frustration simmered. "First, Helgi, you cast my sister into a portal over a decade ago! Second, she has returned, forsaken and grievously wounded! And third, what in the name of the gods is happening?" she exclaimed, tears spilling.

A pang of sympathy struck him for Eden; her sister was a venomous soul, burdened with guilt throughout her childbirth, acutely aware that her sister was denied the joy of motherhood. This knowledge had weighed heavily upon her as the time of labour drew near.

"Silence, my sweet, for I shall mend all that is broken. You know I shall!" he whispered tenderly into her ear. "I truly wish for that, Helgi, for this plight weighs heavily upon Eswella; she has been forsaken! We cannot let this stand! What could have driven Piran to ally with your mother?" she implored, her eyes glistening with sorrow.

"I shall uncover the truth, my love; trust in me! Would you be so kind as to seek out Cador and bid him come to me?" he requested gently. Once she departed, Helgi sought out Amox, knowing he would be with Eswella. "What has transpired, Amox? Speak freely!" Helgi urged.

"I have endeavoured to delve into the depths of her mind, my King, yet I fear she is lost to madness. Her thoughts are scattered, and I struggle to unravel the tapestry of her past twelve years, especially as she endures such torment. I must first attempt to heal her," Amox replied gravely.

"Do so, my friend, for only then shall we glean the answers we seek." As Amox began the healing process of Eswella, Cador sauntered in with an air of casual grace.

"Father, you summoned me," he said, bowing respectfully to the King. Cador was a striking youth, his hair adorned with the exact curls that graced his mother's head. In the dim light of the chamber,

Helgi turned to Cador, his voice steady yet filled with purpose. "Cador, I have a quest for you. Once Eswella has regained her strength, would you accompany her through the portal and return with Piran, Morwenna, and her grandchild?"

"Indeed, my father! I shall strive to fulfil your wish!" Cador declared, his heart swelling with determination. At that moment, Helgi felt a surge of pride for his son. Cador had honed his skills to perfection, becoming a formidable warrior, a feat Helgi himself had never achieved, burdened by his limitations. Yet, there was an unexplainable connection Cador felt towards Eswella, a sense of familiarity that stirred within him.

"You may prepare yourself, Cador," Helgi instructed, noticing his son's gaze linger too long on the frail figure of the woman being tended to. Excitedly, Cador dashed from the room, eager to share the news of his noble task with his mother. He found her seated by the shimmering waterfall in the palace gardens, a shadow of worry etched upon her features.

"Mother, what troubles you?" Cador inquired, concern lacing his voice. "Oh, it is nothing, my sweet child. I merely fret for my sister with Amox," she replied softly. "Fear not, Mother! Father will ensure that Amox cares for her. Once she is healed, nourished, and at peace, we shall journey through the portal to confront the fiends responsible for her plight," Cador reassured her, hoping to ease her troubled heart.

Yet, instead of alleviating her fears, Cador's proclamation only stoked the flames of her anxiety. "What do you mean, Cador?" Eden inquired, her heart heavy with dread, wishing she could turn back time.

"Father has commanded that once the woman Eswella is restored, I am to journey through the portal alongside her," Cador declared with pride. At this, Eden sprang to her feet, striding again toward her husband, but her fury was palpable this time. She would not allow him to diminish her spirit or reduce her to tears. After all, they spoke of her firstborn child, and Eden would go to any lengths for her offspring.

Amox signalled Helgi to Eden's approach, yet when he turned, the woman before him was unrecognisable. She radiated a fierce beauty in her anger, but now she was breathtakingly formidable.

Helgi inhaled deeply, steadying himself.

"What! Eden, what troubles you?" he asked, attempting to mask his surprise with concern. "You intend to send Cador, my Cador, through one of those portals, just as you did with my sister? I refuse to accept it! Just look at how Eswella returned - madness is what she brought back!" Eden exhaled sharply, the words spilling forth in a rush.

"Your sister's mind was already frayed long before I sent her through the portal, and you know this to be true!" he shot back, his voice rising in defence. Eden's voice trembled with desperation as she implored, "Oh Helgi, do not grant passage for Cador, my beloved

Cador! Have mercy, I beseech you!"

Wary of the endless justifications to his wife, Helgi chose a more commanding approach. "I am your sovereign, and my decree is absolute, dear wife," he thundered, echoing through the chamber. "The whims of a mere woman shall not sway me. Is that understood, my lady?!" The weight of his words left little room for response.

"Yes, Your Majesty," she replied, executing a graceful curtsey before hastening from Amox's healing quarters in search of Cador.

Eswella's recovery had surpassed all expectations, even those of Amox himself. Amox already knew Eswella from Gasal, not that Eswella would remember. But Amox knew her, and he knew her past as well. While his arcane arts had mended her leg to a certain extent, the shadows of her mind remained untouched, a labyrinth of confusion. Flickering visions of vengeance against her husband, Piran, danced in her thoughts, a testament to her feelings of betrayal. Amox believed this turmoil stemmed from her recent anguish, yet he was blissfully unaware that the roots of her distress ran far more profound, tracing back to their childhood.

Eswella, being ten minutes the elder, held a sense of superiority in her heart. In contrast, Eden was a radiant infant, a vision of beauty and grace. She was enchanting and possessed a gentle spirit, never shedding a tear when her sister snatched away the toy she cherished. Instead, she felt a sense of joy that Eswella desired her company. Eswella, however, was not blessed with such beauty or kindness; she often devised schemes to ensnare Eden in mischief before their parents, Kelsey and Taran.

Taran found himself ensnared by the beguiling deceptions of Eswella, while Kelsey, with her keen insight, discerned the darkness that festered within her eldest child from the very start. She had borne witness to the malevolence of her daughter, who had mercilessly battered her younger twin, Eden, to the brink of death on numerous occasions. The local healer had become a frequent visitor, tending to Eden's many fractures and shattered bones. Despite Kelsey's desperate attempts to shield her youngest from Eswella's cruelty, the elder twin's strength soon eclipsed her mother's efforts. Taran, swayed by pity for Eswella, chose to stand by her side, recognising her cunning nature, though he could not deny her plainness compared to the vibrant beauty of Eden.

It was different in other countries of Inorac, as only Royals had crystals on Enrac, and some chose for all to have them. On the momentous occasion of their twelfth birthday, when the twins were to receive their crystals, the air was thick with anticipation. Eden's crystal shimmered a radiant light yellow, mirroring the hue of her eyes, and as she grasped it, her flowing red hair seemed to defy gravity, rising in a glorious display.

In stark contrast, Eswella's crystal was a deep tiger's eye, reflecting the same hue as her own eyes. Yet, when she accepted her crystal, no visible transformation occurred. When Taran inquired about her experience, only later that evening did Eswella reveal the truth. With a sense of pride, she described an inward sensation, a surge of warmth coursing through her being. Unsettled by her revelation, Taran implored her to keep this a guarded secret, even suggesting she fabricated a tale. But Eswella, resolute in her pride, refused to conceal her unique bond with the crystal. That night, after the twins had succumbed to slumber, Taran confided in Kelsey about the unsettling nature of Eswella's crystal. A chill gripped Kelsey's heart as she grasped the implications, her fear deepening in the shadows of their home.

"What will the townsfolk think, Taran, if this secret were to slip into the light?" she inquired, her voice trembling with concern. "I cannot say," he replied with a heavy heart. "Our only course may be to flee this place should the truth emerge," he declared urgently. "Let us take each moment as it comes, Kelsey. Perhaps our fears are unfounded."

That night, a weight settled in Kelsey's chest, a foreboding that kept her awake until dawn. She understood the implications of their predicament, and her mind raced with worry. Yet, as the sun rose on the following days without incident, a semblance of calm began to wash over her. Still, she watched over her daughters with a vigilance that did not sit well with Eswella.

When Eden sought permission to gather fruit from the orchard, Kelsey, seeing no harm in the venture, granted her wish. But an hour later, she spotted Eswella emerging from the grove, her dress stained with what appeared to be berry juice, a mischievous grin playing on her lips. A tight knot rose once more in Kelsey's throat as she cried out for Taran, who toiled in the distant fields under the weary sun. Though her voice was but a fragile thread carried on the wind, he heard the tremor in it - and without hesitation, he abandoned his work and dashed toward the house, heart pounding with dread. Eswella perched on the porch, giggling softly as Taran approached, breathless and alarmed.

"Where is your mother, my dear?" he asked, concern etched on his face. "In the orchard, father, searching for Eden's body," she replied, her tone deceptively innocent. Taran's heart sank at the sight of his daughter, her hands and face smeared with crimson, her dress a canvas of horror.

Hendry, a neighbour from the nearby farm, and his son Arthek heard the ruckus and hurried over to help. Taran urgently instructed Arthek to fetch the healer without delay. Upon noticing Eswella's state, Hendry turned to Taran, his brow furrowed with worry. "Where is Kelsey?" he asked, his voice laced with concern.

"Mother sought the lost form of Eden in the heart of the orchard, yet her quest would be in vain, for I had concealed her well." Taran dashed through the dees, calling out for Kelsey. He discovered her deep within the grove, her face a mask of frantic worry, swaying gently as she cradled Eden's lifeless body in her arms, tears streaming down her cheeks.

Arthek returned, accompanied by the healer, sensing his father's presence, drawing him toward the orchard. Kelsey, believing her beloved daughter to be lost forever, initially resisted the healer's approach. Only when the healer revealed that Eden's crystal flickered faintly with life did Kelsey reluctantly entrust her daughter's fate to him.

Jowan, a skilled healer, poured his heart into the magic that would restore the girl. After an eternity, he emerged from the orchard, carrying Eden's revived form, while Kelsey leaned on Hendry and Arthek for support. Jowan entrusted Eden to Taran, instructing him to take her to the chamber and remain by her side as he turned his attention to Eswella, who was stained with blood and in need of examination. However, upon closer inspection, he realised she was not injured.

"Eswella, did you bring harm to your sister?" Jowan inquired with a calm demeanour. "Yes," she replied, a gleam of joy in her eyes. "Do you understand, child, that you have grievously injured her?" Jowan pressed on. "Yes, I do. I wished for her to perish,"

Eswella confessed, her tone shifting to sorrowful. "But now she lives, and that fills me with rage."

At that moment, Jowan stepped back, refusing to offer her further aid, deeming her unhinged. Hendry took Arthek by the hand and hurried home to inform his wife, Rosen. Meanwhile, Jowan the Erland hastened back to share the troubling news with his wife, Gwen, and their young son, Amox.

Amox, a scion of the noble Erland lineage, found himself under the watchful eye of his father, who imparted the ancient wisdom of healing arts. With fervour, Amox engaged in profound discourse with his father for hours, contemplating the plight of Eswella and devising potential remedies for her affliction. Meanwhile, Jowan's wife, Gwen, had taken it upon herself to traverse the village. She spread the word of the recent calamity at Kelsey and Taran's abode, cautioning the villagers about the dangers surrounding Eswella.

The whispers of fear soon reached the ears of Hendry and Rosen, who, gripped by terror, chose silence over speech. They barricaded themselves and Arthek within their home, hoping the storm would pass. The villagers were all too aware of the chaos that could ensue should a distressed child wield a crystal, and dread hung heavy in the air.

A throng of villagers soon gathered at Rosen's threshold, their fists pounding against the door with urgency. Reluctantly, she opened it, fearing the wood would splinter under their assault. With a facade of ignorance, she claimed that Hendry had shared nothing with her, then hastily shut the door, watching as the mob turned their ire toward Taran's dwelling. Just as the clamour faded, a gentle knock echoed through the silence. When Rosen opened the door again, her heart sank at seeing Eswella standing before her.

"Please, spare me your wrath," Rosen implored, trembling. "I bear no malice, foolish woman. I seek refuge, and soon I shall make my escape. You will assist me, yes?" Eswella declared, her gaze piercing. Stunned into silence, Rosen could only nod in reluctant agreement.

Meanwhile, the mob had descended upon Taran's home, leaving chaos in its wake. Taran, Kelsey, and Eden had managed to slip out the back just as the villagers approached, taking only the barest essentials - money, food, and a few cherished belongings. They sought sanctuary in the barn until the mob's fury had waned, only to discover that the family had vanished.

Once the coast was clear, Taran slipped back into the ruins of his home to salvage what supplies he could for the road ahead. There, amidst the charred remains, he resolved to write to Hendry - at last accepting the offer made years ago to purchase the farm.

Taran re-entered the dwelling after the throng of villagers had dispersed, seeking to gather the necessary supplies for their impending journey. He resolved to pen a letter to Hendry in time, intending to sell the farm to him. After all, not long ago, Hendry had made a generous offer for the land. With a purpose, Taran collected garments, provisions, and the essentials for Eden, loading them into the cart. Meanwhile, Kelsey and Eden had prepared two of their swiftest steeds, ensuring they had hay bales for the long trek ahead. Taran manoeuvred the small cart to the barn before returning to the house while Kelsey and Eden secured the horses. Unbeknownst to them, some villagers had returned and ignited the house in flames.

Kelsey and Eden noticed the inferno far too late to save Taran. In a desperate bid for survival, Taran leapt from an upstairs window, his leg shattering upon impact. Gritting his teeth against the pain, he dragged himself along the path toward the barn, where his beloved wife and child awaited him.

The flames consumed the dwelling with ravenous hunger, and soon, the mob dispersed, satisfied that the family had been cast into despair with no refuge to return to. Kelsey was engulfed in sorrow, realising that Taran was now lost to them forever. With all her might, Eden endeavoured to silence her mother's wails, but their plight compelled her to insist on a protective incantation, for she had yet to master the art of spell casting. She tried her best and managed a weak spell to protect them. The sound of her mother's grief threatened to betray their hidden sanctuary. After two long hours of silence from the mob, Eden resolved to lift the spell, allowing them to slip away beneath the cloak of night. She carefully aided her mother onto their modest cart and swung open the barn doors. Just then, a sound pierced the stillness, causing her to gasp.

"Kelsey," the voice called out again. "Father!" she exclaimed, disbelief washing over her as she beheld her father, alive yet wounded. Without hesitation, she dashed back into the barn to share the miraculous news with her mother, urging her to assist as Taran needed their aid. With great effort, Kelsey and Eden lifted Taran onto the cart, and together, they set forth from the village, their hearts heavy yet hopeful.

On the dawn of the third day, the weary travellers stirred from their slumber only to discover that a shadowy figure had infiltrated their camp, absconding with one of their steeds. Eswella's cherished horse had vanished, and an unspoken understanding passed between them, revealing the thief's identity. Henceforth, Eden and Kelsey were bound to traverse the rugged path on foot, for the remaining horse could not bear the weight of their cart and its contents. The journey to the nearest port loomed long and treacherous. One evening, Taran and Kelsey reached a consensus: departing this land was their wisest course, for in a foreign realm, no one would recognise them or their beloved daughter, Eden.

After nine arduous days, they finally set foot upon the shores of Dekhala Port, where they secured passage aboard a vessel bound for a distant land known as Enrac. The ship's captain warned them of the tumultuous seas that awaited, promising a fortnight of discomfort on their voyage.

Upon their safe arrival in Enrac, Taran, Kelsey, and Eden established their camp just beyond the bustling town. The locals greeted the newcomers with warmth and kindness. Eden soon found her place as a handmaid-in-training within the grand Palace, while Kelsey secured a position as a handmaiden to the esteemed Princess Saffran. Having sought the aid of the village healer for his injured leg, Taran took up work as a farmhand. His innovative ideas for improving the farm's operations did not go unnoticed, and the farmer came to appreciate Taran's keen insights. Life unfolded favourably for them, and it would not be long before they amassed enough coin to construct their own humble abode.

Kelsey returned to the camp one evening, her expression heavy with concern. She had bided her time until Eden succumbed to slumber before confiding in Taran about the turmoil that had unfolded that day. A scandal had erupted within the Palace walls, where another servant caught a handmaiden to Queen Morwenna in thievery. That servant was none other than Eswella. Kelsey harboured a deep suspicion that her daughter had orchestrated the theft to secure a coveted position within the Palace. When Kelsey encountered Eswella, the girl had shown no hint of surprise. Kelsey then recounted to Taran the words that had passed between them.

"I stowed away on the very same vessel that brought you here," Eswella had declared. She continued, asserting that she was no longer part of their family. If they kept her identity a secret and refrained from any association with her, she promised that all would be well and that she intended to leave them in peace. "I believe it is time for us to seek refuge elsewhere, Taran," Kelsey urged.

On a fateful day, while Eswella toiled in the Palace, her gaze fell upon the young Prince Helgi. He was concealed behind a marble pillar in the throne room, his striking features illuminated by the soft glow of the chandeliers. Prince Helgi was a sight to behold, with a cascade of dark hair framing his handsome face. Unbeknownst to him, Eswella observed him intently, captivated by his presence. However, her intrigue turned to fury when she realised that he was fixated on none other than her sister, Eden. She fled the throne room in a rage, her heart pounding with betrayal.

As the sun dipped below the horizon, casting shadows upon the land, Eden sought her mother, and together they strolled back to their camp, arms entwined. The night enveloped them in darkness, but Kelsey held aloft a flickering lantern, its warm glow guiding their steps. Amid their conversation about the coins they had gathered, nearly enough to craft a cosy dwelling for their family, a sudden rustle erupted from the underbrush beside the path.

With a flourish, Eswella leapt forth, her voice dripping with mockery. "Ah, Mother, I presume there shall be no space for me in your quaint little abode," she taunted. "Did I not clarify that if you kept your distance, I would do the same?" "Eswella, we have honoured your wishes and kept our distance," Kelsey replied firmly.

"Then pray do tell, why do I catch sight of the man I adore gazing longingly at my cherished sister?" she retorted, her tone laced with sarcasm. Eden bears no blame for the gaze of another - the choice of whom to behold lies solely with the man himself. Indeed, you can see the truth in that, Eswella, Kelsey thought, hoping fervently that Eswella would take her leave.

"I most certainly do not share your view. Keep her from Prince Helgi, or I shall have no choice but to inform the queen of your neglect towards your child," Eswella declared, her voice sharp as a dagger. "Eswella, my dear, you must be reasonable. Even you must recognise the futility of this. If Prince Helgi desires to gaze upon Eden, there is little I can do to thwart his will," Kelsey reasoned gently.

"Simply heed my command and ensure Eden stays far from him," Eswella insisted, her tone laced with menace.

After returning to camp, Eden and Kelsey were still rattled by their encounter, so they recounted the tale to Taran. Tears streamed down Eden's cheeks as she realised she had been unaware of Prince Helgi's interest and felt helpless to change it. That night, she wept herself to sleep, burdened by her sorrow.

Queen Morwenna summoned Kelsey and Eden to her secluded chambers the following day. A sense of dread coiled within Kelsey, for she suspected that her estranged daughter, Eswella, had whispered secrets to the Queen, and a familiar tightness gripped her throat.

"My dear lady, word has reached me of a most enchanting daughter you possess. Might this be her?" Queen Morwenna inquired, gesturing toward Eden, who kept her gaze lowered, hoping to evade scrutiny. She braced herself for the inevitable storm, confident that Eswella had shared tales with the sovereign. "Oh, sweet child, lift your head! You are not in peril, especially not for your beauty," the Queen chuckled, amused by her jest. "Step closer so I may behold the loveliness that has captured my attention."

With trepidation and resolve, Kelsey gently guided Eden forward, inching closer to the regal presence. Eden's red hair cascaded down her back like lava trailing down a mountainside.

"Dearest maiden, I find myself unable to behold your visage. I beseech you, grant me the privilege of gazing upon the face of the one my son has spoken of with such reverence," the queen implored once more.

Kelsey gently prodded her daughter, yet she could see that Eden's eyes shimmered with unshed tears. "Pardon me, my Queen, but my daughter is quite timid and easily startled. Might you allow her a brief moment to gather her courage?" Kelsey requested.

The Queen nodded in consent, prompting Kelsey to turn to her daughter. "My sweet child, I believe the time has come to share the tale of Eswella with the Queen." Eden gasped in dismay but ultimately nodded in agreement.

Kelsey stepped forward, her heart racing. "My Queen, I must make a revelation." "Proceed," the queen gestured with grace. "Before we arrived in Enrac, we resided in a quaint village upon Gasal. It was there that I brought forth twin daughters, one of whom stands before you now," she declared.

"And what of the other?" Queen Morwenna enquired, her curiosity piqued.

In a realm shrouded in shadows and whispers lies a tale of a child whose heart was as dark as the midnight sky. "This wretched soul, a tempest of malice, sought to extinguish the light of Eden on numerous occasions. When my daughters reached the age of twelve, a rite of passage akin to the one you experience here in Enrac, my other daughter was bestowed with a power that surged beyond her grasp. In a moment of fury, she nearly brought about Eden's demise, fleeing into the night without remorse, evading the consequences of her wicked deeds. The villagers, driven by fear and anger, reduced our home and farm to ashes, forcing us to abandon all we held dear. With only a handful of possessions and scant coin, we secured passage on a vessel bound for Enrac."

The Queen raised her hand as she spoke, summoning a servant girl who entered gracefully. Queen Morwenna, her countenance warm and inviting, ordered refreshments for our gathering.

"I sense we shall require sustenance for this unfolding tale, do you not agree?" she remarked, her smile a beacon of comfort. "Come, sit beside me and share the rest of this captivating narrative." Kelsey and Eden took their places at a quaint table while the servant girl busied herself with the preparations. She returned with fragrant, sweet flower tea and an array of exquisite cakes unlike any they had ever encountered. Once she departed, Queen Morwenna gestured for Kelsey to continue.

"We have found work and now rest within our humble cart. Soon, we shall have enough coin to construct a small dwelling of our own," Kelsey shared, hope glimmering in her eyes." "Then I fail to grasp the purpose of your words," declared Queen Morwenna with a furrowed brow.

"The purpose is straightforward, my Queen. My other daughter has ventured into this realm and cast shadows over Eden, warning her to steer clear of Prince Helgi. Thus, you can understand why my daughter hesitates to reveal herself to you," Kelsey explained, her voice tinged with urgency.

"I demand to know the name of your other daughter. What gives her the right to dictate whom my son may associate with?" the Queen insisted, her frustration palpable.

"My Queen, I implore you, do not compel us to speak of her. Remaining here serves no purpose; we must depart swiftly and pray she does not pursue us," Kelsey urged, rising from her chair.

"You shall remain seated; you have not been granted leave. I wish to know the name of your other daughter, for it is evident that she instils fear in both of you," the Queen replied, placing a comforting hand on Kelsey's arm and gently squeezing it.

A hushed tension filled the air in the palace's grand chamber as Kelsey began to speak again. "My Queen, while I…" But before the words could entirely escape, the heavy door to the queen's private sanctum burst open with a thunderous crash, and Eswella, fierce and unyielding, strode into the room.

"Mother, we had a pact! What treachery is this?" Eswella's voice rang out, echoing with indignation. "Ah, so this is your other daughter, my handmaiden," Queen Morwenna declared with a gleam of triumph. "Eswella, come forth! I have heard whispers of your threats against your poor mother and sister. This insolence ends now, do you comprehend?" The Queen's tone was a commanding force, one that brooked no argument. "Your sister Eden was merely about to be asked if she would accept the hand of Prince Helgi when they reach their majority," she continued, her gaze unwavering.

Eswella's cheeks flushed crimson with fury. "But he is meant for me! I laid eyes upon him first!" she cried, her voice trembling with despair.

"Perhaps that is true, but Helgi's heart does not beat for you as it does for Eden. If you wish to retain your position here at the palace as my lady-in-waiting, I strongly advise you to cease this discussion immediately!" The Queen dismissed Eswella with a wave, turning her attention to Kelsey, her demeanour resolute. The Queen's voice rang with a regal certainty as she spoke, "Eden approaches her thirteenth year, a momentous occasion indeed. This signifies that the union shall take place a mere one year before the laws of our realm permit her to wed. Fear not, for I shall ensure you are amply rewarded for the loss of your daughter to my son, bestowing upon you a splendid abode and a yearly stipend worthy of nobility."

Her gaze was unwavering, for she had no desire for responses; her mind was consumed with the preparations for the impending nuptials, and time was of the essence.

"I shall oversee Eden's education from this point forward, enlisting the most esteemed scholars in the land to guide her studies and provide for her garments and any other necessities she may require. Until the wedding day, I must insist that she does not reside within the Palace to safeguard her virtue. Thus, each evening, she shall return to your home, accompanied by a guard for her protection," she declared, her attention shifting to Eswella.

"Your standing in the realm has indeed ascended, yet conditions shall be imposed upon you as they will upon your mother. You shall remain in service at the Palace until the wedding day. In the interim, Eswella, I counsel you to distance yourself from your kin and focus on the quest for a husband of your own. Under the laws of Enrac, you may wed at the tender age of fifteen, for only those of royal blood may marry sooner. Should you discover a worthy suitor and present him to me, I shall endeavour to arrange the earliest union for you once Helgi and Eden have exchanged their vows by royal decree. Upon your marriage, you shall receive a modest dwelling befitting the sister of a Princess, along with a yearly stipend.

Mark my words, young lady: should you so much as raise a hand against your blood, you shall forfeit all claim to my favour and be cast out from Enrac for eternity, your name stricken from its memory as though you never were. Your destination will be of no concern to us as long as it is not within the borders of Enrac. Now, if there are no further matters to address, I must attend to my youngest brother and his wife, who have joyfully announced the impending arrival of their first child. You may all take your leave. Eswella, it is time for you to assess your circumstances. You may depart Enrac immediately or remain, continue your duties, seek a husband, and find happiness. Remember, this is my decision, not your family's, so do not direct your frustrations at them. Now, go. Eden, I ask you to stay; we must deliberate." With that, Queen Morwenna rose and guided Eden from the chamber.

Eswella emerged from the Queen's private chambers, her spirit heavy and her heart burdened. For the first time, she had faced a stern reprimand accompanied by a daunting ultimatum. Desperate, she turned to her mother, rushing and enveloping her tightly. A sense of aimlessness washed over her, leaving her no clear path forward. Kelsey, weary yet nurturing, wrapped her arms around her daughter, whispering soothing words that promised solace. Yet, deep down,

Eswella knew that solace was a distant dream. Eden had captured the heart of Prince Helgi while she stood alone, a mere ten minutes older than her sister, yet bound by the chains of youth that barred her from marriage.

As thoughts swirled in her mind, she contemplated dark schemes to turn Prince Helgi against Eden but quickly dismissed such notions as folly. Countless ideas flitted through her imagination, each one cast aside as unwise. Yet, a flicker of determination ignited within her; indeed, there must be a way to alter her fate. She sensed an inexplicable connection with Helgi, a thread that tied their destinies together, though she could not discern whether it was mere fantasy or a hidden truth. Resolute, she vowed to uncover the mystery while remaining inconspicuous. For the coming months, she donned the guise of a devoted daughter and sister and a diligent worker while observing Helgi with keen eyes.

She noted a troubling pattern in her watchful gaze: when Helgi played with his siblings, particularly with Princess Saffran, his demeanour turned cruel. He would strike her when the shadows cloaked their games, revealing a darker side to the young prince. Princess Saffran, at sixteen, was four years his senior, yet she bore the brunt of his unkindness, a secret that weighed heavily on Eswella's heart.

In the realm of Enrac, at the tender age of seventeen, Saffran found herself delayed in the quest for her destined partner. Tobias, a strikingly handsome young General-in-training of the Royal army, captured her heart with his pride and valour. Yet, Helgi, her brother, harboured a disdain for both Tobias and Saffran herself. In Enrac, the ancient laws favoured the firstborn, granting women the right to ascend to the throne, a notion that irked Helgi deeply.

Convinced of his superiority, Helgi believed he was more deserving of kingship than any woman, regardless of age. He confided his grievances to his mother and, in hushed tones, to his father, Goran, fully aware that his father's hands were tied. Determined to carve out his destiny, he married young and established his own kingdom.

Helgi rose to voice his discontent before the gathered guests on the day of Saffran and Tobias' nuptials. Fortunately, his youth rendered his words primarily ignored, a familiar fate he had come to accept. Thus, the wedding proceeded, and from that moment forth, Helgi immersed himself in his studies while lavishing attention upon Eden, his new bride-to-be. He fulfilled her every desire, leaving her wanting for nothing. This devotion, however, did not sit well with Eswella, who kept a watchful eye on Eden's every action.

One fateful day, Eswella approached Helgi with a mischievous glint in her eye, inquiring if he was aware that her sister, Eden, had woven a spell around him. Helgi found the notion entertaining and decided to indulge in the jest for the afternoon. He strolled about, feigning to be ensnared in a mystical trance. However, his mother soon discovered his antics. Upon learning of his playful deception, she seized Eswella and dragged her to the dungeons. With a stern countenance, the Queen commanded the guards to refrain from offering her food, drink, or conversation for an entire day. Once the Queen had secured the door, she turned to Eswella and declared, "I instructed you to reflect upon your actions, yet you choose to rebel and harbour your spite. The next vessel that arrives shall carry you away, banished from Enrac for all eternity." Just as Morwenna was about to depart, Eswella spoke up.

"But it was merely a game, not a reality, and besides, I no longer desire Prince Helgi; I have found another." The Queen, sceptical of her words, pressed further.

"And who might this fortunate soul be?" Eswella, caught off guard by the inquiry, faltered, for she could think of no other man but Helgi. "He is a lad from the village I pass on my way home, my Queen," she murmured, bowing her head as if cloaked in shame.

"Very well, you shall reveal to me the identity of this young man tomorrow, and as I have vowed, I will orchestrate the union. However, as you so aptly named it, you will remain here for your role in this little game for the night. I shall return at dawn to escort you to the village." With that, she turned on her heel, clutching the key tightly in her grasp. Eswella's heart sank at the thought of being confined with only the scurrying rats for company; their presence filled her with dread. Her mind raced, searching for familiar faces among the recruits in training, yet none stood out to her.

As the first light of dawn crept over the horizon, Queen Morwenna kept her solemn vow and descended once more into the dungeons. In her arms, she carried a fresh gown, a bundle of toiletries, and a finely wrought brush. With quiet authority, she ordered the guards to fetch clean water, nourishment, and a draught for the prisoner.

"Now, Eswella, let us restore your appearance, for we certainly do not wish your future betrothed to behold you in such a state," she declared with a hint of amusement.

Eswella's belly rumbling like a distant thunderstorm devoured every morsel laid before her in silence. Once her hunger was sated, she adorned herself in the exquisite gown selected by the queen. The luxurious silks and satins caressed her skin like a gentle breeze, and at that moment, she felt a radiant beauty envelop her.

Queen Morwenna clasped Eswella's hand, leading her from the grand palace into the bustling village, flanked by a vigilant entourage of guards. Though she was aware that Eswella had yet to choose a suitor, the queen anticipated a splendid display from the young girl and decided to indulge the moment. "Are you excited at the thought of meeting your future husband?" she inquired, her voice laced with curiosity.

"A touch anxious, to be truthful," Eswella replied, her mind racing to escape this unexpected fate. "I know not his name nor anything about him."

"Do not worry, dear one; we shall uncover the truth together," the queen reassured, sensing Eswella's unease. She had been observant of the young maiden within the palace walls, aware that Eswella's heart still lingered for her son, Helgi.

Upon their arrival in the village, Morwenna commanded that all the young men be gathered before her. She sought to find the elusive boy of her vision. Eswella scrutinised each lad as if she were assessing a battalion, her gaze sharp and discerning. At last, her attention fell upon a gentle-faced youth slightly older than herself. In the queen's eyes, he bore a striking resemblance to Helgi. True to her word, the two were introduced, and the queen summoned the boy's father to the palace. The father was briefed on the wedding arrangements for his son, Piran, and the promise of a comfortable home and a yearly stipend upon their union. The queen informed Piran's father that his son would commence training in her army, with the prospect of rising through the ranks upon completion. Grateful, Piran's father hurried home to share the joyous news with his wife. The queen decreed that Piran and Eswella would wed one month after Helgi and Eden's nuptials.

As the day of the grand union approached, the queen's heart grew heavy with concern for her future daughter-in-law. In her wisdom, she resolved to sequester Eswella away from the kingdom's gaze during the week leading up to the nuptials, ensuring her absence on the fateful day.

The wedding of Helgi and Eden was a splendid celebration, a joyous occasion that filled the realm with merriment. Fortunately, Piran had whisked Eswella away to meet his kin, journeying to the estate of his eldest brother, who tended to a sprawling farm a hundred leagues from the bustling town of Enrac. For the first time, Eswella basked in the warmth of attention, though Piran's family regarded her calmly, deeming her indifferent towards their beloved brother. Yet, the queen's decree bound them, and thus, a moon's turn after Eden's wedding, Eswella found herself wed to Piran, as fate had woven.

Eswella basked in joy for a fleeting moment, yet it swiftly became clear that her heart held no affection for Piran. Her sole interest lay with Helgi, and she made it her mission to converse with him daily, nurturing his ambitions of seizing the throne. She aligned herself with his every scheme, becoming a potent influence and a beguiling temptress in his life. With Eden still in her tender years, Helgi was forbidden from sharing a bed with her until she reached the age of fifteen, one year from now. Thus, as a married woman, Eswella graciously offered to fulfil her sister's duties and consummated the bedding ceremony on her behalf. However, the queen soon discerned that Helgi harboured a dark and twisted nature. One fateful morning, she discovered him in the training grounds, attempting to rally soldiers to his cause. To her begrudging admiration, he had garnered a considerable following. She further found that Helgi had been sleeping with Eswella. This thought angered Morwenna greatly.

Before long, an insurrection erupted, and Morwenna recognised it as Helgi's cunning design to eliminate his sister to claim the crown upon her demise. The conflict raged for several weeks, with Morwenna's forces emerging victorious. In the chaos, Helgi abducted Eden and fled the Palace. Eswella yearned to pursue him, but Piran lay wounded and unable to move. Helgi, too, bore injuries from the skirmish and sought the aid of a healer.

The second wave of battles stretched, lasting far longer than the first.

In the shadowed realms of the past, Amox found himself cast out from the land of Gasal, a place that once embraced him but now shunned him for his radical notions of healing. The populace believed that a mind, once twisted by madness, was beyond salvation. Yet, Amox dared to proclaim that, under the right conditions, even the most deranged could be restored. Alongside him, Jowan and Gwen faced a similar fate, driven from Gasal's borders. After the calamity of Eswella, all magical folk were hunted like beasts. In their desperate plight, they lost sight of Amox and stumbled into the nascent realm of Caniax, where fledgling villages were beginning to rise from the ground. There, they found solace, for the absence of a healer allowed Jowan to ply his craft from the moment they set foot in this new land.

Meanwhile, Amox journeyed to Enrac, where he first offered his services to the queen. She regarded him suspiciously, for he was a formidable Erland, brimming with unconventional ideas.

Ultimately, her fears were realised when his attempt to mend the mind of a deranged child ended in disaster, leading to his exile to the mountains, where the vigilant drakÔns kept watch over him. In time, Helgi, a king of ambition, captured many drakÔns, enhancing their might, and in the process, he discovered and freed Amox from his rocky prison.

Amox presented himself to King Helgi as a personal healer, and the king, intrigued by his innovative thoughts, welcomed him. The young Erland proved to be a tireless worker, often found labouring at all hours, earning the king's favour. Amox admired Helgi's dedication to his royal duties, and their friendship blossomed. Amox began to counsel the king on matters of warfare and, more intimately, on his personal affairs. Following Amox's guidance, Helgi resolutely barred Eswella from coming to his realm, for he needed to be seen as a ruler capable of producing a pure-blood heir to secure his lineage.

The war clash continued to echo through the land as Helgi relentlessly dispatched battalions of warriors toward his mother's stronghold, intent on breaching its defences. Among his loyal commanders was one with a cousin embedded within the walls of Queen Morwenna's court, serving as a clandestine informant. This spy had revealed a secret that darkened Helgi's heart: Princess Saffran was with child. The news struck him like a thunderbolt, for it meant another potential heir to the throne, igniting a fierce determination to unleash every soldier.

Despite their fervent efforts, Helgi's forces returned battered and defeated, unable to penetrate the formidable barriers the queen's loyalists erected. Undeterred, Helgi scoured the realm of Enrac, amassing a legion of thousands, with an equal number undergoing rigorous training. After months of relentless preparation, they stood poised for battle, their spirits aflame with the desire for conquest. Helgi would lead this charge, driven by a burning ambition to eradicate his lineage or force them to kneel before him. With Saffran nearing her delivery time, he calculated that she could not join the fray despite her prowess as the finest warrior among them.

Meanwhile, Helgi's wife, Eden, was also on the brink of motherhood, yearning to bestow their firstborn with the kingdom's legacy.

As Helgi unleashed his forces in relentless waves, Saffran gave birth amidst the chaos, her heart heavy with dread for her newborn. The queen's army, weary from the unyielding assault, outnumbered two to one. In a moment of desperation, Saffran entrusted her precious daughter to her mother, the queen, who had managed to escape through a mystical portal just as the storm of battle raged on.

Amox advised Helgi about Eswella and that she yearned to be part of his kingdom. Helgi agreed and soon decided to send Eswella and Piran through a portal to find Morwenna and the child and return them both to Helgi.

CHAPTER EIGHTEEN

Lissa was acutely aware of the urgency that enveloped her mission as they embarked on their journey towards the elusive portal device. Therefore, as a first step, she diligently orchestrated their travel plans to head towards the coastal town of Dover, a historical gateway to mainland Europe, where they would board a boat destined for France. With a determined resolve, she understood the paramount importance of acquiring a detailed world map to aid in navigating the labyrinth of European cities and charting a course towards her ultimate destination. She would go by plane, but that was not feasible, as she hated flying. She tried it on the flight to Sidney from Kakadu. Then, there was a twenty-four-hour flight from Sidney to Heathrow with a short break in Dubai. Upon arriving at Heathrow, she purchased a car and drove directly to Abridge, a small village in Essex, where she bought a house. She preferred to drive rather than fly.

Their arduous voyage unfurled like a tapestry of adventure, spanning diverse landscapes and vibrant cities. Departing to Calais via ferry, their path meandered through the bustling metropolises of Brussels, the enchanting charm of Cologne, the thriving energy of Frankfurt, and the historical allure of Nuremberg before venturing deeper into the heart of Europe and reaching the scenic city of Graz in Austria. Travelling onwards, they traversed the picturesque terrain of Slovenia at Maribor, eventually descending into the cultural tapestry of Zagreb, a city brimming with history and nestled in the embrace of lush landscapes.

Upon reaching their temporary haven in Zagreb, they sought solace in a humble abode, opting for the inconspicuous refuge of the town's least-noteworthy hotel. Lissa's strategic choice reflected her keen awareness of the importance of discretion as she endeavoured to navigate unnoticed through the watchful gazes of potential onlookers. By avoiding the customary luxury accommodations, she aimed to shield her movements from prying eyes and preserve the veil of secrecy shrouding her mission.

Exhausted from their rigorous journey, they succumbed to a deep slumber that enveloped them in a cocoon of peace, allowing their bodies to rejuvenate and their minds to find respite from the relentless pursuit of their goal. Graced by the first light of dawn, they awoke to a breathtaking panorama unfolding before their eyes, with Zagreb's majestic landmarks, such as the iconic Zagreb Cathedral, adorning the cityscape in a regal embrace.

Driven by hunger and a thirst for exploration, they ventured towards Tkalčićeva Street, a bustling thoroughfare teeming with vibrant cafes and pulsating with the rhythmic cadence of life. Enthralled by the melodic symphony of sounds and the kaleidoscope of colours that enveloped them, the children eagerly absorbed the rich tapestry of experiences laid before them. Among them, Jago, with an insatiable curiosity for diverse cuisines, revelled in the myriad flavours encountered along their journey, his palate ignited by the tantalising array of tastes that embraced him.

In the vibrancy of Zagreb's streets, they found a moment of respite amidst the bustling city life, savouring each fleeting instant as they inched closer towards their elusive goal of unlocking the mysteries concealed within the enigmatic portal device.

Jorja, who had fully recovered from her previous physical ailment, diligently engaged in her training routine whenever there was a brief pause in their journey. She eagerly welcomed the opportunity to stretch her muscles after hours of sitting in the car. Despite her renewed vigour, always watchful and protective, Jago stayed by her side, demonstrating his unwavering loyalty.

After intentionally lying low for a few days, they eventually negotiated with a pilot to provide them with transportation to Huangshan Tunxi International Airport in China. Lissa hated to fly but had no alternative, and she sat on the plane, cringing all the way. Once there, they allowed only protection spells for safety measures, with a strict prohibition on any other form of magic. Jorja and Jago intensified their training sessions, focusing mainly on Telm Training. Even with Piran close at hand, Jago remained steadfast beside Jorja, his eyes ever watchful, his distrust of the man unshaken. Lissa, however, held fast to her belief in Piran's loyalty to her cause, quietly suspecting that he had long since betrayed Eswella.

Their time in China was a blend of enjoyment and cultural immersion. While Jago relished the culinary delights, Jorja found solace in exploring the rich heritage and history of the place. On a separate note, Piran and Lissa once again delved into discussions about the mysterious individual who had entered this realm through the portal alongside Eswella. Despite their efforts, Piran, who had spent a similar period on Earth as Lissa, could not offer any substantial insights. Lissa purchased a car for the next trip to the other end of China. Lissa found a little shop that sold tea blends and negotiated with the villagers to buy the necessary tea plants and seeds to grow her own. She was looking forward to the challenge. Piran's shared interest in this concept informed Morwenna of his garden at Widemouth. The notion that they had seen Piran tending to the garden and a memory that Morwenna had forgotten.

According to Piran, Amox was crucial in keeping Helgi's army in peak physical condition. Lissa shared her encounter with Amox, revealing his banishment and subsequent surveillance by the drakÔns. This newfound knowledge left Lissa astonished by the potential consequences of Helgi releasing Amox, aware of the healer's immense power if he had gleaned any vital information on magic from the drakÔns. Thus, she silently vowed to uncover whether Amox had acquired this unparalleled knowledge during his time under the drakÔns' watchful eyes.

They discussed their next move, analysing the situation meticulously to ensure their safety. Both Lissa and Piran agreed that it would be a strategic move to backtrack and check for any potential followers, as evading detection was crucial. With their destination set for the southernmost tip of India by boat, they embarked on this journey urgently, realising that time was of the essence.

As the journey stretched into its fifth month, Lissa could not help but ponder the significance of time and how it seemed to slip away. Despite the risk involved in retracing their steps, they understood that it was necessary to shake off any pursuers who might be hot on their trail.

With Jorja's thirteenth birthday approaching the next day, anticipation mingled with concern in Lissa's mind. She marvelled at her granddaughter's swift progress in Telm Training, acknowledging her innate talent and determination. The passage of time underscored the need for Jorja to hone her skills further and explore new developmental avenues. Aware of the looming threat posed by Eswella and Helgi, Lissa felt a surge of protectiveness towards Jorja, knowing the dangers that lurked. She had purchased small presents on the way to acknowledge the big event and decided to buy a cake secretly.

Lissa's thoughts then drifted to her daughter Saffran, contemplating the grim possibility of her fate in the wake of Helgi's relentless pursuit. The uncertainty surrounding the well-being of her family weighed heavily on her, as she feared for the safety of Saffran, Goran, and even Tobias. The intricate web of familial ties and potential scenarios played out in her mind, casting a shadow over her emotions.

Reflecting on the broader family dynamics, Lissa contemplated the lineage and potential succession in light of Goran and Morwenna's offspring. The intricate balance of power and responsibility within the family structure added a layer of complexity to their already perilous situation. The interplay of survival, duty, and legacy loomed as they navigated the treacherous path.

Setting sail from China towards India in a calculated move, the companions felt a mixture of anticipation and apprehension about what lay ahead. The revelation of Piran sensing his wife's proximity added a layer of intrigue to their journey, hinting at unseen forces at play.

CHAPTER NINETEEN

Eswella's leg continued to ache with a persistent throbbing pain that made it difficult for her to keep up with the relentless pursuit of Morwenna. The frustration of being slowed down by her injury weighed heavily on her, but what pained her even more was the disapproval and anger she sensed from Cador. His impatience matched her desire to conclude their mission and return to Enrac swiftly. Yet, when their journey led them to the foreign land of China, Eswella realised that Cador's frustration had ignited into a fiery anger now directed squarely at her.

His powerful voice boomed with authority as he unleashed a storm of accusations and insults upon her, declaring her useless and unfit for their quest. Despite Eswella's attempts to reason with him, Cador's rage only escalated, fuelled by his belief in his superiority over her. He rejected the bond of kinship between them, viewing her not as an aunt but merely as a servant to his father, a hag unworthy of respect or royal lineage. The derogatory words spewed from his lips stung like venom, poisoning the fragile balance between them and threatening to shatter any semblance of remaining harmony.

As their confrontation intensified, Eswella felt a surge of defiance rising within her, tempered by the realisation that the lingering injury to her leg weakened her magic. She warned Cador not to underestimate her, reminding him that despite her physical limitations, she still retained the power to discipline him if necessary.

But Cador's blind fury clouded his judgment, pushing him further into a realm of hostility and aggression that distanced him from the compassion and understanding Eswella hoped to elicit.

Amid their heated exchange, Eswella braced herself for the storm brewing, knowing that the outcome of this confrontation would not only shape their immediate future but also define the fragile dynamic of their relationship moving forward. The clash of wills and emotions between Eswella and Cador reached a crescendo. This pivotal moment would test the limits of their patience, resilience, and, ultimately, their bond as allies in a treacherous and uncertain world. Cador unleashed his fury upon Eswella—her garments torn asunder, her skin etched with the cruel testament of his wrath. His rage roared like a tempest, a force so fearsome that none dared intercede. It was as if a dark spirit had taken hold of him. Eswella had curled into a tight ball desperately for safety, bracing herself against the relentless storm of blows that fell upon her.

The following day, Eswella woke up in Chengkan village, an ancient settlement rich in historical significance. The majestic Yellow Mountain, also known as Huangshan Mountain, towered twenty-one miles above her. With its captivating beauty and undeniable air of antiquity, the village captured Eswella's attention when she opened her eyes.

However, as she searched for any sign of Cador, she was struck by the deep sense of abandonment that enveloped her. A wave of self-pity washed over her, marking the first time she felt sorrow. Tears streamed down her face as memories flooded her mind, particularly the hurtful actions she had inflicted on her own family over the years, causing her to weep even more intensely.

Amid her emotional turmoil, Eswella recalled Morwenna's advice from years past about reflecting on her life, realising that it might all be too little, too late. The realisation of her past wrongdoings weighed heavily on her, amplifying her cries until they resonated through the village, drawing the attention of an armed policeman who approached her swiftly, commanding her attention.

Before she could fully comprehend the situation, she found herself being forcibly escorted and placed in the back of a police car, swiftly taken to the local police station, where she was confined to a cell. Stripped of all her belongings, including her cherished crystal necklace, Eswella's tears continued to flow unabated, each drop a testament to her regret and remorse for her past actions.

The harsh reality of her confinement set in as she struggled to come to terms with her predicament, the pungent odour of urine from the cell's previous occupant invading her senses. Hours passed with Eswella wrapped in her emotions until exhaustion finally overtook her, plunging her into a deep slumber like she had never experienced before.

The following day, as she stirred from her restless sleep, Eswella was confronted by a small Chinese policeman prodding her ribs, speaking in a language she could not comprehend. "I do not understand you," she uttered, lost in a sea of confusion and uncertainty about her current predicament.

As dawn broke, the soft golden light filtering through the small window of her cell, Eswella's troubled thoughts began to surface. She reflected on her hazy recollections, piecing together fragmented memories. The feeling of abandonment lingered, a bitter taste in her mouth, as she struggled to recall the details of the young man who was once by her side. Was it a dream, a fleeting moment of happiness overshadowed by confusion and pain? Brushing these thoughts aside, she greeted the police officer's inquiries with a careful blend of truth and deceit, a necessary strategy in the face of uncertainty.

Her body, a canvas of aches and bruises, bore witness to a trauma she could not fully grasp. The officer's stern gaze probed, searching for answers she could not provide. Concealing the truth seemed the only escape, a temporary shield from the ominous shadows of the past. Despite the physical agony that gnawed at her, Eswella's mind remained sharp, a beacon of resilience amid chaos.

The officer's departure left her in solitude, a fleeting sense of relief mingling with apprehension. The promise of medical attention offered a glimmer of hope amidst the bleakness of her situation. As the doctor examined her injured leg, a wave of realisation washed over her. The stranger's diagnosis painted a picture of a fall, a heady descent on the slopes of the yellow mountain. Released from the confines of the cell, Eswella faced a new dilemma - a future shrouded in uncertainty, a path fraught with unknown perils.

Yet, amidst the looming shadows of her past, a beacon of kindness emerged in the form of Officer Li. His offer of sanctuary, a humble abode nestled in the heart of Chengkan, held the promise of solace and renewal. Eswella, wary yet grateful, embraced this unexpected gesture, a fragile thread of trust weaving its way into her fractured existence. Li's words painted a vivid tapestry of history and tradition, each thread unravelling the mysteries of Chengkan, a place steeped in ancient lore and whispered legends.

The winding alleys of the village unfurled before her, a labyrinth of secrets waiting to be discovered. Pavilions beckoned, bridges whispered of untold tales, and each corner was a testament to a bygone era preserved in time's gentle embrace. With Li as her guide, Eswella entered this maze of wonders, a world pulsating with echoes of the past and promises of the future.

CHAPTER TWENTY

Meanwhile, across distant seas, Jorja and Jago embarked on a journey fraught with danger and uncertainty. Lissa, their steadfast guardian, navigated the treacherous currents of pursuit, her instincts honed by a lifetime of evading unseen threats. The relentless pursuit of an unknown adversary cast a shadow over their travels, a reminder of the perils that lurked in the shadows of the unknown.

As the plane's engines roared to life, Lissa gripped the arm of her chair, holding tight, carrying them towards their next destination; a sense of foreboding hung heavy in the air. The journey ahead was fraught with challenges, yet amidst the chaos and turmoil, a glimmer of hope flickered in the hearts of the four travellers. Together, they braved the unknown, each step forging a path towards a destiny yet untold.

Upon arriving in Sydney, Australia, they made their way north towards the portal device hidden under a mass of rocks at Jim Jim Falls in Kakadu, the Northern Territory. This remote location required significant effort to reach. Realising that hitch-hiking would not be a viable option due to the risks it posed to others, Lissa decided that the most practical course of action would be to rent a car for the journey ahead.

Indeed, the urgency of their mission compelled Lissa to devise a plan that involved continuous driving, alternating between resting and driving shifts with Piran to ensure they reached their destination in just two days. This strategy meant pushing themselves to the limit, with breaks only for necessary food and refreshments to sustain their energy throughout the arduous journey.

Despite their best efforts, Lissa was puzzled by their inability to evade the unknown pursuer, shadowing their every move. Turning to Jago for help, she implored him to wield his nascent protective abilities to conceal them, an act that provided a brief respite before Jago succumbed to exhaustion and drifted off into a deep slumber.

Lissa had sensed a shift in the magic. A split of sorts, Eswella had parted ways with Cador. In a bid to outmanoeuvre their persistent pursuer, Lissa sought assistance from Jorja, only to sense the stranger's malevolent gaze upon them once more. Engaging in a hushed discussion with the other three, Lissa realised the unsettling truth that their stalker had familial ties. This revelation made it clear that their peril was more profound than anticipated. Only royals could sense royals using magic.

Recognising the need for new strategies, Lissa entrusted Piran with the crucial task of safeguarding them, leveraging his innate strength to shield their vulnerable group from harm. Embracing her role as the steadfast helmswoman of their perilous journey, Lissa navigated the treacherous path ahead with resolve and precision, deftly alternating between bursts of driving and moments of rest to preserve their strength and stay one step ahead of their unyielding pursuer.

Despite the tactical rotation of responsibilities, tensions simmered within the group as Jorja grappled with a sense of powerlessness. Her potent abilities were rendered useless against the elusive adversary tracking their movements. Amidst the challenging dynamics that unfolded, unity and resilience became their allies in a treacherous race against time and a formidable adversary.

"Whilst I have no problem in cloaking us, my queen," Piran began, his expression filled with concern for the safety of all of them, "you say he is family. But how do you know this?" Piran could not shake the worry that weighed heavily upon him, knowing that their lives were now in the hands of fate and uncertainty.

"Piran, whilst I value your input greatly," Lissa responded, her gaze thoughtful and full of hidden knowledge. "There are things at force that we are not completely aware of."

Lost in her memories, she recalled a time from her childhood, a time of innocence mingled with darkness. "When I was very young, just beginning my training at the tender age of five or maybe 6 years old, my mother took me aside to teach me about our family tree." Her voice held a touch of sadness as she recounted the tale of the name that had been crossed out on that ancient parchment. "There was one name, her uncle, a man who once sought to claim the throne through war against the royal family. His story ended in tragedy, struck down in battle by his father, yet he left remnants of his power, a legacy of skills inscribed for those who came after him."

Lissa paused, the weight of history and legacy heavy upon her words. "Before his demise, he had mastered a unique ability granted by his great powers, the ability to seek out his blood and his family. This gift passed down through generations is a mandatory ritual for the royal children to hone their magical talents, a safeguard against unseen dangers lurking in the shadows of the past." Her mother's voice echoed in her memory, guiding her through the twists and turns of their lineage, a legacy tainted by ambition and betrayal.

"If my memory serves me well", Lissa continued, her voice tinged with a mix of reverence and apprehension, "this uncle of my mother's was the last royal descendant to be trained by the enigmatic drakÔns, ancient beings of immense power and wisdom. After his ill-fated rebellion, the drakÔns had turned their backs on the royal lineage until fate led them to me." Memories of her mentor, the formidable and inscrutable Sobex, flooded her mind, a figure of authority and mystery she had once revered. "Under the watchful eyes of Sobex, I underwent rigorous training, his scrutinising gaze probing my soul for signs of darkness. Only after proving my worth, did he relent, opening the doors to a world of magic and wonder that surpassed my wildest dreams."

Deep in the recesses of her mind, Lissa recalled the bond forged between student and teacher, a bond steeped in ancient traditions and unfathomable power. "Sobex, with his infinite wisdom and boundless abilities, unveiled the mysteries of Kitte to me, a mere mortal in awe of the divine. His teachings, a testament to a legacy long forgotten, ignited a fire within me, a spark of potential and destiny intertwined with the threads of history and fate."

Piran was given time to digest this information whilst Lissa drove in quiet contemplation. As they traversed along the winding roads, she marvelled at the changing landscapes unfolding beyond the window, each turn revealing a new vista of rugged beauty. The rhythmic hum of the engine provided a soothing backdrop to Lissa's thoughts as she mulled over the intricate details of the tale she had just shared. The sunlight filtered through the canopy of Dees, casting dappled shadows that danced upon her face, adding a sense of tranquillity to the tense atmosphere within the vehicle.

He protected them with his cloaking magic, a shimmering shield of unseen power that enveloped their vehicle in a veil of secrecy. The mystical energy resonated faintly in the air, giving Lissa a sense of security amidst the unknown dangers that lurked beyond their sanctuary on wheels. Lissa could not feel the young man following them for a long time, his presence obscured by the potent enchantment woven by Piran.

Lissa knew that Piran would not be able to sustain the cloaking magic forever; its intricate weave demanded a toll on his stamina. Yet, as the miles rolled by beneath the wheels, they appeared to have at least fourteen hours' head start on their pursuer. The open road stretched before them like a ribbon of promise, leading to an uncertain destination yet offering a sense of freedom and escape from their troubles.

After seventeen hours of driving, a procession of fleeting moments marked by the changing scenery that blurred into a kaleidoscope of colours, Piran succumbed to the heavy curtain of sleep that draped over his weary frame. The protective magic he held faltered, its glow dimming like a waning ember, signalling the need for respite. Her eyes fixed on the endless horizon ahead, Lissa forced herself to keep driving, the weight of their fate resting squarely on her shoulders.

In her mind's eye, a flicker of awareness stirred as she sensed the young man closing in on their trail, an inevitable convergence looming on the horizon. Fatigue gnawed at the edges of her resolve, a creeping weariness that threatened to overtake her senses. Just as the shadows of exhaustion began to darken her thoughts, Jago roused from his slumber, his young eyes wide with concern as he beheld Lissa's weary visage.

Although he was only twelve, a boy thrust into a world of peril and uncertainty far beyond his tender years, Jago possessed a seasoned intuition, a pragmatic understanding born from a life marked by hardship and survival. With a sense of duty that belied his age, he took over the wheel, guiding the vehicle with a steady hand, a beacon of reliability amidst the storm of chaos that encircled them.

In the ever-changing panorama of their adventure, a rich tapestry spun from the fibres of newfound friendship and collective trials. Jago's eyes were drawn to an extraordinary spectacle: kangaroos leaping elegantly across the wild expanse. Their lithe bodies soared through the dappled sunlight, propelled by powerful hind legs that sent them soaring in effortless arcs, captivating Jago with their fluid grace and nimbleness. Before him, nature's marvels unfolded in a vibrant exhibition of untamed life, a testament to the enduring spirit and breathtaking beauty that flourished in the very soul of the wilderness.

As they embarked on the challenging journey across the vast expanse of Australia during the early days of spring, the relentless heat combined with the arduous nature of the 4,000-mile drive tested their physical and mental endurance with each passing moment. Despite their determination, frequent stops punctuated their progress, leading them to sleep intermittently wherever a moment of respite presented itself. There were instances when the night sky enveloped them in remote locations, prompting them to rely on their limited provisions and the confines of their car for shelter.

Amidst the vast Australian landscape that stretched endlessly before them, the reality of being only three-quarters of the way through their journey after five long days of relentless driving began to weigh heavily on their spirits. The lingering disappointment of not having covered as much ground as hoped for by that point cast a shadow over their aspirations for progress.

Complicating matters was the necessity for one of the individuals to constantly uphold a protective shield, leaving Lissa frustrated by her inability to channel her magical abilities while assuming the role of driver. On the other hand, Jorja found herself in a similar predicament, lacking the skill to operate a vehicle and unable to access her magical powers, contributing to a sense of helplessness among the group. While both Jago and Piran possessed the unique capability to wield their magic while steering the vehicle, Jago's limited stamina in sustaining his magical prowess for extended periods necessitated Piran to intermittently take over, granting Jago the essential respite needed to recharge.

Despite their journey's complexities, their spirits lifted temporarily upon reaching Kakadu. This prompting them to abandon their vehicle and proceed on foot towards their destination marked a symbolic shift in their arduous expedition across the Australian terrain.

Lissa, filled with wonder and familiarity, stepped closer to the magnificent waterfall, its cascading beauty bringing back memories of her past encounters. She felt a deep connection to the natural world surrounding her as she took each deliberate step into the cool, rushing water. Suddenly, her loyal companion, Piran, blinked, and in an instant, Lissa disappeared from his sight, venturing into the heart of the falling water. This mystical place held secrets he was eager to uncover.

Delving into the unknown, Lissa stood behind the waterfall's veil in a hidden cavern. Even as she heard Piran and Jorja's voices calling out to her, she remained focused, channelling the mental link that Sobex had once taught her, weaving their thoughts together effortlessly. With a calm determination, she guided Jorja towards the concealed entrance of the cave, leading her granddaughter into the mysteries waiting to be unveiled using her magic.

Jorja and Jago sensed an unspoken energy guiding them, with Jago following Jorja into the tranquil cave. The atmosphere was excited as Jorja, seemingly entranced, crossed the threshold of the cascading water and into the mysterious cavern where Lissa stood, a beacon of wisdom and strength. With practised ease, Lissa moved aside the rocky impediments, revealing a small yet weighty metal box that piqued the curiosity of all who gazed upon it.

From the depths of her pocket, Lissa produced an enigmatic object, its strange design hinting at untold powers and ancient origins, a key to unlocking the secrets hidden within the box. As the box lid shimmered open, a brilliant green jewel sparkled within, casting a radiant glow that illuminated the cavern's darkness, casting intriguing shadows that danced on the walls.

Touching the jewel gently, Lissa felt a surge of energy coursing through her, intensifying the gem's brilliance as its glow expanded, suffusing the surroundings with an ethereal light. A portal materialised before their eyes, a gateway to realms unknown yet beckoning with promises of discovery and adventure. Focused on ensuring the safety of her companions, Lissa sent the green key through the portal, a symbol of trust and connection to those who awaited its arrival on the other side, ready to embrace the new possibilities it offered. Through this intricate dance of ancient artefacts and mystical energies, Lissa and her allies embarked on a journey to test their resolve and shape their destinies in ways they had never imagined.

CHAPTER TWENTY-ONE

In the quaint Chengkan village, Eswella and Li had forged a bond that blossomed like the rarest of flowers. Their days were filled with laughter and warmth as Eswella took on the duties of their humble dwelling, mastering the art of crafting exquisite Chinese feasts to share with Li upon his return from the day's toils. Li, in turn, cherished her presence, his heart swelling with affection for the enchanting woman who had become the sun in his sky. He resolved to elevate their connection during these blissful moments, contemplating a momentous decision to bind their fates together in eternal union.

Yet, fate is a fickle mistress. One fateful evening, as Li returned home, he was met with a scene that shattered his heart. Eswella was nowhere to be found, and their once-cosy abode lay in disarray, a testament to the chaos that had unfolded in his absence. Though no treasures had been stolen, the absence of Eswella's cherished belongings sent a chill through his soul. His initial frustration morphed into a gnawing dread as he discovered a colossal muddy footprint, a harbinger of dark tidings that hinted at a malevolent force behind her disappearance.

Li's love for Eswella, the essence of his existence, coursed through his veins like a relentless river, carving grooves of undying devotion in his heart. The profound connection they shared compelled him to delve into the depths of her being, endeavouring to grasp the intricacies of her soul by learning the language of her heart.

Each new syllable he mastered served as a stepping stone across the vast expanse that separated them, a testament to his unwavering commitment to bridge the gap and forge an unbreakable bond.

As darkness enveloped his world, despair tightened its grip around his weary soul, pulling him into the depths of despair so profound that it felt like drowning in a sea of sorrow. Utterly shattered, he found refuge in the solace of a weathered chair, tears cascading down his anguished face, silently echoing the ache in his heart. In the deafening silence that consumed him, he yearned with every fibre of his being for the return of his beloved, every heartbeat a resounding echo of his unyielding desire to reunite with her.

In the melancholy shadows of his longing, a solemn vow took root in the depths of his being, blossoming into a fierce determination that no hardship could thwart. He swore, with unwavering resolve, to traverse the treacherous terrain that lay ahead, braving every peril and facing every challenge with unyielding courage. His quest was at once simple and profound: to find her, to draw her once more into the sanctuary of his embrace, to shield her from the tempests that howled beyond their world, and to gently rekindle the light that had faded in her absence. In this odyssey of steadfast love and unyielding devotion, he unearthed a strength deeper than fear, surmounting every barrier until, at last, he stood triumphant against the tide of adversity.

Li meticulously combed through the crime scene, his sharp eyes scanning every corner for any clue that might lead him to the perpetrator. The tranquillity of Chengkan village was seldom disturbed by criminal activities. However, Li's extensive training and experience gained during his formative years in the bustling city of Shanghai equipped him with the necessary skills to manage such situations adeptly. Rising through the ranks to become a Supervisor First Class was a testament to his dedication and expertise in law enforcement. Li deliberately chose to return to his roots in Chengkan Village to further his career, even though there was a police station in Chengkan Village, they all had to report directly to the nearby city of Huangshan.

As he continued his investigation, the only discernible evidence he uncovered was a distinct boot print left at the scene. Li's attention then shifted to a peculiar observation he had made earlier about Eswella. He had always found it odd that Eswella lacked fingerprints on her fingers, initially attributing it to a possible congenital anomaly. However, this anomaly piqued his interest as he realised no fingerprint could be found amidst the shattered pottery and valuables across the room. These trinkets held sentimental value for Li, gifts bestowed upon him by his late mother, adding a layer of personal significance to the crime.

Amidst the debris, the faint sound of the Longxi River cascading down the hillside caught Li's attention, prompting him to contemplate whether the tranquil flow of the river had inadvertently provided an entry point for the mysterious assailant who had left behind the enigmatic boot print.

He dashed through the village, imploring every soul he encountered if they had glimpsed Eswella or any nefarious figure who might have spirited her away. Yet, the villagers were shrouded in ignorance, their faces blank with uncertainty. Only one young lad claimed to have witnessed something, but his tale was so outlandish that even Li found it hard to swallow. "I saw bright lights, Policeman Li! I swear it! Great, flashing lights!" the boy insisted. Li shook his head, knowing well that such wonders were impossible in a place devoid of electricity. His humble abode, with its open windows and simple bamboo walls, could not have harboured such marvels.

Li continued his inquiries, speaking to more villagers and children, but the same bewildering story echoed back to him. Eventually, he succumbed to despair and returned to his empty home as night fell.

The absence of Eswella's sweet fragrance lingered in the air, a haunting reminder of her presence. He longed for her warmth beside him, for the comfort of shared dreams. Though their nights had been innocent, the simple joy of her closeness had filled his heart with contentment. The gentle embraces before slumber and the tender kisses on his cheek had become cherished rituals.

As he slipped into bed that night, the chill of solitude enveloped him, the familiar sensation of loneliness settling around him like a heavy cloak. In the quiet darkness of his room, the echoes of his thoughts grew louder, each reverberating through his mind with a haunting clarity. The cool sheets felt icy against his skin, a stark reminder of the emptiness that seemed to seep into every corner of his being. Despite the weariness that weighed down his body, he knew that sleep would be a distant dream, elusive as the memories that haunted him in the stillness of the night. The room's silence seemed to amplify the echoes of his solitude, each soundless moment stretching out endlessly before him, a vast expanse of emptiness mirrored the void within. And so, he lay there in the darkness, enveloped in the chill of his isolation, navigating the depths of his thoughts as he braced himself for the long night ahead.

CHAPTER TWENTY-TWO

As Helgi arrived on the mysterious planet, he immediately felt a wave of heightened awareness wash over him, signalling Lissa's unmistakable presence. In that pivotal moment of recognition, Lissa could not help but discern that Helgi wasn't alone. Upon closer observation, another figure accompanied his presence, and she realised that Eswella was also with them. Initially, Lissa dismissed any immediate concern; her rational mind deemed them too far away in distant China to pose any pressing threat. However, her perception swiftly shifted like sand in an hourglass as she sensed their energies suddenly shift across vast distances, now settling in Australia, a new figure becoming apparent within their midst. The realisation dawned on her, like the first light of day breaking through the darkness, that the mysterious companion accompanying Helgi was Amox, the enigmatic figure whose actions had caused chaos and disruption.

The fact that they had traversed such immense distances in mere moments left Lissa utterly astonished. Connecting the dots further, she comprehended that they had been using portals for their rapid travel, a feat that showcased Amox was on hand. With a single minded focus, Helgi deftly retrieved Cador right outside Sydney, seamlessly transitioning through another portal and displaying his command over these mystical gateways. In the blink of an eye, they all found themselves standing as one, united in purpose, within the pristine serenity of a shimmering pool of water, the testament to the awe-inspiring power and speed of the portals at their disposal.

Lissa, presiding over the group with an air of authority and wisdom that demanded respect and obedience, immediately issued firm instructions for absolute silence as she directed Piran to activate the cloaking magic that shrouded them in secrecy and invisibility. She understood the limitations of the enchantment in deterring Helgi's relentless pursuit. Still, she clung to the hope that it would grant them a crucial window of opportunity – a slender chance to transmit a vital message through the radiant portal. In a defining moment of urgency, a peculiar key-like object, shimmering in a vivid shade of azure, materialised within the ethereal gateway, serving as the long-awaited signal they had anticipated. "Time is of the essence. We cannot tarry any longer. This is our cue to cross," Lissa commanded urgently, her tone laced with a sense of grave importance and imminent action.

As they commenced their extraordinary trans-dimensional journey, Piran led the way with purposeful strides, his movements defined by a cautious determination, closely followed by a visibly apprehensive Jago, whose nerves betrayed the underlying courage that propelled him forward. Jorja trailed a complex blend of apprehension and resolve behind her expression. Lissa brought up the rear, her atonement to the mystical energies surrounding them, serving as a beacon through the uncharted realms they traversed. The sensation that gripped Jorja and Jago as they crossed through the portal mirrored the unsettling descent of a plummeting elevator, their gravity momentarily suspended before forcefully finding newfound equilibrium as they landed upon the unfamiliar ground, trying to anchor themselves amidst the unfamiliarity that surrounded them.

Meanwhile, back in the realm they called home, Saffran and Tobias eagerly awaited the return of their comrades. Their gestures were imbued with reverence and loyalty, expressed through a deep bow before the revered Queen, a show of deference that spoke volumes of their unwavering dedication.

Amid their grand and solemn homecoming, Lissa swiftly commanded the attention of the assembled warriors, her voice ringing with authority as she emphasised the critical need for unwavering vigilance to safeguard the portal from any lurking dangers that might arise. As her piercing gaze traversed the ranks of her steadfast soldiers, a fierce determination shone in her eyes, indicating that their journey was far from complete. She foretold the gruelling challenges that awaited them, poised to test their strength and fortitude.

Steadfast in their devotion, Saffran and Tobias remained kneeling before the sovereign queen they held in high esteem. At the same time, Lissa rushed to her cherished daughter, enveloping her in a fierce and tender embrace that spoke volumes of her relief and affection. "I feared we had lost you forever," she whispered, tears glistening in her eyes as they spilt onto Saffran's shoulder, a tumult of joy and sorrow intertwining within her heart. In that moment, Saffran, a pillar of strength and fortitude, comforted her mother, saying, "No, dear Mother, I was not lost, merely wounded." She then recounted the harrowing events that transpired during her absence, revealing the treachery of Helgi and the intricate scheme she had devised alongside her father and Tobias to safeguard their family members. The tale of their audacious escape from captivity and Father and Tobia's fearless reclamation of the palace unfolded like a tapestry woven with peril, strategy, and daring resolve. Central to their triumph was Saffran's masterstroke - her feigned injuries, a convincing deception, ensnared Helgi's attention and set in motion the chain of events that led to her salvation at the hands of the gallant Amox.

Mother and daughter, having a deep desire to delve into the stories of the new world that Morwenna had introduced her child to over the past twelve years, decided to reconvene their conversation in the magnificent throne room. Equally intrigued and eager to absorb every detail of the extraordinary experiences and adventures that had unfolded over the years, Saffran eagerly awaited the exchange.

CHAPTER TWENTY-THREE

Jorja stood there in astonishment, entirely overwhelmed by the realisation that she was on another planet and Enrac, an unfamiliar and captivating place. The air felt different, a crispness that she had never experienced before. It was refreshing, almost invigorating. She took deep breaths, trying to soak in every scent that wafted through the air, each distinct and somehow comforting in its purity.

The moment Saffran recognised Jorja, her heart skipped a beat. Seeing the tears of joy streaming down Saffran's face made Jorja's eyes well up with emotion. Saffran's exclamation of recognition and love filled Jorja with relief and apprehension. As Saffran turned to Tobias briefly before rushing to embrace Jorja, the overwhelming sense of belonging and longing bubbled up within Jorja's chest. The way Saffran drew her into a warm, loving embrace stirred in Jorja a long-lost sense of security, one she hadn't felt in years. Each word Saffran spoke - laced with sincere affection and quiet pride - wrapped around Jorja's heart, gently unravelling her defences and bringing tears to her eyes.

"You have grown a little, I'd say," remarked Saffran, her voice hinting at the fun at the sight of her daughter, Jorja. The emotions that filled her were palpable as she introduced the man standing beside her, his presence exuding a sense of quiet strength. "Jorja, I am Saffran, your mother," she declared with a soft smile, gesturing toward the man with a fondness that spoke volumes. "And this dashing man is Tobias, your father," Saffran announced proudly, her eyes shimmering with unshed tears of joy.

Caught off guard by the sudden reunion and the rush of unfamiliar emotions, Jorja found herself at a loss for words. It was as if a piece of her past had suddenly materialised before her, beckoning her to embrace the unknown. In a reflexive gesture, she dipped into a formal curtsy, which felt antiquated and strangely fitting amid this unexpected encounter.

Saffran's melodic laughter filled the air, dispelling any sense of formality with a single sound. Her easy demeanour and genuine warmth enveloped Jorja in a comforting embrace of familiarity and love. Despite the trepidation in her heart, Jorja could not help but feel a glimmer of hope. This was a chance for connection, a moment to bridge the gap that had long separated them.

As Saffran enfolded her in a tender hug, Jorja closed her eyes, allowing herself to revel in the embrace of a mother's love. In that fleeting moment, a sense of peace washed over her, washing away the doubts and uncertainties that had clouded her mind. For the first time in what felt like an eternity, Jorja felt indeed seen and accepted.

Her essence lay bare before those who mattered most.

The embrace between mother and daughter felt like a healing balm, a moment of pure connection after years of separation. Saffran's tears of joy and whispered words of love filled the air with unrestrained emotion. Jorja surrendered to the embrace, allowing herself to be wrapped in the tender warmth and unwavering love that surrounded her. The burdens of the past twelve years seemed to melt away, replaced by a profound sense of belonging and the long-awaited comfort of acceptance.

As night fell over Enrac and the twin moons rose high in the sky, casting a soft, ethereal light over the land, Tobias gently guided

Jorja and Saffran through the Palace. The moment was bittersweet, a mix of reunion and uncertainty hanging in the air. Jorja felt a sense of anticipation growing within her, a curiosity about the new chapter that would unfold in her life in this unfamiliar yet strangely welcoming world.

As Tobias stood by, he looked at Jorja knowingly, silently acknowledging the gravity of the situation. The transition to heightened security was palpable, with twenty vigilant guards stationed at the portal to ward off potential threats while others patrolled the protective walls of the Palace. Jorja could not help but feel the tension in the air, sensing the weight of the impending danger.

Upon being escorted to the throne room, Jago and Jorja were graciously attended to, receiving both sustenance and refreshments. Jorja glanced at Jago, noticing the strain in his expression as he struggled to process the unfolding events. Lissa's words of gratitude for the warm reception were met with a sobering reminder that their trials were far from over.

Amid the gathering, Tobias discreetly slipped away, only to return in the company of a distinguished, older gentleman exuding a sense of kindness. The room fell silent as Lissa abruptly halted her speech and rushed towards the newcomer, Morwenna, with an outpouring of affection. Morwenna's devoted husband, Goran, warmly embraced his wife before his gaze fell upon Jorja, his granddaughter.

Meeting her grandfather's gaze, Jorja rose gracefully and performed a respectful curtsy. Goran's eyes lingered on Jorja, filled with familiarity and curiosity, causing a slight unease to creep over her. As he finally tore himself away from his beloved wife's embrace, Goran approached Jorja, his looming presence evoking a sense of introspection within the young girl.

As Goran embraced Jorja tightly, his touch was physical, deeply emotional, and filled with years of longing and regret. How he held her seemed to convey the love and affection he had been unable to express for so long. Jorja could feel his heart beating fast against her chest as if trying to compensate for all the missed moments and lost opportunities.

In that poignant moment, the atmosphere was filled with sorrow and gratitude. Goran's sobs were a symphony of emotions that reverberated through the room, echoing the pain of separation and the joy of reunion. Jorja, in turn, held onto him as if she never wanted to let go, cherishing the connection they were finally able to share.

The arrival of a guardsman into the throne room shifted the mood. As Jorja acknowledged the seriousness of the situation, her understanding gaze met Piran's offer of assistance. Their unspoken communication seemed to bridge the gap between duty and family, highlighting the complex relationships that defined their lives. Piran's gesture, while simple, spoke volumes about his willingness to stand by Jorja's side, ready to face whatever challenges lay ahead. The silent exchange between the men and Morwenna conveyed a sense of unity and determination as they prepared to confront the trials that awaited them.

Piran followed Goran and Tobias out of the room and towards the wall surrounding the Palace, feeling a sense of familiarity as he navigated the corridors easily due to his prior experience in the army.

Memories of his past life intersected with thoughts of Eswella, prompting a wave of bittersweet nostalgia to wash over him. Despite the physical distance, he could feel her ethereal presence lingering in his thoughts, like a phantom companion accompanying him on his journey through the Palace grounds. Each step he took brought a flood of conflicting emotions - yearning, regret, and a faint hope for the future.

Jago, eyes lit up with eagerness, engaged Jorja in spirited conversation as they sought solace in a quiet corner of the throne room. The opulence of the Palace surroundings, adorned with majestic white columns and regal statues of past monarchs, exuded an air of grandeur and reverence that contrasted with the intimacy the two children shared. Despite the immaculate order and pristine cleanliness that characterised the space, an underlying sense of formality pervaded the atmosphere, making it seem more like a museum exhibit than a lived-in space.

Jago's gaze lingered on the remnants of uneaten food on the table, his unspoken desire for more sustenance palpable as he tried to conceal his hunger behind a facade of nonchalance. Sensing his unspoken hunger, Jorja rose gently with a sly smile, silently inviting him to partake in the fare. Although her stomach was tied in knots with anxiety, she found solace in the simple act of offering Jago a morsel of comfort, a gesture of kindness that transcended their immediate circumstances. Observing the sheer joy on Jago's face as he eagerly reached for the food, Jorja's heart swelled with a mix of compassion and lingering apprehension, uncertain of what the future held for them in this place and this enigmatic world.

Her heart was heavy with the weight of responsibility, and Morwenna sensed Helgi's return to Enrac and immediately sprang into action. Determined to protect her people at all costs, she swiftly made her way to check on the soldiers stationed at the portal. To her relief, the men were still present and unharmed. In a strategic move, she left only two soldiers to guard the portal. She instructed the remaining forces to strengthen the defences along the Palace walls in preparation for the impending confrontation.

CHAPTER TWENTY-FOUR

Just as Morwenna was setting her plans in motion, a thunderous voice echoed through the grand halls of the Palace, unmistakably that of her son, Helgi. His demands rang out with an ominous gravity, challenging Morwenna's rule and threatening the very fabric of their society. Despite the situation's urgency, Morwenna remained steadfast in her resolve, aware of the sacrifices that may be required to protect her people.

With a heavy heart, Morwenna hastened to the throne room, where she stood by her loyal companion, Saffran, ready to face the grim reality of their predicament. In a brave and selfless gesture, she made a decision that would shape the fate of their kingdom. "I will yield to Helgi's demands," she stated, her voice tinged with determination and sorrow. Turning to Saffran, she issued a poignant command fraught with the weight of sacrifice and hope. "Take Jorja and whoever else you can lead to safety through the portal," she urged, her gaze unwavering. "I will do what I must to stall for time. Go now, and may you find freedom and peace with your child."

"Mother, this cannot be how it ends for us," Saffran cried, tears streaming down her face. The desperation in her voice echoed through the dimly lit chamber.

Seeing the devastated look etched into every line of her mother's weary expression like a haunting portrait of anguish, Jorja rose slowly from her seat with a sense of purpose that radiated from her every movement. Her eyes blazed with a fierce determination that seemed to pierce through the heavy silence that enveloped the room. As she stood tall, a pillar of strength amidst the palpable despair, she felt a surge of courage coursing through her veins, emboldening her every word and action. She spoke with a voice that carried the weight of unwavering resolve, her words cutting through the air like a sharpened blade, "No, Mother, this is not how it ends." At that moment, her voice resonated with a strength that filled the room, pushing back against the shadows of doubt and fear that threatened to suffocate the air they breathed.

In the face of adversity, Jorja refused to be defeated, her spirit unyielding in the face of the challenges ahead. With a steely gaze that held a promise of defiance, she made a bold declaration that echoed with a sense of unwavering purpose. "Helgi will wish he never started this war when this night is through." Her words hung in the air like an unspoken vow, a testament to her unwavering determination to see justice served and peace restored.

At that moment, Jorja seemed to embody a force of nature, a beacon of hope amidst the darkness that threatened to consume them all. Her unwavering resolve breathed life into the sombre room, infusing it with a flicker of light that refused to be extinguished. As she stood there, a solitary figure framed by the looming shadows of uncertainty and fear, it was as if she had drawn upon the very essence of courage itself. Her presence, both defiant and resolute, challenged the forces that threatened to unravel everything they held dear. The return of her formidable crystal to Enrac rekindled her confidence, fortifying her resolve like steel tempered in flame.

With each passing moment, Jorja's resolve only seemed to grow stronger, her spirit unbroken despite the despair that lingered in the air like a heavy shroud. In her eyes burned a fire that refused to be quenched, a flame of determination that blazed brightly in the face of adversity. And as she stood there, her very being seemed to resonate with a power that transcended words, a silent vow that spoke of a resolve that would not be swayed.

In that moment of defiance and determination, Jorja stood as a warrior in her own right, ready to face whatever challenges lay ahead with courage that knew no bounds.

The throne room was filled with a hushed silence, broken only by the sharp inhalations of the attendees as they bore witness to an incredulous scene unfolding before their very eyes. Jorja, the epitome of grace and power, stood bathed in a shimmering light that seemed to emanate from deep within her soul. This radiant glow, a stark reminder of the mystical energy she had previously wielded with her crystal hidden in her rucksack, cast a mesmerising aura that left those gathered in a collective state of awe. The vibrant blue crystal vibrated upon her back as if it had been dormant for years away from the planet, and now, full of purpose, it came to life once more.

Her transformation was a sight to behold, a testament to the magical forces at play, and in that moment, all eyes were riveted on her. Confidence exuded from her very being with each step she took, resonating like a palpable force. It was a mesmerising sight that etched itself into the memories of those who bore witness, a moment that transcended mere spectacle and touched upon the profound.

As she approached her grandmother and mother, her strides purposeful and unwavering, Jorja's voice rang out clear and steady, a beacon of determination amid uncertainty. "Fear not," she spoke, the weight of her words carrying a promise of resolution, "I will deal with this. By the end of the day, Helgi will wish he had not started this war. I promise you that." With those simple yet resolute words, she set forth on a path that would forever alter the course of their lives, a destiny intertwined with power, magic, and unwavering strength within her.

Jorja felt an overwhelming sense of power surging within her for the first time, yet her demeanour remained eerily calm, like the quiet before a storm. With a graceful yet determined stride, she moved past them, traversing the unfamiliar halls of the palace as if she had always belonged there. Jago, caught in her wake, struggled to keep pace with her swift steps, his gaze fixed on her as though he were witnessing a miracle unfold before his eyes.

Upon reaching the towering palace gates, Jorja commanded their opening, her voice resonating with authority as she made it clear that no one else was to accompany her on her journey. The heavy gates swung wide, allowing Jorja to step out alone into the cool night air, her figure silhouetted against the moonlit sky. With a final glance back to ensure the gates were securely closed behind her, she ventured forward with unwavering determination.

Positioned at the edge of the gates, Jorja surveyed the formidable white walls surrounding her. Their sheer size and pristine appearance cast an intimidating shadow over her petite frame. The task ahead loomed before her, but she stood resolute, a beacon of strength in the face of uncertainty.

Eswella, consumed by a deep sense of desperation, was endeavouring to distance herself from Helgi. She had finally realised that he was not the man she had once foolishly believed him to be. In her deluded state, she clung to the hope that Piran might have filled the void. Jorja could sense everything around her, and Eswella's feelings were palpable. The only man she found herself genuinely drawn to was Li, the one she longed to be reunited with in China. Li had a reassuring presence that could calm her just at the thought of him. A profound sense of emptiness engulfed her whenever she was separated from him.

As Eswella observed the grandeur of the palace gates opening, a solitary figure emerged - a woman. Helgi, convinced that it was Morwenna, pressed Eswella into the task of intercepting her and escorting her back to kneel before the true King of Enrac. Eswella, still nursing her injuries, voiced her reluctance to undertake the mission. Unmoved by her protests, Helgi commanded a horse to be brought forth for her to hasten to Morwenna.

For the first time in her tumultuous journey, Eswella found herself gripped by genuine fear. Nevertheless, she mounted the horse and commenced her journey towards the apparent Morwenna. As the horse painstakingly advanced, Eswella's mind raced with schemes for evasion, myriad stratagems unfolding before her. Approaching the figure she had mistaken for Morwenna, Eswella discerned that it was not her. Glancing up at the palace, she spotted the genuine Morwenna, flanked by Saffran. Eswella realised that she needed to devise a signal to reveal her allegiance to Morwenna, but the daunting question lingered of what course of action to take.

Jorja rapidly closed in on Eswella despite deep resentment toward her, sensing a glimmer of goodness within her. When the two women converged in the expanse, Eswella broke the taut silence, her voice trembling with anticipation.

Jorja nodded slowly, her brow furrowing in intense concentration as she braved the unfamiliar challenge of sending a message across a great distance. The task's weight was not lost on her, but a sense of empowerment surged within her, bolstering her resolve. With unwavering determination, she focused on reaching out to Nanny on behalf of Eswella.

"Nanny, I am with Eswella, and she has a message for you. It is sincere and full of love. May I connect you to her, please?" Jorja communicated telepathically, her voice resonating in Morwenna's mind with surprising clarity and purpose.

Encouragement and gentle guidance flowed back from

Morwenna, her words laced with a quiet confidence in Jorja's latent abilities. "Child, you have a gift like no other that enables you to breach the barriers of the mind and connect me with Eswella. Trust in yourself, Jorja; you possess the strength to accomplish this feat."

Upon relaying the message successfully, Jorja, her gaze unwavering, announced to Morwenna, "Nanny, Eswella is ready to communicate directly with you at this moment."

Beneath the veil of the mental connection, Eswella, her voice tempered with hesitance and vulnerability, spoke up to her queen. "I... I have heeded your advice, my queen. I have reflected upon myself as you instructed and realised my changes. I hope it is not too late for me and that you will not forsake me for my lateness. I beg forgiveness for the delay in my revelations; my heart no longer beats in unison with your son."

In response, Morwenna, though surprised by Eswella's confession, thinking it may be another trick of deception, acknowledged the sincerity in her words. "Eswella, your allegiance wavers at a pivotal juncture, yet a flicker of faith stirs within me.

Return to Helgi with my granddaughter by your side; together, you shall find a way to safeguard your freedom."

With mounting desperation, Eswella voiced her apprehension, pleading, "My queen, I implore you, spare me the torment of returning to Helgi's clutches. He embodies pure malevolence; I cannot face that darkness again."

Firm yet compassionate, Morwenna elucidated the necessity of preserving appearances for their plan's success. "Eswella, we must maintain the façade of delivering Jorja to Helgi to avert suspicion. Endure this momentary hardship; Jorja shall be your guardian amidst the shadows that loom ahead."

As their connection faded, Jorja extended a comforting hand to Eswella, her promise of protection ringing true in the tumultuous air that enveloped them. "Trust me, Eswella, I shall shield you from harm," Jorja affirmed as they ventured toward Helgi, the sinister presence awaiting them.

Helgi stood transfixed, his gaze alternating between the unexpected arrival of a resolute young girl and the quiet turmoil brewing in Eswella's eyes. "Uncle, you summoned us to surrender," Jorja declared, her voice resolute against the silent tension in the room. With unwavering determination, she challenged Helgi, compelling him to confront the consequences of his actions.

Caught off guard by Jorja's unyielding resolve, Helgi hesitated momentarily, his usual composure faltering in the face of this unforeseen defiance. Beside Jorja, Eswella fidgeted nervously, her gaze flitting fearfully between Helgi and her newfound protector.

Helgi then spoke with a commanding presence that demanded attention and submission. "Niece, you have finally returned," he declared, his voice resonating with authority. He instructed Jorja to kneel before him, a gesture symbolising the allegiance he expected from her. Despite the moment's seriousness, Jorja found amusement in Helgi's demeanour as she heard a whisper in his ear, signalling the influence of someone nearby.

Jorja had never observed this unfamiliar creature before and assumed it to be Amox, unlike anyone she had encountered. Amox warned Helgi to tread carefully, acknowledging the immense power he sensed emanating from her. The intensity of this power surpassed anything he had ever felt, leaving him in awe.

As Helgi continued to assert his dominance, disregarding any hint of fear from Amox, Jorja decided to play along with his demands. She chose to kneel not out of genuine subservience but to prolong the façade. She understood that the more trust she earned from Helgi, the more time she had to accomplish her goals.

Doubts arose within Helgi regarding Jorja, leading him to question her courage publicly. Amidst the tension, Amox interjected, urging Helgi to recognise the latent power residing within Jorja. However, Helgi's pride and authority overshadowed Amox's warnings, dismissing them with contempt and ordering him away.

Unbeknownst to the unfolding drama, a pulsating crystal nestled in Jorja's backpack seemed to respond to the escalating energy around her, hinting at a hidden significance that had yet to be revealed.

As her power surged, the energy flowed through her being, and

Jorja could feel its invigorating warmth enveloping her in a radiant, ethereal glow that seemed to emanate from the very core of her existence. With a sense of awe and purpose filling her soul, she slowly raised her arms in a graceful, almost ritualistic manner, tapping into a wellspring of ancient strength that lay dormant within her until this very moment. The sheer intensity of the force she was wielding left even Helgi, the seasoned warrior, momentarily stunned and strangely apprehensive, as if some primal instinct within him recognised the raw power she was harnessing.

Meanwhile, amid the swirling currents of magic and energy dancing around her, Jorja felt familiarity as her crystal hummed. Yet, in this pivotal moment, she knew without a doubt that she was tapping into that cosmic energy, drawing strength from the enigmatic crystal.

As Jorja's arms arced gracefully upwards, a wave of energy radiated outward from her, causing a ripple in the fabric of reality that seemed to bend and twist at her command. To her astonishment, she watched as Helgi's entire army, one hundred thousand strong, previously brimming with vigour and battle-readiness, succumbed to a sudden, deep slumber, their bodies falling limply to the ground in a surreal display reminiscent of the enchanting tale of Sleeping Beauty. The parallels between the ancient story she had cherished since childhood and the scene unfolding before her eyes were uncanny, almost as if the lines between myth and reality were blurring in this extraordinary moment.

Despite the sheer magnitude of the power she wielded and the awe-inspiring spectacle that had transpired, Jorja managed to maintain a façade of calm composure, refusing to betray any hint of surprise or vulnerability in front of the few individuals who remained unaffected by her spell. It was a testament to her inner strength and unwavering determination, the formidable, enigmatic figure she had become. And as the echoes of the legends surrounding her continued to reverberate ominously in the minds of those present, she stood poised and resolute, ready to face whatever challenges lay ahead with a courage born of ancient wisdom and indomitable spirit.

Among those still standing were Amox and Helgi, with Eswella still at her side, their expressions a mix of disbelief and curiosity. They stood in awe of the unfolding events, their eyes betraying a blend of emotions that mirrored the intense energy crackling in the air. As Jorja gathered her inner strength, her focus shifted towards her uncle, a man whose countenance exuded a combination of paternal pride and enigmatic wisdom. In that pivotal moment, a realisation dawned upon Jorja, illuminating the profound depths of her innate power and the unbreakable bond she shared with the ancient lore.

As she surveyed the faces of her uncle and the remaining witnesses, a profound sense of duty settled upon Jorja's shoulders, a duty she recognised as a sacred responsibility bestowed upon her by the universe. She understood the grave implications of her newfound abilities, knowing that they carried the weight to shape not only her destiny but also the destiny of those who surrounded her, intertwined in the intricate web of fate. While the air buzzed with a heady mix of anticipation and uncertainty, Jorja maintained a serene composure, bracing herself for the unforeseen challenges.

Helgi and Amox knelt before the young girl without hesitation, acknowledging her prowess with utmost reverence. Meanwhile, her grandmother's palace gates swung open, releasing a flood of guards swiftly apprehending and confining the perpetrators. Asserting her authority, Jorja intervened, ensuring that Eswella was safeguarded and not subjected to restraint. With a steely resolve, she kept her powers trained on the captured men, wary of any possible deception, as they were escorted and imprisoned beneath the opulent halls of the palace.

The evening unfolded in a spectacular display of festivities, with Jago revelling in the sumptuous feast before him. Laughter and merriment permeated the atmosphere, tinged with affection for the ravenous young lad who had endeared himself to all with his unbridled hunger for food and life.

The break of dawn heralded the return of the ancient drakÔn and the aged Sobex, Morwenna's venerable mentor, who appeared weathered by the passage of time. Tears of joy welled in Morwenna's eyes at the sight of her revered friend, a reunion that stirred the depths of her soul with profound nostalgia and gratitude.

In a heartfelt conversation between Sobex and Morwenna, a solemn decision was reached - both Helgi and Amox were deemed too perilous in their possession of magic and were to have their powers stripped from them. Confusion clouded Morwenna's features as she grappled with the revelation that such a feat was possible. With unequivocal authority, Sobex led the delegation to address the palace denizens and set in motion the irrevocable fate that awaited the two once-powerful sorcerers.

But Sobex felt the urgent need to have a personal conversation with Jorja. Realising the importance of ensuring their plans were communicated directly to her, he kindly requested Morwenna accompany him. This thoughtful gesture demonstrated Sobex's respect for Jorja and his desire to involve her in their discussions. As they approached Jorja, Sobex's voice softened with a hint of vulnerability as he began to express his request. "I have a small favour to ask of you, youngling," he started hesitantly. His words carried a sense of humility as he acknowledged his limitations.

Despite his age and weakened magical abilities, Sobex hoped that Jorja's assistance could boost a particularly challenging spell. He cast his gaze upon her, his eyes reflecting trust and a deep-seated belief in her capabilities. "There is none other I trust to take on this task, youngling. Will you lend your aid to an old drakÔn?" Offering the opportunity for Jorja to contribute to his magical endeavours seemed to ignite a spark within her as she eagerly agreed to assist. Overwhelmed with a sense of honour and responsibility, Jorja marvelled at the idea that a drakÔn like Sobex would turn to her for help. Recollections of tales depicting Sobex's unparalleled magical prowess raced through her mind, causing her to feel a mixture of astonishment and unwavering determination. The realisation that she had willingly accepted to aid a being of such esteemed magical stature filled her with awe and intrigue. Despite the initial surprise at being chosen, Jorja's inner resolve and curiosity spurred her to eagerly delve into this newfound alliance with Sobex, embracing the unexpected journey that awaited her.

Not wanting to miss a moment of the magical experience, Jago remained by her side, reassuring Jorja as they ventured towards the dungeons alongside Morwenna and Saffran.

As they embarked on their journey, the group were enveloped by a sense of purpose and camaraderie, their steps echoing with determination and curiosity. Sobex led the way, his aura radiating wisdom and vulnerability that tugged at Jorja's heartstrings. The weight of his request hung in the air like a delicate tapestry of trust and possibility, weaving the bonds between them even tighter.

Upon their return, the group was met with warm smiles and cheers, a chorus of relief and pride washing over them. The successful completion of the task was evident in the glimmer of satisfaction in Sobex's eyes, a silent acknowledgement of the bond that had formed between them during their shared endeavour. Still reeling from the awe-inspiring display of magic, Jago could not tear his gaze away from Jorja, a deep admiration and affection blossoming within him with each passing moment.

Ignoring the feast before them, the group basked in the afterglow of their achievement, their spirits lifted by the tangible sense of unity and accomplishment that filled the room. Jago, sitting beside Jorja, felt a surge of emotions welling up within him, a tide of adoration and respect for her that transcended mere words, solidifying his unwavering devotion and admiration for the courageous young woman who had proven herself a faithful ally to Sobex and a beacon of light in his own life.

EPILOGUE

In the wake of an overwhelming surge of affection and resolve, Eswella's destiny shifted wondrously. Fuelled by an unyielding bravery and a deep faith in Sobex Jorja's wisdom, a dormant power stirred within Jorja. With every essence of her being, she summoned the ancient lore to command the elements and reshape reality. The fabric of existence responded to her summons, manifesting a radiant portal of shimmering light. In that crucial instant, poised at the crossroads of fate and possibility, Jorja poured her most profound spirit into the portal, igniting its energy with fervent emotions and steadfast determination. The barriers of time and space quivered, opening a passage to a realm where love knew no limits. From this fleeting threshold, Eswella stepped forth, her gaze illuminated by a profound yearning and recognition. Deep within her heart, she understood that this reunion was no mere happenstance but a testament to the unbreakable bond she shared with Li. As the celestial forces converged, weaving them together in a symphony of cosmic unity, Eswella found peace in Li's embrace, the resonance of their love echoing through the infinite reaches of the cosmos.

As they settled in the opulent surroundings of the throne room, Lissa, with a nurturing gesture, passed the tea plants and seeds to her servant, emphasising the importance of their proper utilisation within the palace greenhouse to enhance the kingdom's botanical offerings further. In a thoughtful gesture of sharing a piece of her cherished memories with Saffran, she handed over a prepared box of PG Tips tea bags, knowing well how she had developed an extreme liking for them. She instructed the servant to bring her a pot of boiling water, a small milk jug and some sugar.

When the items arrived, Lissa made a pot of tea with skilled hands, and everyone tried it. They were all eager to have one of the seedlings when grown, so they could make this decadent drink.

Lissa also asked to see the pot maker and instructed him on making teapots, cups, and saucers. She would need hundreds of pots and thousands of cups and saucers. She showed him pictures on her phone, to which he gasped, and she laughed, of the items he needed, to which he scribed notes. She showed him the holes required to allow the liquid to be poured out.

A thick tension enveloped the realm, almost as if it could be grasped with a hand. With each breath Morwenna drew, she sensed the heavy anticipation coiling around her like a serpent ready to strike. The air shimmered with vibrant energy, as if the world itself held its breath in anticipation. A transformation of great magnitude loomed just beyond the horizon. Morwenna stood motionless, attuned to the delicate patterns unfolding around her. Her instincts stirred, soft and insistent, whispering of a coming shift, a quiet unravelling of fate. The silence was not empty but alive with unspoken possibilities. Each heartbeat carried the weight of promise, each breath drawn with quiet resolve. As she looked ahead into the unknown, she understood with sudden clarity - the journey was not ending but awakening into something greater.

THE END

CHARACTERS AND PRONUNCIATIONS

Jorja	It is a form of Georgia. Jor-Ja
Saffran	Jorja's mother, Princess of Enrac, is a wife to Tobias. Saff-ran
Morwenna/Lissa	Saffran's mother, grandmother to Jorja. Mor-when-a
Goran	Morwenna's husband, grandfather to Jorja.
Tobias	Saffran's husband and father to Jorja.
Helgi	Son of Morwenna and Goran, Bother to Saffran
Enrac	The home planet is also referred to as the realm. En-Rac
Eden	Wife to Helgi, mother of Cador and sister to Eswella.
Piran	Husband of Eswella.
Cador	Son of Helgi.

Erlend	Fairy-like creatures, but devoid of wings, in this world.
Undines	Elf-like creatures with wings in our world.
Amox	An Erlend. Son of Gwen and Jowan.
Telm	It's a form of martial arts, but so much more. Tel-m
DrakÔn	A small dragon that we would know. Drakon
Jago	James in Cornish.
Gasal	Taran & Kelsey's home country
Kerra	Morwenna & Goran's daughter Ker-ra
Baron	Morwenna & Goran's son
Treeve	Morwenna & Goran's son Tree-ve
Elestren	Morwenna & Goran's daughter El-lest-ren
Sobex	Eldest of the DrakÔn's
Sodux	Son of Sobex a Kasa
Kasa	Sobex's mate and mother to Sodux

Dees	Dees
Dees Ygrene	Small wood in DrakÔn language
Minglegroves	Minglegrove in DrakÔn language
Nyana	Queen of the Undines Ny-arna
Helio	King of the Erlends Hel-io
Carantok	King of Enrac Morwenna's father
Sagira	Queen, Wife of Carantok, Mother to Morwenna
Lanrah Grikor	DrakÔn Mountain
Oighodit	Helgi's DrakÔn
Nitte	DrakÔn Magic

REFERENCES AND ATTRIBUTES

The Lady of Llyn Y Fan Fach:

Copyright 14 January 2015

- Myddfai – Wikipedia, the free encyclopaedia

- The Physicians of Myddfai, History of the 12th century

1000s: The Lady of the Lake and the Physicians of Myddfai The Physicians of Myddfai

Thanks to Wikipedia for its historical knowledge of the City of Durham and its Cathedral.

Thanks to cornishbirdblog.com for the information on Cornwall.

And Wikipedia for its knowledge of dragons.